THE
JOURNALIST

THE JOURNALIST

A Paranormal Thriller!

David Gardner

Encircle Publications
Farmington, Maine, U.S.A.

The Journalist © 2021 David Gardner

Hardcover ISBN 13: 978-1-64599-168-7
Paperback ISBN 13: 978-1-64599-144-1
E-book ISBN 13: 978-1-64599-145-8
Kindle ISBN 13: 978-1-64599-146-5

Editor, Encircle Publications: Cynthia Brackett-Vincent
Book design, cover design and digital illustration by Deirdre Wait
Cover images © Getty Images

Published by:

Encircle Publications
PO Box 187
Farmington, ME 04938

Visit: http://encirclepub.com

Printed in U.S.A.

Acknowledgments

So many people have contributed to my writing over the years that I don't know where to begin. Their feedback, patience, and encouragement has been invaluable, and I owe much of my success to them. I want to thank Bill Regan, Jane Roy Brown, Richard Bolt, Vicki Sanders, Peggy McFarland, the late Steve Gordon, Alyson Miller, Erica Harth, Arlene Kay, Kevin Symmons, Elizabeth Lyon, Judy Giger, David Gallant, Ray Anderson, and especially my wife, Nancy, also a writer, who understands my need to write, and understands me (as much as I'm understandable). I would also like to thank Cynthia Brackett-Vincent and Eddie Vincent for bringing me into the Encircle Publications family, and Deirdre Wait for her clever cover design.

Dedication

To the memory of Steve Gordon, a fellow writer and dear friend.

Chapter 1

SCORPIO Oct. 23 - Nov. 21

Your ancestors are the raw material of your being, but who you become is your responsibility alone. Learn to turn your troubles into opportunities. Today is a good day to defrag your hard drive.

He hovers in the doorway at the far end of the newsroom, his feet not touching the floor. When he spots me, he glides forward, trailing diaphanous versions of himself that become smaller and smaller until they disappear. He wears leather chaps, an oversized black cowboy hat and high-heeled boots that almost bring him up to five feet. He has leathery skin and a drooping gray mustache.

It's my great-great-grandfather Hiram Beekle, back for another ghostly visit.

He first showed up when I was six years old, right after I shot and killed my stepfather.

I'm the only one who can see him, hear him, talk to him.

As a kid, I would wet my pants and run away whenever Hiram showed up. Now he's just a pain in the ass.

I turn back to my keyboard, hoping he'll go away. I'm not in the mood for advice, taunts, prods, complaints, boasts.

He showed up last week to tell me to quit my job and find

something better. Same thing the week before and the week before that. Probably why he's back today.

I have to admit he's right, but I'm sure as hell not going to tell him that.

Just four months ago I was a hot-shot investigative reporter for the *Boston Globe*. Now I write for a tacky supermarket tabloid, the *Boston Tattler*. Its newsroom is an open bay on the second floor of a ratty building that once served as a cheese warehouse that on humid days still smells of Camembert. Out front are the marketing and distribution people, along with the office of the publisher, my Uncle Sid. Only he would hire a disgraced journalist like me.

I churn out fanciful tales about creatures from outer space, Elvis sightings and remedies for double chins. Some readers believe my stuff and some don't. Those in between ride the wave of the fun and nonsensical and don't care whether the stuff they're reading is true or not.

Our larger rivals concentrate on noisy Hollywood breakups and soap-opera stars with gambling addictions. The worst of our competitors traffic in fake political conspiracies. But Uncle Sid stays with alien visitors, kitten pictures and herbal cures for chin wattles. He likes to point out that kittens and spacemen don't sue. He's been sued too often.

I type:

> Although many local sportswriters puzzle over the inconsistencies of Red Sox hurlers, the shocking truth is that—

"That's crap, Jeff."

Hiram has drifted around behind me to peer over my shoulder.

"Try 'terrifying'," he adds. "'Shocking' is overused."

Hiram pretends he'd been a cowpoke, but in fact made a living writing pulp westerns.

I look around to see if anyone is watching, then turn back to

Hiram and whisper, "Is that why you're here, to dispense advice on adjectives?"

"That and to let you know I sense danger."

"You're always sensing danger. Just last week, you told me than an earthquake was…"

I stop whispering when Sherwood shuffles over, coffee cup in hand. He's a doughy, middle-aged man who reads the dictionary for pleasure. "Another tale about space critters, Jeff?"

"A follow-up to last week's. It's Uncle Sid's idea. He loved the national exposure."

Sherwood nods. "You knocked that one out of the ballpark."

Sherwood loves sports metaphors but hates sports.

One of my stories from the week before somehow got into the hands of a particularly dim U.S. Congressman who scrambled onto the floor of the House of Representatives to fume against the government agency for hiring a mob-controlled construction company to build a prison for creatures from the planet Ook-239c.

I kick off my sneakers, tilt back my chair and put my bare feet up on my desk. "What're you working on today?"

"I've got a TV chef who's gone on a hunger strike, identical twin sisters in Chattanooga who've been secretly exchanging husbands for fourteen years, and an eight-year-old boy in Brisbane who can predict the future by licking truck tires—the usual stuff." Sherwood takes a gulp of coffee, shrugs, sighs. "Do you ever wonder what you're doing with your life?"

"Sometimes. But who doesn't?"

Again Sherwood sighs. I've never known anyone to sigh so often. His wife ran off with a termite inspector a few years back, and soon afterward he lost his professorship and his house. Sherwood was put on the earth as an example of what I don't want to become.

"You should look for another job," I say.

Sherwood shrugs, then ambles back to his desk. He doesn't want another job because it would make him feel better.

But I want a better job so badly that I dream I've found one, then wake up to reality.

Hiram floats around front and shakes his head. "The little guy's right—you should get a better job. And for that, you need to get that darn Pulitzer back."

I delete 'shocking' and type 'terrifying.' "Think I'm not trying?"

"Try harder. Young people these days—"

"...don't know the meaning of hard work," I contribute. "Yeah, I know. Now go away."

"No, you go away. You're in deep trouble, young man. Two black-hearted sidewinders have ridden into town to—"

"That's the ridiculous opening line from *Rise From Ashes*. A dreadful novel."

"*Dreadful?* Do you know how many copies I sold?" Hiram says.

"The protagonist was an idiot who shot his own big toe off."

"That had a solid plot purpose. And at least he shot himself, not a member of his own family."

Whenever I piss Hiram off, he brings up the shooting.

"Screw you!" I whisper and turn back to my keyboard.

Green Monsters on the Green Monster!

Late last night, a sharp-eyed Boston Red Sox guard spotted a pack of green, three-eyed space monsters in Fenway Park. Authorities believe them to be the aliens who escaped from the secret government prison first brought to the public's attention in last week's *Boston Tattler*. The guard reported seeing the creatures scrambling up the wall that Red Sox fans have lovingly dubbed 'The Green Monster.'

Green monsters attracted to a green wall? A coincidence? Unlikely. In fact, experts on the subject of aliens from outer...

"This little piggy—"

"Hey!" I jerk my foot back.

Melody has sneaked up on me. She likes to do that.

She wiggles my little toe again. "This little piggy went to market, this little piggy—well, you know the rest of the narrative." She lets go of my toe.

"Actually, that felt good. Don't stop."

"That's as much wiggling as you get, Jeff. You're married."

I pull my feet off my desk and rest them on the floor. "Separated."

"That's still married."

Melody is my editor. She's thirty-seven—three years older than I am. Her face is narrow and pretty, her hair red and wavy. She likes hoop earrings and has long feet.

She shuffles through the printout in her hands. "You sent me eight stories this week but promised me nine."

"I'm still working on the last one. Did you know that a space creature has replaced the Red Sox mascot and has put a hex on the top of the batting order?"

"They're already hexed," Melody says. She eyes me for a long moment, then screws up her mouth. "I'm concerned."

Here it comes again. "About my articles? About my bare toes? Or my collection of metal toys?" I reach across my desk, pick up the *Spirit of St. Louis* and fly it back and forth overhead.

Melody puts her hands on her hips and rolls her eyes. "Yes, all those things, Jeffrey, but in this instance, what I meant was I hate to see you wasting your talent writing this garbage. You're the best writer I've ever edited. You deserved that Pulitzer."

"Which they took back twenty-seven days later."

"Most journalists would kill to have one for even twenty-seven days."

Melody said that with a smile. She says most everything with a smile. It's a pretty smile, but sometimes forced, as if she were trying to make herself happier than she feels. She's the opposite of Sherwood, who wallows in gloom and wants to pull everyone down with him.

I say, "You always see the best in every situation."

"Thanks."

"It drives me batshit."

Melody raps her knuckles on my desk. "I need the copy by two o'clock." She raps her knuckles on the top of my head. "At the latest."

I watch her go. I shouldn't tease her the way I do. Melody's not the hard-ass editor she pretends to be. She's in fact a softy, smart and thoughtful. Also curvy.

Hiram says, "That young lady has a fine carriage."

"I hadn't noticed," I say and pick up my typing where I left off:

> Space lizards have the ability to slow down fast balls, strip the spin from curves and send knuckleballs off in...

Hiram says, "'Slow down fast balls' is flabby and clumsy because 'slow' and 'fast' interfere with each other."

"Uh-huh." I keep on typing.

"Clementine's coming to visit."

"Oh?"

"She's worried about Ebenezer."

I look up from my keyboard. "What is it this time?"

"He's missing."

"Grandpa Ebenezer is always missing," I say.

"Clementine thinks he's in trouble."

I delete 'slow down fast balls' and type 'retard fast balls. "How can Ebenezer be in trouble? He's dead."

"I don't like that word—and now you're the one in trouble."

I look up to see Uncle Sid coming toward me. Two burly guys walk with him, one on each side, clutching his arms.

My uncle looks scared. I hate to see that. I love the guy.

"Jeff," he says with a quiver, "these two gentlemen want a word with you."

I've watched enough local news to recognize the Ramsey twins—Hank and Freddie. Not gentlemen. Mobsters.

I get to my feet, pull Sid free from the pair's grasp and wrap my arm around his shoulders. They're trembling. "What in hell do you two want?

Hank steps closer and blows his cigar breath in my face. He has big ears and black hair combed straight back. At six feet three, he stands eye-to-eye with me, but he's half again as wide. He says, "Did you write that idiotic story?"

"Which idiotic story? I write lots of idiotic stories."

Freddie says, "Asshole!" and steps forward.

Hank reaches out to hold him back. "Easy."

Although the two were born identical, no one has trouble telling them apart because Freddie had the front half of his nose lobbed off in a knife fight. This gives him a piggy look.

Hank says, "You know what I'm talking about, wiseass. Who told you about that government prison for space monsters?"

"Who? No one. I made it up."

"You made it up?"

"I make up everything I write."

Hank tilts his head back and half closes his eyes. "You made the story up?"

"Isn't that what I just said?"

Hank pokes me in the chest. "Then how come it's true?"

Chapter 2

SCORPIO Oct. 23 – Nov. 21

Life's problems are never as bad as they seem. Be ready to make new friends. Vinegar will get rid of that pesky earwax.

"True?" I say.

"Yeah," Hank says. "Except for that crap about green aliens from outer space. It's a prison for aliens but like the foreign terrorist kind."

Terrorists? *Terrorists!*

He's gotta be kidding.

Hank points at my feet. "How come you got no shoes on?"

I ignore him. "If parts of the story are true, then it's pure coincidence. Stuff like that happens all the time. For instance, haven't you read about people who've won the lottery more than once?"

Hank doesn't answer. He pulls a folded copy of last week's *Boston Tattler* from an inside suit pocket. A frog-faced alien stares back from the cover. 'Feds Hire Mob to Build Secret Prison!'

Hank rattles the magazine. "We gotta talk."

"Go ahead."

"Down in the alley," he says.

"I'm happy here."

Hank tilts his head toward Melody, Sherwood, and Janet the

Horoscope Lady, motionless at their desks, wide-eyed and staring. "On account of witnesses," Hank says.

Witnesses?

I don't like the sound of that.

I also don't want others involved in this, whatever this is. "Okay, but leave Uncle Sid out of it. He hasn't read the story because he's been out of town visiting a cousin in Chattanooga. Besides, you know you can trust him from the old days."

By that I mean my uncle used to chauffeur Hank's mobster father around in a big white Cadillac.

And—as Mom once let slip—he sometimes served as a getaway driver.

Uncle Sid says, "I'm coming along, Jeff."

"No, you're not."

"Yes, I am."

Hank shakes his head. "We don't need you, Sid."

My uncle looks at me, Hank, me again, then slinks away, disappointed to be left out. Uncle Sid likes to drop hints about his heavy connections back in the day, but in fact was never much more than a gofer.

I lead Hank and Freddie down the rear steps. At the bottom of the stairs, Freddie pushes past me, slips his hand inside his jacket and says, "Wait." He peers importantly up and down the alley, grunts, and steps outside. Hank and I follow.

This is the quiet section of Boston's North End—few restaurants, shops or tourists. The brick buildings on each side of the narrow alley are three stories tall and a couple hundred years old. The air smells of car exhaust and urine. Across the alley, Hiram sits atop a zigzagging fire escape, swinging his little legs, waving at me and grinning his best 'I-warned-you' grin.

Hank lights a cigar. He's in no hurry to start the conversation, his way of showing who's in charge. He wears an expensive gray suit and a blue tie. Freddie has on pegged black slacks, pointy black shoes and a black leather jacket that's way too hot for summer. The retro punk look. He keeps touching what's left of his nose.

Freddie's not the brightest bulb. Something about oxygen deprivation at birth, I once heard Uncle Sid tell Mom. Hank runs the outfit. Freddie breaks knees.

Hank blows smoke my direction.

I pretend not to notice. "Okay, what in hell is this all about?"

"You still sticking with that bullshit story about a once-in-a-million coincidence?"

"Why wouldn't I? It's the truth."

I in fact modeled the site on the place where my buddy Willy had worked construction before doing time for stealing a backhoe. He's out now, so I have to warn him about this conversation as soon as Hank lets me go. If he lets me go.

Hank snaps the magazine open to my article and dangles it in front of my face. "Read."

I squint at the page. "'The *Boston Tattler* has learned that a secretive government agency has hired a mob-controlled construction company to build a prison to house a dozen green inhabitants from Planet Ook-239c, and that—'"

"Not that, asshole," Hank says, shaking the magazine. "Two paragraphs down."

"'Constructed to resemble a self-storage facility, the massive building in western Massachusetts contains dozens of lead-lined cells that—'"

"Enough," Hank says, lowering the magazine. "Lead-lined cells? That's pretty damn specific. You couldn't have pulled that out of your ass. So who talked to you?"

I raise my hands in surrender. "Okay, I got a tip."

"Let's go back inside so you can show me the email."

"It was a phone tip."

"Convenient," Hank says. He drops his cigar, scrunches it under his heel and looks up at me. "What if I tell Freddie to beat the shit out of you?"

"What if I beat the shit out of Freddie?"

Freddie steps forward and chest-bumps me.

I feel the weapon in his shoulder holster.

"Back off, Freddie," Hank says. "The jerk's just messing with you."

Freddie snorts, glares, steps back.

Hank crumples the magazine and tosses it onto a stack of flattened cardboard boxes next to the rear door. "The story's out already, so I guess the source no longer matters."

Uh-huh. And Freddie's going to grow a new nose. "I suppose you're here to ask me to write a retraction."

"I don't ask people to do things, shithead, I tell them to do things. But in this case, it's too goddamn late. Anyway, I'm really here because I got a job for you."

"You want me to whack somebody?"

"You?" Hank says. "Whack somebody? Give me a break. Anyway, I don't whack people. That's old school. I checked you out after I read your goddamn story and found out you're good at what you do." Hank taps his temple. "So I want to use your brain. You're going to do some investigating for me, just like if it was a regular story. Isn't that right, Freddie?"

Freddie's been shuffling his foot all this time. He looks up, pleased to be consulted. "Right. Maybe they'll give you another Wurlitzer."

Hank looks pained. "A Pulitzer, idiot!"

Freddie winces and lowers his head, hurt written all over his face.

I almost feel sorry for the guy. He just got out of prison for trying to hijack a Buick with an FBI agent behind the wheel. The expression, 'He's his own worst enemy' was invented for Freddie Ramsey.

Hiram waves at me from high up the fire escape across the alley, grinning and swinging his little legs. He's greatly enjoying himself.

Hank pokes me twice in the chest. "What I got to say to you goes nowhere right? Otherwise… well, you can guess."

I can guess.

Two summers ago, a runaway city bus toppled an angel statue in front of a children's hospital and uncovered the skeletal remains of two soldiers from a gang warring with the Ramseys. Since Hank's construction company had poured the base, he and Freddie were brought in for questioning, but released for lack of evidence.

Hank says, "By now you must've figured out that the terrorist prison was built by my construction company. I operate it through a middle man in Providence. He got the contract from a private company that calls itself OASIS. That stands for... uh... 'Organization for Auditing Special Independent Systems.' I figure they get money from the Department of Defense or the CIA. I'm telling you all this because I want to find out who at OASIS has just started throwing lots of extra money around."

"Why?"

"Because I do, that's why."

"How in hell could I find that out?" I say.

"Check the OASIS parking lot for a shiny new BMW, or search through real estate records for someone there who just put a big down payment on a condo, or break into a few houses and look for hidden piles of cash, that sort of thing. Shit, do I have to tell you how to do your job?"

"That's not how I do my job."

Hank ignores this. "You also gotta make a contact inside OASIS. You know, meet someone at a bar, get them drunk and talking. That's what you big-time investigative reporters do, isn't it?"

On TV. "Sure. Exactly. But what in hell makes you think I'd ever work for you?"

"You won't be working for me. If you was, I'd have to pay you. You'll just be doing me a few little favors."

"Why not just give the job to your go-between in Providence?"

Hank lights another cigar. "Him? He'd be worthless. Besides, he's never even seen his contact at OASIS, some jerk who calls himself John Smith and does all his business by courier. He doesn't even phone or use email."

"If I did find out who at OASIS has just come into a pile of money—which I'm sure as hell not going to do—what would you do about it?"

"Nothing," Hank says, lifting his hands. "I'm a legit businessman who likes to know who he's dealing with, that's all. What in hell do you think I'd do?"

Probably something involving fresh concrete. "Why can't you do your own investigating?"

Hank studies the glowing end of his cigar. "I can't snoop around myself on account of how my picture gets in the papers so much." Hank glances over at Freddie, who for the past few minutes has been digging his little finger into his left ear. "And the goobers I got working for me can barely read stop signs. So I gotta use you, a big-time investigative reporter who's won a Wurlitzer."

Freddie stops mining for earwax and looks back and forth between us, confusion written all over his truncated face.

"When you're in my particular line of work," Hank adds, "it's hard to hire outsiders and even harder to trust them."

"I'm an outsider. What makes you think you can trust me?"

"I can't trust you, but I know you won't screw up because I've got you by the balls." Hank opens his hand and squeezes it closed. Hard.

My testicles scramble up into my groin. "I'm not afraid of you."

Hank chuckles. "I get that a lot from guys just before they shit their pants." He tilts his head back and examines the upper floor of the *Tattler* building. "Your uncle raised you after your mother died, right?"

I don't answer.

"You must owe him a lot, right?"

Again I don't answer.

Yes, I do owe my uncle a lot. He treated me like a son, took me to movies and one time dislocated his little finger catching a foul ball for me at a Red Sox game. And I remember how patient he was with Mom after she slipped into her own world. And then there was how he handled the shooting.

Hank points his cigar at the building. "I'll bet the wiring in an old shit box like this is dangerous. What do you think, Freddie?"

"A fucking fire hazard."

"Dying in a fire is a painful way to go," Hank says and tosses his cigar onto the flattened cardboard boxes by the door. They start to burn. "But you know that better than anyone."

Hank is baiting me.

Dad died in a fire.

Nothing would feel better than to smash Hank's teeth down his throat, and nothing would feel worse than to get shot by Freddie.

So I shuffle over and stamp out the fire.

Hank chuckles. "I guess that means we got a deal?"

I'll do anything to protect Uncle Sid.

I nod.

"Good," Hank says. "For your uncle's sake, don't even think about skipping town, talking to the cops or screwing with me in any way." Hank scribbles a phone number on a slip of paper and hands it to me, then reaches into a side pocket for a phone. "This is a burner. When you get a call on another line from someone asking for Reggie, hang up and get me on this one, got it?"

Hank gives me the phone and a long hard look, then leads Freddie to the black SUV at the end of the alley. A bald oaf opens the front passenger door for Hank but leaves Freddie to open his own. They roar away.

I take a deep breath and for the first time notice the sounds of traffic, see the sunlight slicing obliquely across the bricks on the far side of the alley, and smell the garbage, cat urine and my own nervous sweat.

If I work for Hank, someone at OASIS gets hurt. If I don't, Uncle Sid gets hurt. And maybe me. No, sure as hell me.

Hiram floats down from the fire escape and settles lightly in front of me, his wrinkly grin extending from ear to ear.

He says, "See? You should have listened to me and left town, and you should have…"

I step into the building and pull the door closed in his face. That makes me feel good even though I know damn well that Hiram can pass right through solid objects.

On the way up the stairs, I call Willy and get his voice mail. "Call me ASAP. I've got you in a shitload of trouble, old buddy."

Chapter 3

SCORPIO Oct. 23 – Nov. 21

Heed your own advice: Only you know what is best for you. Today you will have a lot on your mind. Oft-told tales are often the best-told tales. Each day drink eight glasses of water.

The minute I set foot in the newsroom, Melody jumps up from her desk, rushes over and gets in my face. "What did those awful men want?"

I plop down at my desk. "Nothing much."

"*Nothing much? They* wanted *nothing much?*" Melody puts her hands on her hips.

I turn to my screen and read Janet's newest horoscope. *A lot on my mind?* It's spooky how Janet so often gets things right. She sends me personalized horoscopes several times a day. Too much time on her hands.

Melody leans closer. "What did they want?"

"The one with the unabridged proboscis asked why I was barefoot."

"Don't be cute," Melody says, straightening up. "You're in some kind of trouble, aren't you?"

I pull on my left shoe. Trouble? "No, of course not."

"*No, of course not,*" Melody says. She watches me tie my sneaker.

"A problem shared is a problem halved."

I pick up my right shoe. "Uh-huh."

"That's it—*Uh-huh?*"

"Uh-huh."

Melody rolls her eyes and drifts back to her desk.

I shout, "Sorry, Melody. I have a lot on my mind right now!"

She doesn't turn around.

Melody's well-meaning and deserves better. We bicker a lot, but it's never serious, more like adolescent flirting. I'll make things up to her later by getting her talking about her daughter. That always puts her in a good mood.

Sherwood, who's basically a nice guy but lacks all social skills, once asked Melody who Dawn's father was. Melody said nothing, went back to her desk and sniffled into a tissue. I hurried over and made cheery small talk. It didn't seem to help, but she gave me a sweet smile anyway. She has a great smile.

I pull on my other shoe and look up. Uncle Sid is coming toward me. His walk is jerky, his features tight.

I say, "We have to talk."

"We sure as hell do."

"Tell me everything you can about the Ramsey brothers."

Uncle Sid glances around the newsroom, then turns back and lowers his voice to a low whisper. "Not here. There might be bugs. Let's walk."

He likes to think that the police, the FBI and the mob still take an interest in him after all these years. Or that they ever much did. Making his living as a magazine publisher doesn't fit his self-image. But I love my uncle and always play along. "Of course," I whisper. "Bugs."

We head down the backstairs to the alley and turn onto North Street. In a few minutes, we're in front of the Paul Revere house, one of Uncle Sid's favorite spots. We take a bench across from the site in a minuscule park enclosed by narrow cobblestone streets.

I say, "What's the story on Hank and Freddie?"

"The father trained Hank as the heir apparent and mostly ignored Freddie. Hank took over after a rival gang gunned down the old man about four years back. Technically, Freddie's his second in command, but he's mostly muscle. Anyway, why did they come to see you?"

"Hank wants me to investigate a shadowy company called OASIS. They gave him the contract for the building I mentioned in my article. He thinks they have ties to the government."

"How did the contract go to a bunch of mobsters?"

"Until my article came out, OASIS apparently thought they were dealing with a legit construction company in Providence. But its real owner is Hank."

We both turn to watch a woman across the street leading a dutiful line of preschoolers toward the entrance to the Paul Revere house, each clutching a rope.

Uncle Sid stands up. "Don't cooperate."

"Hank threatened to torch the magazine office."

Uncle Sid sits down. "Not good."

"Not good."

Uncle Sid pats my knee. "Okay, then you have to leave town until this blows over. I'll keep your salary coming. In fact, I'll even—"

"I'm not abandoning you to deal with the Ramseys alone,"

"I can handle them."

Yeah, sure. "I'm staying. End of discussion."

Uncle Sid falls silent and watches the school children across the street. "You got a plan?"

"No, but I'll string Hank along until I have one."

Uncle Sid pats my knee again. "I'm always here if you need advice."

"Thanks."

But I get lots of that. Too much of that. And I listen when I shouldn't.

Speaking of advice-givers, I spot my great-great-grandmother Clementine Beekle in front of the Paul Revere House, hovering a few inches off the ground and surrounded by school kids. She smiles at them and now and then touches a child's head, or tries to, her hand passing right through. No doubt she's reliving her days as a teacher back on the frontier. She wears a long black dress with a white bonnet laced tightly under her chin. I've never seen her in anything else.

I of course say nothing about Clementine to Uncle Sid. Over the years, I've wanted to tell him about my ancestral visits, but I never have because I knew I'd sound crazy. Which I might be.

Clementine has been showing up every few days to exhort me to get back together with Adele. "You get married and you stay married," Clementine scolds. "You've made a compact with God and with society. So you stay with your spouse, even if that person is a drunken, scheming, cheating lout who can go a whole year without even once telling the truth."

No secrets who she has in mind, married as she is to Hiram.

Clementine is a person—or ex-person—of strong opinion. Over the years, her advice has been as dicey as Hiram's—sometimes useful, more often disastrous.

What a couple Clementine and Hiram make: An ersatz cowpoke who wrote pulp novels, and a bossy schoolmarm with a peg leg.

Uncle Sid takes off his right shoe, massages his toes, puts the shoe back on. "How'd your private eye work out?"

"He turned out to be a dud. His replacement was worse. So I'm acting as my own PI."

Uncle Sid nods, falls silent.

He was proud when I won a Pulitzer, devastated when it was taken away. I'd written a series of articles on domestic-violence shelters in Massachusetts. The man who ran them had provided substandard care, embezzled funds and filed fake reports. But the four former employees I'd interviewed went on to recant their stories on the witness stand, each insisting I'd never talked to them. It couldn't be proven that the shelter owner had bribed the witnesses, so he got off free.

I didn't. I lost my Pulitzer for supposedly fabricating the interviews, then my job, my wife, my reputation and my dignity.

I have a special interest in shelters. When I was five, Mom checked us into one after my stepfather Mike gave her two black eyes. I wanted to stay there forever, but after a week Mike drove up and took us home. He and Mom chatted all the way home as if nothing had happened. I sat in the back seat and cried.

Uncle Sid said, "You still think the shelter operator bribed those people to lie on the witness stand?"

"Who else would have a motive?"

"No one, I guess."

"It was a monumentally stupid move," I said. "What made the jerk think he could bribe all nine witnesses? Besides that, his lawyer must have told him I'd recorded all the interviews."

Uncle Sid nods absently. He's heard this story too many times. "You still haven't got the recorder chips back?"

"Not yet. Adele says she has no idea where they are, and she won't let me into the condo to look for them."

Uncle Sid opens his mouth, then closes it. He's never liked Adele but has always kept it to himself.

We watch a school bus pull up in front of the Paul Revere house and deposit two dozen of the world's happiest and noisiest ten-year-olds.

"Kids have all the fun," Uncle Sid says. "Speaking of which, remember when you were about their age, and I'd just gotten back in circulation and took you to eat at that place near here? You gobbled down two whole plates of lasagna and four cannoli."

I know where this is going. An oft-told tale. "I remember."

"Then we toured the Revere House, and you upchucked right on the great man's rocking chair. There were slimy hunks of cannoli and lasagna all over the place." Sid tips his head back and chuckles. "The asshole guide just stood there and screamed at you."

"He screamed louder after you kicked him in the balls."

That was four-and-a-half years after the shooting, a few weeks after Uncle Sid got out of prison, and a couple years after I'd started talking again. I say, "Maybe by now they'll let us back in."

Uncle Sid shakes his head. "Better give it a little more time."

Chapter 4

Uncle Sid and I head back to the magazine office, neither speaking, lost in our own worlds. I keep checking over my shoulder for Clementine but don't see her. I do spot Hiram, however. Now and then he stops to tug up his baggy leather chaps. Hiram, the rodeo clown.

Uncle Sid heads to the office, but I continue on across Atlantic Avenue and settle onto a bench in Columbus Park, a grassy half circle facing the harbor. I need time to settle my nerves and figure out how to handle Hank and Freddie. If that's even possible.

Who'd have thought that one stupid article could get Uncle Sid, Willy and myself into such a shitload of trouble.

Boston's tall buildings rise off to the right. Behind me sit the three-story brick buildings of the North End. To my front, a blue tour boat pulls away from the dock. Passengers press against the railings, their smart phones raised to snap pictures. They're happy and carefree. Mobsters aren't chasing them.

I call my housemate Willy and leave another message: "Wait for me at home. We have to talk. This is important."

Willy treats few things as important, and probably won't take this seriously either. Willy's stubborn and independent and irritating. Also my best friend.

I'm reluctant to call Adele at the *Boston Globe* because we always end up arguing. Still, I need information, and she knows a lot, although less than she thinks she does. I get voice mail and leave a message. "When you worked in Washington, did you ever hear of a secretive outfit called OASIS, which is short for the 'Organization for Auditing Special Independent Systems'? Call back as soon as you can. Also, I'm dropping by tonight to search for my voice recorder's memory cards."

I keep bugging Adele for them, but she insists she doesn't know where they are. "I'm just so disorganized," she said the last time I called. "You know that, Jeff."

I do know that. But I also know I can't trust her to tell the truth.

I tap in the number of a former colleague at the *Globe* who once worked at the Washington bureau. Voice mail again. "Charlie, I'm trying to find out what I can about a privately held company called OASIS, which stands for the 'Organization for Auditing Special Independent Systems.' Please get back to me ASAP."

I start to Google OASIS when something hits my sneaker. A pacifier. A round-faced toddler in a stroller gives me a blank look. I pick up the pacifier and hand it to the mother, who wipes it on a tissue and stuffs it into the girl's mouth. "Cute kid," I say.

The mother nods—she already knew that—and moves on.

I watch them until they disappear. Adele didn't want kids.

"Cute?" Hiram says, settling down next to me. "The kid's got a face like a mule's rear end."

I slide to the far end of the bench. "I spotted your wife a few minutes ago."

"You always say that to get rid of me."

"I always want to get rid of you, but this time it's the truth."

Hiram grunts, pulls off his pointy-toed boots and massages his feet. A big toe pokes out of a hole in the left sock.

My ancestors wear the same outfit every time they appear. But I've never noticed a hole before. Can Hiram get a replacement? Are there clothing stores Back There? Or do new clothes materialize magically? Over the years, I've pretty much figured out the rules of ancestral visits, but have learned absolutely nothing about the place my ancestors refer to as Back There.

Dad went Back There when I was two years old.

"Hiram, whatever you have to say, I don't want to hear it."

He slides closer. "Here it is anyway: Some dark night, you're going to have to bushwhack Hank and Freddie in some back alley and blow their brains out."

"No."

"No?"

"No."

Hiram shakes his head. "Then there's nothing left but to hop on your horse and gallop out of town."

"I'm not shooting anyone, and I'm not running away."

Hiram takes off his hat and wipes the inside sweat band with a big red handkerchief. "Okay, then come up with a plan to get Hank and Freddie sent off to the hoosegow for a long stretch. Fabricate a crime. Or better, commit it yourself and lay out clues implicating the brothers."

"That," I say, "is straight from *Bill Bart Turns the Tables.*"

Hiram puts his hat back on. "One of my best efforts."

"Which isn't saying much. The trick was contrived in your novel, and in real life would get me killed. By the way, I read all your stuff as a kid. When I was a teenager, I picked up one of your novels and recognized it for the dreck it was."

Hiram snorts, then pulls his boots back on. "What do you know about writing fiction?—you're a journalist for cripes sake. Now listen to me: Either shoot those two hooligans or skedaddle." Hiram gives me an evil grin. "After all, you sure as heck know how to fire a gun."

"Shut the fuck up!"

The woman with the baby has looped back. She glances at me, lowers her eyes and breaks into a trot, the stroller jouncing over the seams in the sidewalk.

Hiram laughs and watches her hurry away. "One more thing: Before those two sidewinders kill you, you gotta get off your butt and get your darn Pulitzer back."

"Think I'm not trying? I've been bugging the attorneys who defended the shelter owner, but they won't talk to me. Same for the four witnesses who lied on the stand."

"Try harder," Hiram says and adjusts his gun belt. "Kids these days don't know what hard work is."

"Lecturing the boy again, are we?"

Hiram and I look up.

It's Clementine.

Hiram says, "That's your schoolmarm voice."

"That's your drunk voice. Have you been—"

"Heck, no. You're always accusing—"

"If I am it's because—"

"Be quiet!" I say. "Both of you."

They glare at me but do stop arguing.

Clementine nudges Hiram on the shoulder. "Move over."

He doesn't budge.

Clementine pushes him aside, sits down and tugs the hem of her dress down over her peg leg.

Hiram stands up.

She grabs his elbow and jerks him back down. Hard.

Hiram winces.

Ancestors can't feel us, and we can't feel them, but they do feel each other, talk to each other, and in general behave like the living, for good or for bad.

Clementine is a husky woman, a head taller than Hiram and in her late thirties. She looks his age even though he's twenty years older, the price she paid for marrying him. She looks concerned. Clementine lives in a perpetual state of concern. Again, the price for wedding Hiram.

She says, "Has either of you seen Ebenezer?"

"I haven't seen Grandpa for over a year," I say. "He doesn't visit much."

Hiram scratches his mustache, releasing a cloud of white flakes.

"Not for quite a spell."

Clementine closes her eyes and shakes her head. "He's cutting it close. He knows what happens if he doesn't get Back There in time."

Clementine's scared, something rare for this tough frontier lady.

She and Hiram worry about getting Back There late, but won't tell me why.

Clementine opens her eyes. "I'm afraid Ebenezer has once more strayed from the path of righteousness and in doing so has lost all sense of time. She takes off her bonnet, shakes her head and lets her gray hair fall to her shoulders. "I suppose I shouldn't be too hard on him, though. He had spotty parenting."

By that Clementine means Hiram. The two raised Ebenezer after both his parents died of cholera.

Hiram looks up at her. "Don't be so hard on yourself."

"Ha, ha," Clementine says dryly. She jerks her bonnet back down over her head, tucks her hair up inside and ties a tight bow under her chin. "You think you're funny, don't you?"

"I am funny," Hiram says. "My novels are hilarious. They—"

"You only *think* they're funny. No one else—"

"Is that so? Well just—"

I tune out.

I've always wondered why these two ever married and how they managed to stay together. They nevertheless look happy enough in the wedding picture on the wall of the old family home in Concord, where I've been living since my breakup with Adele. The picture hangs alongside a couple dozen other daguerreotypes, photos and painted portraits of my ancestors. Mom dubbed it the Ancestor Wall. She revered her forebears as well as Dad's. When I was five, she led me by the hand to the Ancestor Wall and told me that these were some of the smartest people in the whole world. She said that she wished they could talk so they could impart their wisdom to us.

I took that to heart. I would stand in front of the wall and make up lavish tales of heroism and noble deeds about my extraordinary grandparents and great-grandparents and the generations beyond. Most of all I was enthralled by the portrait of Hiram in a black cowboy hat and a string tie, his right hand clutching the reins of a palomino. A famous writer, Mom always said. When I got a little older, I read and reread his novels until the bindings gave out. His books appealed to me as a child because Hiram has the mind of a child. I soon wanted to become a famous writer like him.

After I learned to read and write, I made up a story about how Hiram single-handedly captured a gang of black-hatted outlaws, another of how he and his loyal wife Clementine—in spite of her peg leg—stopped a stampede from destroying a Kansas town, and another story of how my great-grandmother Colette made audiences swoon when she sang like a canary on the stages of Paris (Mom had not yet let slip that her grandmother was in fact a high-kicking dancer at gentlemen's clubs). I would show my writings to Mom, who always had high praise for them, although after I was ten her attention span had deteriorated so badly that she could no longer concentrate on the page and I had to read to her.

I wrote one story about Dad, but it made Mom cry, and that was the last.

Dad wears his firefighter's outfit in his photo on the Ancestor Wall, a red helmet tucked under his left arm. He's never visited me, nor did Mom after she died. Hiram said that parents never do. When I asked why, he said that's just the way things work Back There.

When I was a kid, I'd stand in front of Dad's photo and tell him what I'd done that day, hoping he'd approve. He died a hero, my mom would always tell me. Someone you should grow up to be just like.

I'm trying, but not doing much of a job of it.

Chapter 5

SCORPIO Oct. 23 – Nov. 21

Take time to smell the roses. A good friend is worth more than a pot of gold. Love is all around. Put a dish of soap and vinegar on your kitchen counter to drown those pesky fruit flies.

I call my housemate Willy on my way to the office and leave another message, then remember he took off work to attend a Red Sox game with his girlfriend. He's fixing up my old family home in exchange for free room and board and a modest salary while he looks for full-time work. Jobs are scarce for someone fresh out of prison.

I hurry up the backstairs to the office, plop down at my desk and grab my keyboard. I owe Melody a story. And an apology. I shouldn't have been so flippant with her earlier.

Sherwood brings me coffee. I thank him, but set the cup aside. My stomach still churns from the meeting with Hank and Freddie.

I delete the story about green space monsters invading Fenway Park—no need to piss off Hank even more—and type: "Unbelievable, but…" then stop. Okay, what's unbelievable? Well, faking an article that turns out to be almost true is unbelievable. I could write about that. And earn a pair of concrete shoes and a trip to the bottom of Boston Harbor. I continue typing. "Unbelievable, but the news from…"

From where? And what news?

Writer's block.

I can't get Hank and the murderous Freddie out of my head.

Melody edges over and stands next to my desk. She smells of roses. I look up at her. "Sorry I was so grumpy with you earlier. You deserve better."

"You're forgiven… this time." She taps her watch. "But I'm still waiting."

"It's almost finished."

She bends down and looks at my monitor. "Uh-huh."

"It's finished in my head."

"Uh-huh."

Ideas come easily when I'm relaxed but never when pressured. I could try to slip an old story past Melody with different people and different settings, but she remembers everything she's ever read.

She straightens up and puts her hands on her hips. "Well?"

She's still put out because I wouldn't tell her what Hank and Freddie wanted with me. Melody fusses over my wellbeing. Which is annoying. And sweet.

"Well?" she says again.

I take off my sneakers, line them up next to my chair, catch Melody's expression, put them back on.

I'll go with something I won't have to make up. I delete the few words I've written and type:

Ghostly Visits!

Thousands of Americans receive visitors from dead ancestors! During a year of intensive interviews and research, the *Boston Tattler* coaxed this shocking discovery from dozens of reluctant subjects. Highly skeptical at first, our crack team of reporters eventually turned into believers as a result of the absolute consistency among the persons interviewed.

Melody draws in her breath.

I look up. "What?"

She shakes her head. "Nothing."

Sherwood wanders over, coffee cup in hand, and peers at my screen. I continue:

These individuals turned out to be normal in every way. In fact, they tended to be highly intelligent, witty, personable and...

"Bonkers," Sherwood says. "Totally bonkers."

"No they're not, damn it!"

Sherwood steps back. "Just an observation."

I point at his desk. "Do your observing over there."

He shrugs and leaves.

Melody says, "Someone got up on the wrong side of the bed this morning."

"I always get up on the wrong side of the bed," I say, turning to look up at her. "I'll have this ready in a few minutes. You don't need to stick around."

She doesn't budge.

I type:

All the subjects interviewed testified that, as children, they had at one time or another seen pictures of the ancestors who visited them. In addition, only the ancestors in a direct line appeared, such as grandfather, great-grandmother, etc., but never a father or mother.

Melody leans closer. "That's incredible."

"I'm an incredible writer."

"That's not what I meant."

"So, I'm not an incredible writer?"

Melody straightens up, says nothing.

I decide that her perfume smells more like lilac than rose. I can hear her soft breathing, feel her warmth. I turn back to my keyboard:

> The deceased ancestor and the descendant they visit can carry on normal conversations but cannot make physical contact. Outsiders can neither hear nor see the ghostly apparition. However, ancestors can interact with each other just as they had in real life—through speaking, listening, touching. There remains much speculation as to where an ancestor dwells when not visiting a descendant, just as there is a great cloak of mystery surrounding...

I finish in thirty-eight minutes—eight hundred and fourteen words in thirty-eight minutes. A new record. I do a quick reread—twice changing 'shocking' to 'terrible' for Hiram's sake.

"Okay?" I say to Melody. She's been watching me the whole time. It's nice having her around.

She nods.

I slap my forehead, then tap the screen. "Oops, I hyphenated a proper noun."

I do that from time to time to get a rise out of Melody.

She doesn't react, apparently not in the mood for games.

I lean back in my chair. "I'm keen on learning everything I can about hyphenation. Are you free for dinner?"

Melody is absorbed in something and at first doesn't register what I've said. She blinks her eyes, takes a step back and shakes her head. "I have to pick up Dawn from day care."

"Bring her along."

Melody turns to leave. "She doesn't go out with married men."

I send her the article, which she'll devote much more attention to it than it deserves. Melody is bright, hardworking and kind, and knows more about the English language than anyone I've ever met. In fact, she might know more about anything than anyone I've ever met. I'm guessing she remains at the magazine only because Uncle Sid gives her—a single mother—lots of flex time to be with her four-year-old daughter. I also suspect that he pays her a fat salary, just as he pays all of us fat salaries. None of us understands how he does that and keeps the magazine afloat—or why he became a magazine publisher in the first place, this man who never reads.

While waiting for Melody to edit my article, I call Adele at work and get voice mail. I phone again and listen to the phone ring. She avoids my calls—out of sadness over my lost Pulitzer, she claims. She always says she was devastated after she found out I'd lost the prize, absolutely devastated.

Uh-huh.

Finally, Adele answers. "Oh, hello Jeff. I was at a meeting."

Uh-huh.

Her voice is sweet, unctuous, false.

I say, "While you were on assignment in Washington, did you ever hear of an outfit called OASIS, the Organization for Auditing Special Independent Systems?"

Long pause. "No, I don't think so. I'm sure I'd remember an untidy name like that."

That's her calm voice when she's telling the truth.

"Who might know?" I ask.

"Um… let's see. Try Charlie Miller."

"I've already contacted him. Anyone else?"

"Not that I can think of."

Again, her truth-telling voice.

"Also, as I mentioned in my earlier voice mail, I'm coming by this evening to search for my recorder's memory chips."

"No, you're not, Jeffrey. This is *my* home now. And I've been telling you for weeks that I can't find them."

"Because you're so messy, right?"

"No… on account of the burglary."

I let this sink in. "Burglary? What burglary?"

"The one I told you about."

"You never told me about a burglary," I say. "Were you home at the time? Are you okay?"

"I was away, and yes, I did tell you about it. You weren't listening. You never listen to me. In fact—"

"Let's hear your tale about the burglary."

"It is *not* a tale," Adele says. "It was devastating, just devastating. I was so absolutely devastated that I'm still not sure what else they took."

"So," I say, "you're telling me that, on his way out the door, your rascally intruder paused long enough to scoop up a half dozen cheap memory chips?"

"Something like that," Adele says, her voice distant.

"Why don't I come over and look for them anyway? Just in case the burglar didn't take them after all and you missed them in all the clutter."

"Don't even think about it. You're not allowed to set foot in my home. I said that just a minute ago. See, you never listen."

I take a couple of deep breaths. "You're right. Forget about it. But if you do find my stuff, be sure to give me a call."

Fat chance that'll ever happen.

I hang up and dig out my keys and check that I still have the one for our Beacon Street condo.

●   ●   ●

I leave work early to be home by the time Willy gets back from the game. If there's any chance he'll take my warnings about Hank seriously, I'll have to confront him face-to-face. I get my pickup from the lot, then head west toward Concord. The truck shimmies and smokes, which means it's running normal. Carless after the separation, I picked the truck up for $410. Both doors announce in bright red, 'Larry's Portable Latrines. Free Delivery and Instalation.' I refuse to paint over the lettering or even correct the misspelling. My transportation fits my budget, my state of mind, and my way of giving the finger to the world. The truck doesn't smell, but that didn't stop Adele from holding her nose the first time she saw me drive up in it.

She bought a shiny silver Lexus after she cleaned out our joint bank account. My lawyer's working on that.

A mile east of Concord, I turn up the driveway to the family home. It's a large white colonial that sits alone on a hillock looking across a reedy marsh. My missing Grandfather Ebenezer—Dad's father—had the place built before he went to prison for running a Ponzi scheme. He was a man with no moral compass, Mom once told me, always scheming, always looking for a way to make a fast buck, always loads of fun.

Mom died when I was fourteen, and Uncle Sid moved into the house to look after me. He went back to Boston after I left for college, and I rented the place out to one unpromising tenant after another, each one leaving things in a worse condition than when they moved in. Mom loved the house. She'd lived there for her entire adult life. The week before she died, she made me promise never to sell it. Eventually, I wasn't even able to find renters. Too much to heat in the winter, prospects said. And where's the dishwasher? And is that mold in those ceiling stains? And why is that room sealed off? ("A rotting floor" I replied. "It gave way two summers ago, and my cousin Gomer fell through and fractured his tibia.")

In fact, it was the room where I shot my stepfather. It's been nailed closed for decades.

So the house stood empty until I moved back in after losing my Pulitzer and my job at the *Globe* and after Adele kicked me out. She claimed I'd become impossible to live with.

The Concord house is packed with memories, good and bad.

I unlock the front door, follow the hallway to the kitchen, grab a Heineken from the fridge, and plop down at the table. Willy's phone sits on top, recharging.

Willy forgets to carry his phone, doesn't pay bills on time, lets his driver's license expire, and gets arrested trying to sell a stolen backhoe on eBay, having not bothered to paint over the construction company's name. He never plans, never worries, never regrets. Which means in most ways we're opposites. He hates to exercise, and I'm a fanatic. He never reads, and I read too much. He hunts and I don't. He drives fast, and I drive slowly. The list is long. We're best friends.

Willy and Uncle Sid are the only people alive who know I killed my stepfather, and Willy is the only person who knows that ancestors visit me. I was ten when I broke down in tears and told him about the killing and about my ancestors. I made him swear not to tell anyone. I said I was afraid that I was crazy and would get locked away forever because I talked to dead people and had murdered someone. All Willy said was, "Shit happens," and we never talked about the subject again.

I'm halfway through my second beer when I hear the front door open. Willy saunters into the kitchen. He's short, wide-shouldered and muscular, with a round head covered in wavy black hair down to his shoulders. He wears a purple T-shirt that reads "Not Sorry." He grabs a beer from the refrigerator, drops down across from me and says, "You look like shit."

"I feel like shit."

He taps his bottle against mine. "Cheer up. The Red Sox kicked Yankee ass."

"I got you in trouble."

"I doubt it," Willy says. He tilts his bottle back and takes a long swig.

"You doubt it?"

"You're always talking about trouble," Willy says, and scratches his two-day-old beard. "You're a worrier."

"Goddamn it, Willy, this is serious!"

"Uh-huh." He stands up. "Bring your beer. I want to show you what I'm going to fix up next. Do your talking on the move."

I watch him go, then get up and follow him into the living room.

Willy thumps the wall. "See how it bows out here?"

"Two mobsters threatened to kill me."

"No shit?" Willy says. He thumps the wall again. "I think the studs have rotted."

"Willy, listen, goddamn it!"

He looks up.

I tell him about the article I wrote, about Hank and Freddie's threats and about how they've forced me to spy on OASIS for them.

"That's gnarly," Willy says. He gets on his knees and pries the baseboard off with a screwdriver. "But what does all that have to do with me?"

"The mobsters wanted to know who told me about the site."

Willy examines the back of the baseboard. "Did you tell them it was me?"

"Of course not. I said I made everything up."

Willy lies on his side and pokes the studs with the screwdriver. "It's all good."

"What's all good?"

"I don't see signs of rot."

"Goddamn it, Willy, if Hank finds out you're living with me, he'll know you're my source!"

Willy shakes his head. "The whole eight months I worked at the site I never once saw Hank or Freddie or anyone else from the mob, which means they never saw me. They don't know I exist."

"You're sure?"

Willy bangs the board back in place with the side of his fist and scrambles to his feet. "On paper someone else owns the company, not a bunch of gangsters. Which means they don't want to be seen at the construction site."

"I still want you to get out of town."

Which is what Hiram told me to do.

"Can't leave," Willy says, rolling his eyes and taking on a look of woe. "I'm too busy. My boss is a son-of-a-bitch who's always busting my ass. Fix this, fix that. A real bastard."

"The mob will spot you if they're watching the house."

"Yeah, but like I said, they don't know I worked at the site. Follow me."

He leads me into the study and points at the ceiling above the Ancestor Wall. "Rain is coming in through the siding and seeping into the ceiling. That's gotta be fixed next, or those pictures are going to get wet." Willy climbs onto a chair and pokes the screwdriver into the ceiling stain.

Grandpa Ebenezer stares at me from his photo on the wall. He's about fifty in the picture, the same age as when he visits me. He's a handsome, big-bellied man with a curled black mustache. He, too, appears to be fretting over the condition of the ceiling of the house he'd built. Or is he worried about being away too long from Back There?

In the photo to Grandpa's right, Hiram wears a tall cowboy hat and holds the reins of a palomino, no doubt rented for the occasion. He shows up again in the wedding portrait directly below, with Clementine beside him, a head taller, both legs still intact. In the photo below, she holds a stunningly ugly baby.

Nearby, my great-grandmother on Mom's side wears a coy look, her head turned partially sideways, her forehead half hidden under a mass of dark curls. Colette looks about forty in her photo and forty on those rare occasions when she visits. We communicate easily since she's fluent in English and French because her father was a Parisian and her mother British. Colette was a dancer until the Germans occupied France in 1940. During her whirlwind visits to me, she brags about affairs with Henri Matisse, with the 1936 winner of the Tour de France, two French presidents and with Simone de Beauvoir.

Colette's a chatty woman, sultry and boisterous, and was decorated for her work with the French underground in World War II. A hero like Dad.

Her daughter, Giselle, married a GI in the late 1950s and moved to the States two months before Mom was born. Giselle visited me when I seven, but things were awkward because I hadn't started talking again, so she never showed up again.

Dad's photo hangs below Colette's, a firefighter's helmet tucked under his left arm. My dad was six foot three, like me. I inherited his big jaw, wide eyes and curly brown hair. Mom would always tell me how much I looked like him, then start to sob. Mom cried a lot, especially in her last years. I'd try to cheer her up—pratfalls, jokes I'd heard at school, fictional deer sightings in the backyard. Sometimes it worked, usually it didn't.

I lean closer to the photo. Dad looks concerned. Is he seeing his early death? Or is he judging me? Does he see a failure? A loser? A fraud? A crazy person? All those things?

I look up at Willy, still standing on the chair and poking the ceiling with his screwdriver. "What if I fire you and kick your ass out of my house?"

"You'd do that?"

"I sure as hell would if it saves the Ramseys from coming after you."

Willy looks down at me, grins and spreads his arms. "Okay, go ahead."

I say nothing.

"Thought so," Willy says. He gives the ceiling one more jab, then hops off the chair. "Follow me." He leads me down the hallway toward the Shooting Room.

That's what it's always been in my mind—the Shooting Room. And what it always will be.

Three days after the shooting, Uncle Sid phoned a friend from jail and got him to drive out to the house, slap plywood over both windows and nail the door shut. The room's been sealed ever since.

Willy taps the bottom of the door with his toe. "It's time to open up this room. We'll turn it into a man cave—you know, a huge mother of a TV, a screecher sound system, a floor-standing popcorn machine on big red wheels, two fat leather sofas and a bar. We'll start with the bar."

I shake my head.

Willy reaches up, puts his hand on my shoulder and gives it a squeeze. "I know what you're thinking, but I'll fix the place up so you won't recognize it. I'll strip the wallpaper, paint the walls, tear up the carpet and sand the floors. Shit, it'll be beautiful. You'll love it. Face it, Jeff, it's time to move on."

I see blood pooling on the carpet. I see blood dripping down the green flowered wallpaper. I see blood leaking from the hole in my stepfather's forehead.

That day my great-great-grandfather Hiram was wearing a black cowboy hat and a string tie, just like in his photo on the Ancestor Wall. But this time he wasn't in the photo. He was standing right there beside me.

"Not yet, Willy," I say, shaking my head. "Not yet."

Chapter 6

SCORPIO Oct. 23 – Nov. 21

Embrace strangers as old friends. Surprises make life worth living. Wash your sneakers at least once a month.

It's midmorning before I get into work. Sherwood is sitting at his computer, with Melody standing behind him. She looks upset, but he wears a big smile. Rare for him.

He looks up from his monitor. "Hey, Jeff. Come on over. You've hit a home run, bases loaded, bottom of the ninth."

"What's so funny?"

"Your article. Or better, our readers' reaction to your article."

"Which article?"

"The one about people conversing with their ancestors."

"It hasn't gone to print yet," I say.

"No, but it went online last evening."

"Right."

Normally, I don't pay attention to feedback from my readers. They consider me either a fool or a genius. I don't know which is worse. This time in particular, I'm reluctant to hear from them. "Not interested."

"Come on, take a look," Sherwood says, waving me over. "You're in for a surprise."

I hesitate, then sidle over and stand next to Melody, who gives me a look I can't interpret. Disbelief? Concern?

Sherwood opens an email from someone named Gloria:

> Elvis visits me and we talk and he's a real sweet fellow. He looks just as scrumptious as he does in his photos. I have them everywhere on my walls. All along I thought he was just being nice to come and see me but it turns out he's my very own ancestor! Me? Related to the World's Greatest Singer and the World's Greatest Human Being? Thanks! Thanks! Thanks! Love you!
> Gloria G.

Sherwood says, "A nut case."

"Maybe," I say, "but I made her happy. What's wrong with that?"

Sherwood glances up at me, shrugs, rotates back to the screen and opens a new email. "Here's one in bad need of Melody's editing."

> I talk to grandpa Alfred like he's right their standing acrost from me and what he says makes me feel well again and thanks to the lady and or gentleman whose wrote that fine article to make me feel well again.
> Marvin P.
> Thanks again.

Sherwood says, "We bought Marvin some books and sent him to school, but all he did was chew on the covers."

"Show some humanity, for Christ sake," I say. "If Marvin thinks his late grandfather visits him, and if it gives him comfort, then what the fuck's the problem?"

Janet the Horoscope Lady gets up from her desk and limps across the room. She started working at the magazine the same day I did. She's a soft, short, vinegar-scented woman who wears the same long black dress and purple neck scarf every day. No one knows if it's the same outfit, or if she has a closet full of matching clothing. She's everyone's aunt, grandmother, kindly third-grade teacher. She's constantly inquiring about my welfare and is always ready with soothing advice. For my part, I know nothing about her, where she lives, where she grew up, and whether she has a family. A sweet mystery.

She writes the horoscopes and the advice column and creates a weekly crossword puzzle from scratch. She's a bundle of energy.

Melody and I step aside for her. I pull out a chair.

Janet sits. "Jeff's right, Sherwood. You should be ashamed of yourself for making fun of our readers. And who knows? Maybe ancestors do sometimes return for visits?"

Janet lives in a world of prophesies, magic crystals, kindly elves.

"I agree with Janet," Melody says, starting back to her desk. "We shouldn't make fun of our readers."

Good for Melody. If I were to tell anyone besides Willy about my frequent visits from Back There, it would be her or Janet. Janet would probably believe me. Melody maybe not, but in any case she'd comfort me in my nuttiness.

The next email comes from twin sisters in Kansas City who "frequently share delightfully long ancestral dinners with Napoleon."

A chuckle from Sherwood, but it's a quiet one for fear of upsetting Janet and pissing me off again.

He says, "Read this one. The lady's as loony as the others, and she's way too wordy, but at least she can write a decent sentence."

Dear Sir or Madame:

I wish to thank the lovely person who wrote that wonderful article about ancestors who visit the living. You cannot begin to understand how relieved I was when I read your piece online last night and discovered that there are others out there in the world just like me. For the past forty-seven years, I have clutched my secret tightly to my chest, living with the fear that I am insane, living with the fear that the day would come when I could no longer contain my painful secret, living with the terror that some Sunday morning I would lose control and stand up at church and—right in the middle of the preacher's sermon—announce that my great-grandmother Anna visits me almost daily.

"Crazy but literate," Sherwood says.

"Dial it down," I say.

"Someone got up on the wrong side of the bed," Sherwood says.

That's one of Melody's favorite expressions. Sherwood likes to make fun of her because she sends his articles back covered in corrections. He never mocks her in her presence, however, because he's afraid of her. Sherwood is afraid of everyone.

He says, "The lady has more."

Just as you described, my great-grandmother appears first as a mere shimmer, then becomes a semi-transparent outline, then turns full color. She disappears in the reverse order.

Stuff from my article, nearly word-for-word, only I used 'disturbance' and she used 'shimmer,' hers the better word choice. She goes on:

I would like to add that my great-grandmother looks exactly the way she does in her portrait on my bedroom wall. She often visits at moments when I most need advice, comfort and friendship.

Whoever you are, you have changed my life. Although I will guard my secret to my grave, I have the satisfaction of knowing that there are others like me. You are a wonderful journalist and a wonderful person.

Thank you.

Eleanor Peterson

P. S. I am confident that you will not make my name public.

Sherwood rotates his chair toward me. "Gosh, Jeff, I always knew you were a wonderful journalist, but as for your being a wonderful person, I—"

"Give it a fucking rest," I say. "And stop making fun of Eleanor. And Melody. And everyone else."

Sherwood turns back to his screen.

I return to my desk in a fog. Are all those people who responded to the article insane? Putting us on? Or could they actually…?

No, that's impossible. Sherwood's right that most of our readers are bat-shit crazy. Every day we get emails about trips on space ships that involved untidy bodily probes, poodles fluent in French, rock-solid proof that LBJ killed JFK, and designs for aluminum-foil headgear that prevents government thought rays from penetrating the skull.

It would be nice if I weren't alone. No, a hell of a lot better than nice. It would be great. Soothing. And wouldn't it be fun to talk to others like me? To compare notes? To make fun of our ancestors? To discuss our scars even?

My mind wanders a while longer, then I start a new article:

Squeezebox Duchess

Last week one of our sharp-eyed reporters spotted a heavily disguised Kate Middleton, the glam spouse of Britain's Prince William, in a Houston bar playing the accordion in a Lawrence Welk tribute band. Sources close to the Royal family insist that…"

I stop typing and look up from my monitor. Eleanor talked about when and why her ancestors visit. My piece said nothing about that.

Or have I forgotten? I reread the article. Nope, no mention of the subject.

A coincidence? Coincidences do happen. After all, I cooked up a story about a mob-built prison for aliens that turned out to be true—or at least almost true. And haven't I read about people who've won the lottery more than once? In fact, each of us experiences a thousand events a day, and billions of people inhabit the Earth, each experiencing a thousand events a day. That means that it would be impossible for bizarre coincidences not to be a common occurrence.

I let out my breath. How long have I been holding it?

Still…

I open a reader's email forwarded from the receptionist at the front desk. It's mostly chatter, but one paragraph stands out:

> What surprises me is that my ancestors show up as mature adults but before the age when disease or accident brings their life to a close. And another thing is that I can never get a straight answer when I ask about where they are when they're not visiting me. They call the place 'Back There.'

Back There?

I sit up straight.

You gotta be kidding!

That sure as hell wasn't in my article!

I push my keyboard aside and jump to my feet.

I am not crazy!

My heart speeds up. I feel warm all over.

I am not crazy! I am not crazy! I am not crazy!

I close my eyes, breathe slowly, smell lilacs, open my eyes. Melody is standing beside me.

She says, "Sid will be as happy as a calf in clover about all the attention your article about ancestors is getting."

"Uh… right."

"Hmm, you're flushed." She reaches up and places her hand on my forehead. "What's going on?"

Her hand is soft and cool.

"I'm trying to remember whether or not Kate Middleton can play the accordion."

"That's *not* what you're thinking," Melody says, and pulls her hand away. "Something's got you in a tizzy. Tell me what's really bothering you."

I wish I could. I wish I could tell her about the visits from my dead ancestors and about the gangsters who are threatening my uncle if I don't do what they want. And I wish I could tell her about my joy at discovering that I'm not alone in my madness.

"Nothing's bothering me. In fact, I feel great, buoyant, ecstatic, joyous, giddy."

Melody tilts her head to the side and squints. "Your response to a well-received article usually makes you come up with something smarty and cynical."

"This one's special."

"How?"

"It just is."

I feel happy for myself and happy that one of my loopy tales has brought relief to my readers. I've pulled together a community. I think of how much better Gloria will feel the next time Elvis visits, Marvin when his grandfather shows up, the twins dining with Napoleon, Eleanor and her great-grandmother Anna.

I feel free, floating, capable of flapping my arms and taking to the air.

The newsroom is tight, the air stale, the room gloomy. I need sunlight and open spaces. Freedom to fly.

I switch off my monitor. "After my uncle gets in, tell him I'll be back in a couple hours. I'm too antsy to work right now. I need to get outside, go for a walk, maybe jog along the Charles."

"Are you sure you're feeling okay?"

"Never been better."

I bound down the backstairs, trot down the alley, turn left at the sidewalk and keep on going. I head one direction, then another, and on a whim turn around and go back. It's a bright and sunny day, a beautiful day. People are beautiful. Life is beautiful. It's a day of flowers and puffy white clouds, of gentle warm breezes and bird song. I whistle—when was the last time I whistled? I smile at everyone, shove my hands into my pockets, whistle louder.

It's not a day to worry about Hank and Freddie, Hiram and Clementine, my crappy job, my dismal finances, a destroyed marriage, a lost Pulitzer, a leaky roof, and maybe most of all the absent Ebenezer, who has Hiram and Clementine worried in a way I've never seen.

I am not alone. I am not alone. I am not alone.

As soon as I get back to the office, I'll set up interviews with the readers who've responded to my article. I'll tell them I'm doing a follow-up that might interest the scientific community. It'll be a chance to meet my kind, face to face.

My kind.

I haven't been this blissed-out since the Pulitzer board called to say I'd won, since Adele agreed to marry me, since getting accepted into Cornell, since I was ten and Mom drove me to the prison gate and I rushed into Uncle Sid's arms. Sweet memories.

I smile at a petite blonde in a Harvard T-shirt who smiles back. I smile at a pensive tall priest who nods, at a teenage boy on a skateboard who grunts, at a wrinkly faced man in a dark suit who blocks my path and pulls his jacket aside to show me a holstered pistol.

I step back.

He steps forward.

His hair is an unconvincing black, his face tanned and wrinkled, his eye bags enormous.

I half raise my arms, take another step back, bump into someone.

A hood comes down over my head, everything goes black, a pistol presses into my gut, someone pins my arms behind my back, drags me to a vehicle, shoves me inside, pushes me down, slams the door.

We screech away.

Chapter 7

SCORPIO Oct. 23 – Nov. 21

Adventure is the spice of life. You can never have too many pals. A thick layer of vinegar will get rid of that closet mold.

"Where in hell are you taking me?" I ask.

"Shut up."

"Who in hell are you?"

"Shut up."

I lie sideways on the back seat, my wrists tied behind my back, my knees crunched up against my chest, soaked in a nervous sweat and my gut in a knot. The hood scratches my nose and smells like dirty socks. We stop after a half hour. Two men drag me from the vehicle and push me through a door. They plop me down on a hard chair, untie my hands and jerk the hood off.

I blink and look around. I'm seated in the middle of a large empty warehouse that stinks of rodent droppings. A rusting yellow forklift sits nearby, and wooden pallets lie in piles all over the place. A hoist hangs from an overhead track. Will I end up dangling from it?

The guy with the big eye bags says, "I'm Drucker Ames." He nods toward a buff, bald younger man standing nearby. "That's Johnny."

Drucker looks about fifty. He smells of cigarettes and wears a pricey Breitling watch and a suit costing a couple thousand dollars. Adele bought me one like that soon after we married, but I was too embarrassed to wear it. I wonder if I'll ever see the suit again. Or her. Or anyone.

Johnny opens a folding chair for Drucker, who sits down opposite me. Johnny pulls up a chair for himself but stands behind it. He takes off his jacket, folds it with great care, and lays it on his chair. There's a pistol in his shoulder holster.

"This is a cliché," I say, "the victim tied to a chair in a warehouse by mobsters in expensive suits."

"You're not tied to the chair," Drucker says. "And we're not mobsters."

He speaks slowly, choosing his words with care. An educated voice.

I say, "When I talked with your boss, I promised I'd cooperate. So why in hell did you snatch me?"

"What boss? What in hell are you talking about?"

"Hank Ramsey."

Drucker snorts. "He's not my boss. What makes you think I work for a mobster?"

Of course he wouldn't admit it.

Sparrows chatter in the overhead beams. I smell mold, rotting wood, and my toxic sweat.

Drucker takes fingernail clippers from his pocket. He reads my expression. "No, I'm not planning on ripping out your nails."

"I didn't think you were."

I did think he was.

He trims the little fingernail on his left hand, slowly and with great attentiveness. *Click, click, click.* He glances up at me. "This is just an ordinary nail clipper," he says, holding it up and snapping it shut a couple times, then getting back to work. "You have too much imagination."

Probably. But that's how I make my living. "I don't know who you think you've abducted, but you got the wrong man."

Drucker looks up again. "Now that *is* a cliché. No, we got the right guy. You're Jeffrey Henry Beekle. You're thirty-four years old, six feet three-and-a-quarter inches tall, and you weighed 220 pounds at your last annual checkup. Your fireman father died in the line of duty in… let's see… in 1985. Your stepfather was killed when you were six. That's when you went mute. Your mother home-schooled you until you started talking again two years later. You went through the Concord public school system, then to Cornell and on to the Columbia School of Journalism. Afterward, you got a job at the *Boston Globe*. Your mother died in 1997, you married Adele Throckmorton in… uh… 2013, and she kicked you to the curb about three months ago. Sound about right?"

Drucker goes back to clipping his nails.

My pulse pounds in my temples. "How do you know all this?"

"Because I do," Drucker says.

"Why do you want to know it?"

"Because I do," Drucker says. "Notice I didn't bring up the Pulitzer you lost? That's because I wanted to spare your feelings. It can't be fun losing a Pulitzer. In fact, it must hurt every time you hear the word 'Pulitzer.'" Drucker looks up and gives me a big smile. "So I won't say the word 'Pulitzer' again."

"You're all heart." I glance over at the door. Much too far away. "Who are you?"

"You asked that before."

Again I look at the door.

Johnny grins at me and pats his pistol.

If he got close enough, I could probably drop him with one punch and make a try at Drucker. But Johnny is staying a safe distance back. A pro.

Drucker says, "We brought you here just for a friendly little chat."

"Yeah? Then why all the drama—the hood, the abandoned warehouse, the guns. Why didn't you set up an appointment like a civilized person?"

"First of all, because I like drama. Second, I'm not all that civilized. Third, I don't want to be seen talking to you. Finally, if I had gone to your crummy magazine to talk to you, would I have had your full attention the way I do now?"

I say nothing.

Drucker says, "I thought so."

"Tell Hank I won't write any more stories about the site."

"I told you already he's not my boss. You have to learn to pay better attention. But I'm glad you mentioned the fellow, because he's the reason we're here having this nice little tête-à-tête. I saw your colorful piece about the secret government prison and the mob connection."

"You read the *Tattler?*"

"Normally not. I have better taste. Now shut up and let me talk— we've got the guns, remember? What prompted you to write that piece?"

"Why do you care?"

"Because I do. Answer my question. Why did you write it?"

"I was under a tight deadline, so I made the thing up on the spur of the moment."

Drucker shakes his head. "Someone talked to you."

"No, they didn't. But even if someone had—which they didn't—I would never reveal my source. It's my right as a journalist."

Drucker snorts. So does Johnny.

Drucker says, "You write for a cheap rag and don't get to call yourself a journalist anymore. Did someone in the Ramsey gang tip you off about the OASIS site?"

"Of course not. I don't consort with mobsters."

"That's funny," Drucker says, scratching his left ear. "Because I'd swear we spotted you chatting up Hank and Freddie Ramsey in the alley behind the magazine office."

Uh, oh.

"Were you following me?" I ask.

"No, we were following Hank and Freddie."

"Why?"

"Because they're gangsters," Drucker says. "It was a coincidence that you were there."

"Do you have a habit of following gangsters?"

"I ask the questions, remember?" Hank says. "Why did Hank come to see you?"

"He… wants me to write something about how the FBI unfairly treats honest businessmen like him."

"That's bullshit. Did the visit have something to do with your mobbed-up uncle?"

Mobbed-up uncle?

"My Uncle Sid's been straight for years."

Drucker grins, exchanges looks with Johnny, then pockets his nail clippers.

"No, really, he has. He's—"

"What did Hank say about the construction contracts?"

"What contracts?"

"The five follow-ups that were canceled after you wrote your goddamn article."

I settle back in my chair to let this sink in. Hank lost five contracts? No wonder he was so ripped with me. Did Drucker snatch me because he's afraid of Hank? Probably. People fear Hank. I sure as hell do.

"You had something to do with Hank and the site's construction?" I ask.

"Could be," Drucker says, "but you didn't answer my question."

"Hank never said anything about any contracts. Why would he? And who in hell are you? Do you work for the feds?"

Drucker turns his chair around, sits backward on it, rests his forearms on the back and studies me for a long moment. "What I have to say stays with just the three of us, got it?"

"Do I have a choice?"

"No," Drucker says. "To answer your earlier question, I work for a private company that's contracted to a government agency. We're called OASIS, which stands for the 'Organization for Auditing Special Independent Systems.' You've probably never heard of us."

Actually, I have—from Hank when he coerced me into spying on OASIS. Small world. Small and dangerous world. What a goat rodeo. "Why did OASIS give a building contract to Hank Ramsey?"

Drucker watches a sparrow circling overhead. "We didn't know he owned the construction company. We got burned." He turns back to me. "We want you to do a little investigating for us."

"Investigating? Aren't there people at OASIS who can do the job better than I can?"

"None of them has a connection to Hank Ramsey."

"I've only met him once," I say.

"Once more than they have."

I let this sink in. "You want me to work for OASIS?"

Drucker shakes his head. "Not directly. You'll be working for me, and I work for OASIS. That's all you need to know. Now shut up and listen. Your first job will be to find out what Hank Ramsey thinks the site will be used for."

"I can tell you that right now. He said it's to hold foreign terrorists."

Drucker pushes his tongue around inside his mouth, the right cheek, the left, the right again, then nods, satisfied by my answer.

"Okay," he says. "Here's the deal: You're going to find out if Hank's got plans to make a move against OASIS. Losing those contracts didn't put him in the best of moods. That's not a comfortable situation when one is dealing with a mobster."

"That's your problem," I say, again glancing at the door. Again Johnny pats his pistol. "What makes you think I'd work for you?"

"We have the guns."

"Shoot me," I say, spreading my arms, "and I won't be worth anything to you."

Drucker looks up at Johnny. "Think we should?"

Johnny screws up his mouth, shrugs, shakes his head.

Drucker turns back to me. "Johnny's a softie, so I won't take you up on your offer as long as you do what I tell you to do."

"Sure, no problem. I shouldn't have any trouble infiltrating the mob and becoming best buds with Hank. He'll be glad to discuss his criminal activities with me, right before he puts a bullet through my head."

"You know what I'm talking about, wiseass," Drucker says. "Sniff around and get chummy with some low-level sleazeball in Hank's organization, some guy with a gripe. Get the goon drunk in a bar and start him talking. That's what you're good at, right? You won a Pulitzer, after all. Or at least for about a month, anyway." Drucker examines his nails, first the left hand, then the right. "Oops, I said 'Pulitzer' again."

"And let me say this again: There's not a chance in hell I'll cooperate with you."

Drucker stands up, yawns and presses his hands against the small of his back. "My girlfriend's an FBI agent. She specializes in money laundering."

"Good for her."

"And bad for your uncle."

I don't like the sound of that. "Why?"

Drucker tilts his head. "You're telling me you don't know?"

"Know what?"

"About twelve years ago, there was this dumb jerk who ran up a fat gambling tab with the Ramsey gang that he couldn't pay back. So Freddie broke both the guy's wrists, then the mob took over his magazine and forced your uncle to run it so they could wash their gambling and prostitution money through it."

"That's bullshit. My uncle owns the magazine."

"That's what everyone thinks," Drucker says. "In fact it's part of a corporation the Ramsey's secretly control."

"I don't believe you."

"Believe me."

"That doesn't make any sense," I say. "People launder money

through cash-intensive businesses like strip clubs, car washes and casinos. Who ever heard of laundering money through a magazine?"

"That's the point. It doesn't raise a red flag with the IRS."

That does make sense. I wish it didn't.

So that's why Uncle Sid has been able to pay us so well, and that's why he became a magazine publisher, a man I've never seen reading a book, a newspaper or a magazine except for the *Tattler*.

Some investigative reporter I am. I should have figured this out long ago. Does Melody know of the mob connection? Sherwood? No, because both have too much integrity to stick around if they did. Where's my integrity? Should I quit my job? Not yet. For now I can't leave Uncle Sid alone to deal with the Ramseys. He took the fall for me after I shot my stepfather, and he raised me after Mom died. I owe him more than I can ever pay back.

Drucker starts filing his left thumbnail. "Personally, I don't give a rat's ass about your uncle's shady dealings, but the Feds do. With your uncle's prison record and his long association with the Ramsey mob, it wouldn't be hard to get the charges to stick. He'd do a shitload of hard time."

I see my Uncle Sid outside the prison that day twenty-four years ago, sad and thin, holding up his baggy trousers with one hand, and with the other gripping his personal effects in a brown paper bag.

That's not something I want to happen again. Uncle Sid wouldn't survive a long term in prison.

"Well?" Drucker asks.

I nod.

Drucker waves the nail file and grins. "You and me, I can see us becoming real good pals."

Uh-huh.

I've just made a deal with the devil.

No, with two devils: Drucker has blackmailed me into investigating Hank, and Hank has blackmailed me into investigating Drucker.

"Right," I say. "Pals."

Chapter 8

SCORPIO Oct. 23 – Nov. 21

One of life's great joys is making new friends. A heart is won with kind words. Reflect on what the world would be like if you were never born. Get enough fiber.

Drucker's goon pulls the hood down over my head, ties my hands behind my back, steers me to a car, pushes me into the back seat and orders me to curl up and lie down. We drive in silence for a half hour, then stop.

Drucker unties my hands, jerks the hood off and says, "Have a nice day."

I climb out of the car. It squeals away. I recognize Lewis Street, just a few blocks from the magazine office. I squint in the bright sunlight and start walking.

What a clusterfuck—mobsters, an abduction, threats, spying and counter-spying.

"You looked like you were ready to wet your pants."

I swing around. It's Hiram in his silly leather chaps and high-heeled boots. "Have you been waiting here for me?"

Hiram shakes his head. "I was sitting with you in the back seat the whole time. On top of you, actually. Didn't you see me?"

"I had a goddamn hood over my head."

"Right," Hiram says. "Anyway, you handled things pretty darn badly back there. You should have—"

"Go away."

I turn and start toward the office.

Hiram follows. "There was this one time when I was caught like you between a rock and a hard place. I'd gotten myself involved in a little cattle rustling, and I had the sheriff as well as a gang of outlaws breathing down my neck, and—"

"Go away."

"…and both parties told me that, if I didn't cooperate and give up my accomplices, I could expect—"

"You've told me that story before. Besides, it wasn't you who got caught, but the bumbling hero from one of your novels. If I remember correctly, it was—"

"*The Twisted Trail,* one of my best."

I speed up.

So does Hiram.

I say, "Okay, I've heard what you wanted to say. Now go away."

"Actually, I really came by to ask if your granddaddy Ebenezer has visited since the last time we talked."

"I haven't seen him." I break into a trot.

Hiram does too, his little legs churning. He says, "Clementine blames me for his disappearance, of course. I'm hoping he's just hiding out in some whorehouse Back There, but I haven't mentioned that to Clementine. Ebenezer spends a lot of time in them."

I slow down. "You have that sort of thing where you come from?"

"Of course."

"No kidding? What about bowling alleys, pet hospitals, Starbucks?"

"Of course," Hiram replies with the grin he uses when he's making something up, which is most of the time.

"What's it's like Back There? Do you live in a house? Do you eat? Sleep? Go to the bathroom? Tell me."

"What do you think?" Hiram asks.

"I have no idea. That's why I keep asking."

Hiram spreads his arms. "Make of it what you want—Heaven, hell, hades, Valhalla, Elysium, a really swell shopping mall."

"Goddamn it, Hiram, just for once can't you give me a straight answer?"

"To find out what you want to know," Hiram says, tipping his hat up in front and grinning wickedly, "you'll have to wait until you're in my situation."

I stop walking. "*Situation?* You mean dead?"

"I don't like that word."

"Does that mean that, like you, I'll come back to visit—"

"Too many questions," Hiram says, raising his hands. "You irritate me sometimes."

"I irritate *you? I* irritate *you?*"

Hiram falls quiet and his expression turns dark. "If Ebenezer does stay away from Back There for too long, it becomes a matter of life and death."

"Life and death? What are you talking about? Ebenezer's already dead."

Hiram winces at the word, then says, "I shouldn't have said anything, so forget about it."

"*Forget about it?* Is Ebenezer actually in danger of... well... dying?"

"Not just him."

"What does that mean?"

"You ask too many questions."

Then Hiram disappears.

• • •

I climb the backstairs to the *Tattler*. The newsroom looks changed because my life has changed. I'm now working for the mob as well as a sleazeball who threatens to dime out Uncle Sid to the FBI. I've also been told that if Ebenezer doesn't get to Back There in time, it's a matter of life and death—whatever that means.

Also, was Hiram fibbing when he intimated that, after I die, I will turn into a visiting ghost? Or was he toying with me? He loves to do that. Hiram possesses a cruel sense of humor. His readers probably appreciated it, but his great-great-grandson sure as hell doesn't.

I try to type, but can't because my fingers are trembling. I rest my hands on my knees.

A few days ago, my worries revolved around a lost wife, a lost job and a lost journalistic prize. Stuff that seemed important back then.

I want to go back in time.

But who doesn't?

Melody looks up from her screen and turns to me. "You were certainly gone longer than you said you'd be."

"I was out making new friends."

Melody narrows her eyes. "You look like a cat that's trapped in a dog pound. What's wrong?"

"I need more fiber."

Melody pouts.

"Sorry," I say. "I slept badly last night."

She doesn't buy that either.

Uncle Sid steps into the newsroom. "Melody, you got a minute?"

She gives me a concerned look, then follows Sid into his office.

Should I come right out and ask my uncle if he used to launder money for the Ramseys? Or still does?

Do I want to know?

I Google 'OASIS' and am informed that it's an English rock band, also an acoustic company, also an online dating service, also a thousand other things. After many dead ends, I come to a Web site that calls itself 'The Federal Snooper':

The highly secretive Organization for Auditing Special Independent Systems (OASIS) was established in 2010 by former employees of the Central Intelligence Agency. OASIS is headquartered in Washington, D.C., with satellite installations in Chicago, Los Angeles and Boston. Although OASIS purports to be privately owned, it is in fact funded entirely by the CIA and the Department of Defense. OASIS undertakes projects that agencies of the federal government are reluctant to lend their names to— telekinesis, teleporting, mind reading, etc.

I lean back in my chair. Telekinesis? Teleporting? Mind reading? Drucker's mixed up in stuff like that? Unbelievable.

It's also unbelievable that he would have given me his real name, but I check anyway. A row of photos of men named Drucker Ames appears on my screen. Big surprise: One is my baggy-eyed Drucker. I find two bios of him, plus links to three newspaper articles dating back several years.

I learn that Drucker has a degree in criminology, was a military police officer in the U.S. Army for six years and worked for the CIA until he was released after eight years on suspicion of embezzlement, with the charges later dropped.

Drucker then set up a one-man security firm in a suburb of Washington, D.C., with most of his work done for OASIS. After two years, he closed up shop and took a full-time job with them.

Drucker has had several disputes with the IRS and reportedly paid heavy fines.

I shake my head and grunt.

"Mr. Grumpypants is starting to make more-or-less human noises," Melody says, standing beside me. "That's an encouraging sign."

She and Uncle Sid have slipped up without my noticing. Uncle Sid lays his hand on my shoulder. "How's the research on that special set of articles coming?"

He means my job with Hank. "I have a long way to go."

"I figured. That's why I'm having Melody work with you."

"I don't want help."

Melody screws up her face. "Just *what* is wrong with my help, Jeff?"

"What I really meant was that you're too busy."

"It didn't sound like that's what you meant."

"No choice, Jeff," Uncle Sid says, giving my shoulder a squeeze. "Melody's on the project. Period. And that's coming from your uncle, not your boss. Uncle trumps boss."

He's always pulling that. "If you say so."

Melody watches Sid leave, then turns back to me. "When your uncle gave me this assignment, he was as nervous as a teenage groom at the altar, but he wouldn't say why."

She shifts from foot to foot while waiting for me to explain what's worrying Uncle Sid. When I don't, she lifts *The Spirit of St Louis* off my desk and gives the propeller a spin. "Does my new assignment have something to do with why you've been so distracted and cranky lately?"

"Could be."

"Whenever you use that expression, you always mean yes."

"Could be," I say, pulling a chair up for her. "As a start, I'd like you to go online and search for anything you can find out about U.S. prisons built to house foreign terrorists. Also, check out a small company in Washington, D.C. that calls itself OASIS, which stands for 'Organization for Auditing Special Independent Systems.'"

Melody sets the airplane down, sits beside me and scribbles into her notebook. "Working at a place like OASIS sounds as dull as dishwater."

"They're into paranormal activities. They might even be spooks."

Melody looks up, eyes wide. "No kidding? That sounds exciting."

"Not too exciting, I hope."

She twirls her pen. "This'll make me feel a bit like a spy."

"You'd make a terrible spy because you're incapable of telling a lie."

She screws up her mouth.

I hurry to add, "But an exceptionally fetching one—a genuine femme fatale."

She tilts her head to the side and purses her lips, pleased by the compliment. In truth, she's pretty enough to play the role of femme fatale, but way too wholesome.

I say, "Since we both have busy schedules doing our day jobs, maybe we should get together after work to continue on the project. It doesn't have to be in the office, of course. Someplace more comfortable."

"'More comfortable?'"

"Uh, well, I meant…"

She picks up *The Spirit of St Louis* again. "This looks like an antique. Where did you get it?"

"It was my father's when he was a kid. His father—Grandpa Ebenezer—gave it to him, along with the other metal toys on my desk."

I think of Ebenezer and his troubles. I'd like to share my fears with someone, especially Melody.

"These toys are darling," Melody says, giving the propeller another twirl.

I picture my dad as a child sitting on the floor, buzzing the airplane back and forth overhead or pushing his red toy firetruck around and around in a circle. I played with the same truck, sat on the same red oriental carpet, made the same engine sounds. Grandpa Ebenezer bought the rug in Istanbul, the toys in a Miami shop. The firetruck's the biggest of them, over a foot long, its wheels of real rubber, a grimy yarn hose wound around a yellow drum, one ladder missing, the other bent from when I tried to pry open a tin of marbles.

Melody waves her hand in front of my face. "You're off somewhere."

"I was thinking about my father."

"Oh? You never talk about him."

"You're right, I never do."

Melody studies me for a moment. "That was an invitation to say something about him."

"I know it was."

Her expression softens. "Maybe some other time." She grazes her hand across my bare forearm, smiles and walks away.

The touch of her hand lingers, warm and tingly. No woman has touched me in months. Melody's a toucher like Uncle Sid, but she's also a hugger, a kisser, a smoother of bad moments. Adele was none of those things.

Adele. I lean back in my chair. Will I ever work things out with her? Do I even want to work things out with her? She slips farther and farther away as the days go by. I tell myself that it's all for the best, just give up on the marriage and move on. That's what Hiram advises. Clementine, however, tells me to stick it out through thick and thin. But look where it got her—a lifetime with Hiram and an afterlife of the same.

An email from Melody pops up. I open it.

> I started researching ancestral visits after you got such a strong response to your article. I'm pointing you to something along those lines that I found on the Internet. Hope you'll find it as thought-provoking as I do!

It must be thought-provoking for Melody to use an exclamation mark. I click the link. The site calls itself 'Ancestor Visits: The Definitive Truth.' It opens with three paragraphs of unintelligible psycho-babble. I'm about to give up when I read this:

> An individual who experiences a visit from an ancestor can without difficulty see and talk with said ancestor, but cannot feel them or be felt by them (although in the case of multiple visitors, those ancestors do interact with each other in a normal fashion through speaking, touching,

etc.). Only the person visited is aware of the presence of their ancestor (or ancestors). No one can see or hear another person's ancestor or is in any way aware of their existence.

I sit up straight. Whoever maintains this site knows their stuff.

Ancestors make their visits when—in their opinion, at least—a descendant is in trouble and needs advice. Although those visited are not required to heed the proffered guidance, they often do, usually in spite of their efforts to resist. On occasion, however, it seems that ancestors show up for no other reason than simply to taunt a descendant, to boast or to create mischief.

"Boasting? Mischief?" Hiram says. "That's not—"

"I thought you'd left," I whisper. "What do you want now?"

"I found out about your article on ancestor visits. You shouldn't have written it. The topic isn't for public consumption."

"Why?"

"Because it isn't, that's why."

I tap my screen. "Tell it to the guy who maintains this Web site." I continue reading.

Visiting ancestors refuse to answer questions about their other existence (if 'existence' is an applicable term for their unique situation). Many appear to delight in misleading their descendants with wild tales about what they refer to as 'Back There.'

I say, "It sounds like the writer has you in mind."

Hiram grunts.

The visited subject regularly puzzles over the capriciousness often exhibited by ancestors in that they (the ancestors) may not show up at those times when a descendant actually is in most need of comfort and advice. There exists speculation that the ancestors are instead visiting other descendants at the moment, ones with even more pressing needs.

"Do you visit others?" I ask.

"Blah, blah, blah," Hiram says. "He could have said all that in a single sentence."

"That's not an answer."

"It's all you're getting."

I keep reading.

For reasons unknown, deceased parents never visit their offspring.

Hiram says, "Reasons unknown? I'll tell you why parents never visit—it's because it's a terrible idea. Back in the old days it sometimes happened, but the results were catastrophic. The parents got too emotional and gave terrible advice, and at the sight of their parents, the children were often… well… spooked."

Hiram smiles at his word choice.

I shudder at the thought of Mom or Dad visiting me.

Although it appears (highly speculative, one admits) that anyone is capable of receiving ancestral visits, only those predisposed to such an event have this experience. Often (and possibly in all instances) the person visited lives with a deep psychological scar.

Hiram snickers. "Maybe like plugging a stepfather through the forehead?"

"Give it a rest, damnit!"

Melody looks up.

I tap my screen. "I'm arguing online with a whacko conspiracy theorist."

Melody gives me a doubtful look, then goes back to typing. I go back to reading.

> Surprisingly, the ancestors who visit with advice do not always represent the best of humanity. Although many are (were) fine and upstanding citizens, a handful of others are fibbers and scoundrels, egotists and braggarts.

I chuckle.

Hiram says, "The writer's an idiot."

> There are reports of the occasional visiting ancestor who can blend in with the living and lead (more-or-less lead) for extended periods of time a normal day-to-day life (for want of a better term for their singular condition). These ancestors do not make themselves known to other visiting ancestors and are said to possess the power to make short-term predictions. They offer their advice obliquely, never directly (which means that the subject never recognizes them as their ancestor).

> Such long-term and corporeal visiting ancestors are considered wiser and more stable than the other type, and they appear when a descendant is going through a particularly bad period in their life (and when other ancestors seem to be failing in their duties).

I whisper, "Hiram, is that true?"

"The guy should be horse-whipped for so many parentheses."

"That's not an answer. Is it true?"

"What do you think?"

"I don't know what to think. That's why I asked. Is this true?"

Hiram shrugs, yawns, says nothing, which he often does when he doesn't want to say yes.

There are two types of visiting ancestors?

Unbelievable.

I read on:

> WARNING: The following is so shocking and disturbing that you may want to stop reading. (I have long hesitated to include this material.) However (after many sleepless nights of tossing and turning), I have decided that the subject simply cannot be ignored.

> Should an ancestor remain absent beyond a certain (as yet unknown) period of time, returning to Back There becomes impossible! The horrifying consequence is that the ancestor in question and all his or her descendants disappear forever! It will be as if none of them had ever been born!

I reread the last paragraph, then lean back in my chair. "Hiram, is that true?"

He looks away.

"Is it?" I ask.

He keeps his head turned.

"Well?"

"The guy should have his head shoved into a bucket of sheep dung for all those exclamations marks."

"That's not an answer, Hiram. Is this true?"

Long pause, then he produces a faint nod.

Unbelievable!

"Hiram, how would anyone even know if someone else's whole

family line disappeared?"

"They wouldn't," Hiram says. "They can't. It's impossible."

"Then how do you know?"

Hiram tilts his hat back and wipes his forehead with his big red handkerchief. "Things work differently Back There."

Again I reread the warning paragraph. It's even more gut-churning this time. I say, "No wonder Clementine's so worried about Ebenezer's absence. You must be, too."

No response.

I look around.

Hiram has disappeared. No goodbye, no reproaches, no parting words of advice. That's not like him.

Unbelievable!

If Ebenezer disappears, he'll take Dad and Uncle Sid with him.

And me.

And any children I might have, and their children, and the children after them, and so on forever.

Maybe right this minute, there's an ancestor visiting one of my relatives somewhere, and that ancestor will stay away too long and wipe out our whole family line.

Has this happened to other people? Have others been born and then not born? It seems so.

I get up and circle the newsroom. My existence is fragile. Everyone's existence is fragile.

How would the world change if Ebenezer disappeared and caused me to disappear? Ebenezer's not Mom's relative, so she'd still be around, but with me gone, who would have taken care of her after she started losing her grip on reality? A different son? A daughter? A husband who didn't die in a house fire?

But at least Mom would have been spared the sight of her six-year-old son shooting her second husband.

All this is hard to get my head around.

I make another swing around the newsroom.

Melody cocks her head to the side. "Is there something you want to talk about?"

I shake my head and keep going.

My third time past Sherwood, he looks up from his screen and says, "You're as nervous as a pinch hitter who's just up from the minors, bottom of the ninth, bases loaded. What's up?"

I lay my hands palms down on his desk and lean in close. "Have you ever asked yourself what the world would be like if you'd never been born?"

Chapter 9

SCORPIO Oct. 23 – Nov. 21

A day in the open air cleanses the body and the mind. Troubles come in twos. Solutions come in fits and starts. Fight for what you believe is right, no matter the odds.

Still in a daze, I spend another hour searching for other Web sites related to ancestral visits, but find nothing. Melody keeps glaring prettily in my direction. Four articles are overdue, which is okay because writing them will keep my mind absorbed for a few hours. I close my browser and type:

North Koreans Abduct Two-Headed American Hacking Genius!

The *Boston Tattler* has just learned of an alarming abduction that could change the nuclear balance of power in Asia. Our crack team of investigators has discovered that...

I stop writing. The word 'investigators' triggers something. Drucker said he wanted me to investigate the Ramsey gang because he was afraid they'd come after him for canceling their building contracts.

Okay, that makes sense. But why ask me for help? OASIS works for the Feds, and if Drucker's in trouble, he could turn to the FBI. So why hasn't he? Is there something he doesn't want them to know? Maybe that he signed a building contract with mobsters? No, that's no longer a secret. Is there some reason that OASIS is afraid to let the FBI snoop around their outfit? Maybe. Or is Drucker hiding something from both the FBI and OASIS?

My cellphone chimes. Speak of the devil.

"What do you have for me?" Drucker asks in his scratchy high voice.

I walk to the far corner of the office and say in a low voice, "Hello to you, too."

"Talk."

I tell Drucker what Sid said about Hank and Freddie, the abusive father, the crappy childhood.

"I'm not writing their weepy biography, for Christ sake. I want to know about Hank's next move."

"Damn," I say. "I guess I forgot to ask."

"You don't ask him, dickhead, you—"

"I have another call coming in."

"Sure you do," Drucker says.

"It's Hank."

Long pause. "Are you making that up to get rid of me?"

"Do you want to take the chance?"

Drucker grumbles and hangs up.

I take the other call.

Hank says, "Reggie?"

"He's out."

"I'll call back later," Hank says.

That means I'm supposed to phone him on the burner phone he gave me.

I go down to the back alley, lean against the building and make the call.

Hank says, "What'd you find out about OASIS?"

I summarize what I'd read online.

"Good enough as far as it goes," Hank says. "But what I really want is info on the OASIS employees, in particular the dickhead who won't meet us face-to-face. Find out where he lives and if he has a family.

If he has a family!

Not a chance.

"I've spent hours and hours online," I say, "but the world has a million John Smiths, if that's even the guy's real name. So it won't be easy getting info on him. It's not as if he's going to just walk up to me on the street some morning and introduce himself."

"Fuck the excuses. Keep working, asshole. I'm getting impatient. Freddie, too. No, especially Freddie, and you sure as hell don't want that."

No, I don't want that.

The line goes dead.

I head for the lot where my pickup is parked. Melody and a sparkling article about abducted two-headed programming gurus will just have to wait. If I don't find out more about OASIS, then Hank will turn Freddie loose on me or on Uncle Sid. As for Grandpa Ebenezer, there's not a damn thing I can do about him. It's not as if I can go looking for the guy. If he shows up, he shows up. Those are the rules.

I call Willy.

"Hey Jeff, how the hell are you?" His standard greeting.

"Want to drop work and go for a long ride?"

"I always want to drop work and go for a long ride. Where to?"

"Somewhere that can us get into a load of trouble."

"Sounds about right," Willy says. "Anything's beats scraping wallpaper."

"I mean real trouble. You've got a record, so give this some hard thought."

"I'll take my chances. Like I said, anything's better than scraping wallpaper."

I drive to Concord, pick up Willy, and we head out on the interstate toward Fort Robbins, two hours west of Boston. It's a miniscule army base built during World War II and closed for decades. This is the OASIS site where Willy worked construction until he and a friend stole a backhoe and tried to sell it on eBay.

Willy dozes off for a few minutes, wakes up, rolls his window down and shakes a cigarette out of his pack.

"Willy, have you ever thought about what the world would be like if you were never born?"

"Your house would be falling down around your ears."

"I'm serious. How would your non-existence affect the people you know? Would they miss you?"

"Nope," Willy says, "because they'd never know I existed." He flicks ash out the window. "Everyone thinks about their non-existence sometime in their life, then shoves it aside. It's just a mental exercise."

"What if it weren't?"

"Now you got me spooked. What's—"

My phone chimes. I pull it from my shirt pocket. It's Charlie from the *Globe*. I forgot that I'd left a phone message asking him what he knew about OASIS from his stint in Washington.

"Hey Charlie," I say.

"What're you messed up in?"

"What's the problem?"

"That message you left on my phone is the problem," Charlie says. "I don't know what you're up to, but I'd advise against it in the strongest terms. That's all I've got for you. And as they say, this conversation never took place."

"Just a couple quick questions, Charlie. Is OASIS legit, and if so, what—"

The phone goes silent.

Not good.

Charlie did two tours with Special Forces in Afghanistan. Not the type to scare easily.

Willy lights another cigarette. "OASIS is a Brit rock band. Pretty good, too."

"This OASIS is a mysterious outfit that unknowingly contracted with the Ramsey mob to build the site where you worked before you went to the pokey."

"No shit?"

I tell him everything I know about OASIS, Drucker, and the Ramsey brothers.

Again Willy says, "No shit?"

Nothing bothers him, nothing scares him. Willy grew up a ragged kid in a family of drunks. During the two years after the shooting, when I still wasn't talking, he was the only kid who would play with me. We hiked, fished, and blew up stuff with illegal firecrackers, him talking nonstop, me saying nothing. In later years I got into fistfights for Willy, who was small for his age, and I tutored him through high school. From Willy I learned about courage, loyalty, unquestioning friendship, and how to produce explosive armpit farts.

We drive a few minutes without speaking, then Willy says, "So, it sounds like you want to get inside the OASIS building."

"Yup."

"I don't like the sound of that."

"Neither do I."

Willy glances around the cab. "Uh… I've been wondering. Are there any…?"

"Ancestors riding with us? Not today."

"Don't they usually show up when stuff like this goes down?"

"Not necessarily," I say. They're capricious. Today they might be visiting other descendants, or just not paying attention to me. Or even sleeping."

"They sleep?"

"Who knows? In any case, I'm pretty sure we won't see Hiram for a while because I pissed him off."

"Weird," Willy says. "Definitely weird." He pulls his Red Sox cap down over his eyes and goes to sleep.

Nothing fazes him, nothing surprises him.

I drive for an hour and a half, then turn down a bumpy gravel lane that leads through the pine forests surrounding Fort Robbins. I shut off the engine, and Willy wakes up.

We each grab our binoculars, water bottles, and a handful of granola bars, then spray ourselves with insect repellent and climb down from the pickup.

A sign reads, "U.S. Government Property. Keep Out!"

I take a compass reading, and Willy takes a leak up against the sign.

We start up the hill. Back at the office, I Googled a map and saw that the old army base lies in a valley on the far side of this slope. We don't find a trail through the woods, which is good because we won't run into hikers, bad because we have to climb over rocks and fallen trees and rip our way through thick, waist-high brush.

Willy gingerly pulls a thorn from his sleeve. "Gnarly going."

"Makes it even more fun."

The air smells of pine and decaying plants. Squirrels bounce from branch to branch, and birds warble. Up ahead a deer freezes, stares at us, then bounds into the thicket. I think back to when Willy and I were kids and hiked a lot. He would steal two bottles of his father's beer, and Mom would make us a dozen chocolate-chip cookies.

She rarely cooked a meal, just once in a while opening a can of beans or peas and serving them cold, so most of the time I'd heat up frozen dinners for us from the supply Uncle Sid would bring during his Sunday afternoon visits. I would help him lug the packages to the freezer in the garage. Before we carried the other groceries into the house, Uncle Sid would always sit me down on the front steps and ask how the week was going. Do you need money? (No.) Are you getting enough to eat? (Yes.) Do you need new clothes? (No.) Do you get lonely? (Sometimes.)

Mom didn't make meals, but she loved to bake chocolate-chip

cookies. I can still taste them. I would slide a whole one into my mouth and let it sit there until it dissolved into a sugary cloud. When I was about eight, I said my first words in over two years: "Can you make more cookies?" Mom burst into tears and hugged me. "Yes, I can," she said. "Yes, I can, dear." She sobbed and squeezed and forgot all about making another batch of cookies.

We climb for ten more minutes, then lie on our stomachs just below the crest. Here the trees are scrubby and sparse. I whisper, "From here on we have to crawl."

"I was afraid you'd say that."

We each drink a bottle of water and wolf down a granola bar. Willy starts to light a cigarette. I say, "Don't."

"I was afraid you'd say that."

We squirm over the crest, stop at the tree line and peer through our binoculars at the abandoned army base spread out below us. A ring road and a torn wire fence surround it. Two dozen wooden barracks sit inside a grid of broken, blacktop streets. The buildings date back to World War II. They're two stories tall, with broad shingle roofs and peeling yellow paint. Several have burned to the ground. The rest are covered in graffiti, with most of their windows broken. The new OASIS building sits on our side of the base, a trailer out front.

I say, "Did you ever go inside that trailer?"

"A few times. It's the construction headquarters. It's filled with plans and drawings."

"I'd like to get in and look around."

"How?" Willy asks.

"No idea."

I shift my binoculars to the main building. A wide red sign over the front door reads, 'Spirit Storage.' The building is concrete, windowless and four stories tall, with a wide steel front door. A row of spotlights peer down from the front edge of the roof. Surveillance cameras hang off the corners of the building. "When you worked here, what did they tell you they were building?"

"A self-storage facility," Willy says, "but we all knew that was bullshit because who'd put one way out here? Everyone figured it was a prison of some sort. But from my subsequent experience inside a prison, I realized that this sure as hell wasn't one. At least not the usual kind."

I lower my binoculars. "No?"

Willy rolls on his side, pulls three sheets of paper from his jeans pocket, and spreads them side-by-side on the grass. "Here are my sketches you wanted of the interior." He taps the leftmost sheet. "See that?"

"It looks like a row of cells."

"It is. But what's missing?"

I study the drawing, then shake my head. "Don't know."

"Toilets. Cells have toilets. You think they'd risk letting a con out of his cell every time he has to take a piss?"

"Probably not."

Willy slides the middle sheet closer to me. "Where's the mess hall?"

I point at the largest room. "There?"

"Nope. There's no water or gas hookup, just a million wires running back and forth under the floor. I think it's for some kind of lab or computer center. As for a mess hall, there isn't one, at least not one big enough for dozens of inmates. If the place really is a prison, then it's a prison for freaks who don't eat or crap. So tell me, what in hell is it?"

"No idea. But it rates some heavy security." I point down the hill. "Check that out."

Two men in black uniforms have just stepped from the construction trailer. One is tall, and one is short. Both have holstered pistols and binoculars. They turn them in our direction. The taller guard points up the hill, right at us.

Willy says, "Oh, shit!"

"Well put."

We scramble backward on our stomachs, cross over the crest, jump to our feet and tumble down the other side of the hill, leaping over fallen trees and rocks, ignoring the bushes snagging our sleeves. We run to the truck and jump in. I start the engine, throw the gear into reverse, lay my right arm over the seat, turn to look out the rear window and back up as fast as I can.

Willy lights a cigarette. "This reminds me of that time we were kids and snuck into the Johnson farm to steal watermelons."

"The good old days."

"Except when we got caught. Do you remember the time—"

I slam on the brakes.

The back of Willy's head thumps against the rear window.

A Jeep sits sideways across the lane. The short guard we'd seen earlier stands next to the driver's door. He holds a pistol in both hands, aimed right at us. He shouts, "Come out with your hands up!"

Willy says, "Just like in the movies."

We climb out of the pickup but don't raise our hands.

The guard eases forward and stops just three feet away. He points the pistol at me, at Willy, at me again. His name tag announces that he's Cedric. He's a short, skittish, soft kid with narrow eyes and small ears. "You're trespassing," he says.

"No we're not," I say. "This is government land, and we're tax-paying citizens."

"Didn't you read the sign?"

"Sign? What sign?"

"That one," Cedric says, turning toward the no-trespassing sign. "It says right there that... ouch! Goddamn it!"

Now I'm holding the pistol, and Cedric is holding a twisted wrist. Willy smiles. "Smooth move."

"Cedric," I say, "didn't they tell you in training to keep back a safe distance?"

"You bastard! You broke my wrist!"

"It's sprained at worst," I say. "Now listen up. You're going to hand the Jeep's keys over to my buddy so he can drive it off the road. Then he and I will leave peacefully. You'll find the keys and your pistol in the ditch at the spot where the road turns onto the highway."

"Nope," a man behind me says in a rumbling low voice. "I've got you covered, as they say on TV, and I'm not stupid enough to get too close. So lay the pistol down slowly, big guy."

I glance at Willy, then set the pistol on the ground.

Cedric scoops it up in his good hand.

"Now step away from the gun and turn around," the man says.

Willy and I do.

It's the other guard we saw earlier. He's tall and buff and about twice Cedric's age. His name tag reads 'Quincy.' He has a sharp nose and a long jaw. He looks calm, almost sleepy. He says, "We spotted you two on surveillance."

I should have checked the trees for cameras. "We're just a couple of hikers."

"Hikers hike," Quincy says. "You crawled. So what's the real story?"

I screw up my face. "Okay, I guess I have to tell the truth. We own a self-storage facility, and we're out here checking on the competition."

Willy says, "Yup."

Cedric peeks from around behind Quincy. "They're lying," Cedric says and points at the writing on the side of my pickup. "They're just a couple of shit-house haulers who don't own—"

"Just a side job," I say.

Quincy slaps the back of his neck. "Before the mosquitoes drink all my blood, I think it's time for you two fellows to start telling the truth."

I look at Willy. He shrugs his shoulders. Your call, he's thinking.

I search around for the right story. I could tell them that a guy who does in fact own a self-storage facility hired us to scope out the place. Or that we were lost. Or that we're bird watchers. Or that we're here because a mobster has pressured me into working for him and that a sleazeball from a mysterious company has pressured me into working for him.

"Okay," I say.

Quincy whacks a mosquito on his forehead and studies his bloody palm. "Okay, what?"

I look at Willy. He raises an eyebrow, which is about all the emotion he ever shows. I turn back. "We're burglars."

Quincy raises his eyes. "Burglars?"

"We specialize in self-storage places."

Quincy shakes his head. "You gotta be kidding."

"I never kid."

Quincy lowers his pistol. With his free hand, he lifts his cap and scratches his scalp. "You've got about as much chance of breaking into this place as into Fort Knox."

"Which is exactly what we concluded. So if you'll let us go, we'll—"

"Not so fast!" Cedric says, stepping around from behind Quincy, his pistol wavering in his uninjured hand. "You two are—"

"Ease off, kid," Quincy says, pushing Cedric's pistol down and holstering his own. "They haven't broken any laws except for a little trespassing."

"But they're burglars. They said so."

"Yeah, well, by the looks of that thing," Quincy says, nodding toward my beat-up pickup, "they're not very damn good at it and can't be much of a problem to society. Besides, we're private guards, not cops. It's not our business." Quincy scratches his scalp again. "You boys better get moving."

We scramble into the pickup.

Quincy orders Cedric to move the Jeep, then strolls over and studies the driver's side door of my pickup. He rests both hands on the open window and leans in close. "Just one more question before you go."

"Uh… okay."

"Aren't there two 'l's' in 'installation'?"

Chapter 10

SCORPIO Oct. 23 – Nov. 2

Every romance has its ups and downs. Learning the truth hurts, but not knowing it hurts worse. Violence never solves a problem. For ingrown toenail relief, soak the affected foot in a gallon of lukewarm water and a cup of apple cider vinegar.

The next morning I come downstairs in a T-shirt and jogging shorts to find Willy sitting in front of two fried eggs, three strips of bacon, four slices of toast and a bottle of Budweiser. His standard breakfast. I say, "Want to join me for a run?"

Willy nips off the end of a piece of bacon. "Tomorrow." His standard response.

Willy has never jogged and never will. He makes fun of my Fitbit, my stretching, my weightlifting, my shiny blue jogging shorts.

I leave the house and set out along the road toward Concord center. Hiram joins in, his chaps flapping. He often runs with me and has no trouble keeping up. He's light on his feet.

We swing onto Lexington Road and jog past the house where Louisa May Alcott wrote *Little Women*.

Hiram says, "I'll bet Louisa May wouldn't have let some sidewinder steal her literary prize."

"That again?"

"I know your mind's elsewhere because Hank and Drucker have the dumplings scared out of you, but—"

"The hell they do." I speed up and pull ahead of Hiram.

He catches up. "You need to forget about them for a while and take care of your own needs."

"When did you start worrying about my needs?"

"When did I not?" Hiram says and spreads his arms. "It's my mission in life."

"Life?" I ask, slowing down. "You're dead."

"You know what I mean. And stop using that word. Listen: You shouldn't be out here running around in your undies. You should be looking for those memory cards. By the way, you're as dumb as a donkey for not taking notes when you interviewed those shelter workers."

"I did," I say. "Of course I did. But without the cards, the Pulitzer Board had no proof the notes weren't written after the fact."

"Okay, so go get them."

"Adele says a burglar stole them."

"You believe that hussy?"

I swing to the right at the Colonial Inn and head down the road toward the Revolutionary War battle site.

"Well?" Hiram says.

"No, I don't believe her. But she's probably hidden them where I can't find them."

"Have you looked?"

I pull up my T-shirt and wipe my face.

"Have you?" Hiram asks.

I don't answer.

Hiram snorts. "You're a pussy."

"Shut up!"

A man on the sidewalk stops walking his dog. Both stare at me.

"How long would it take to search her place?" Hiram asks. "Two hours? Three? You can sure as heck take that much time away from this OASIS business so you can—"

"I don't want to hear this."

Hiram swings around to my front and runs backward, pumping his arms, hovering a foot off the ground, showing off. "Before Drucker snatched you," he says, "you were ready to break into Adele's place. Now you've chickened out." Hiram tucks his thumbs under his armpits and makes flapping chicken wings. *"Puck! Puck! Puck!"*

"I have more important things to worry about," I say, then jog across the Old North Bridge. "Do you know how silly you look?"

"You're the only one who can see me, and I don't care how I look to you because you're a loser."

"No, I'm not!" I shout.

Two startled boys jump aside and let me pass.

I whisper, "No, I'm not."

"Loser!"

"No!"

"Loser!"

But Hiram's right, I am a loser. And as for his advice, there actually have been times when it was good. He told me to apply to Cornell, and he was right. He told me to become a journalist, and he was right.

And he's right that a couple hours stolen from investigating OASIS won't make a difference. I've taken off time to jog, after all, and last night Willy and I watched *Attack of the Killer Tomatoes* for the hundredth time.

I reach the North Bridge Visitor Center on the hill overlooking the battlefield, jog in place for a minute, turn around and start back down. I stop at the Old North Bridge, lean against the railing and call Adele at the *Globe*. She doesn't pick up. I try five more times. Nothing.

Gritting my teeth, I phone the odious Beckworth Parker-Primgate, Adele's editor and my former editor. Beckworth Parker-Primgate is a fake, a scheming bastard, a snob, an oozing lump on the ass cheek of journalism. I get his voice mail and his phony Brit accent. He says he's out of the office but will get back as soon as he can. "Cheerio."

Cheerio? Give me a fucking break.

Janet's horoscope recommends that I control my impulses today, which is the only thing keeping me from leaving a message reminding Beckworth that he's a flaming asshole.

I hang up and get through to Marge, Adele's only friend at the *Globe*. Maybe her only friend in the whole world. Marge tells me that Adele and Beckworth are at an all-day off-site meeting.

I shower, change clothes, eat breakfast, drive to Boston, and park in a Back Bay lot that charges more per week than I paid for my pickup. I start toward Adele's place—our old place. Flowering pink trees line the brick sidewalks, just as they had the day we moved into the condo. I think back to the excitement Adele and I felt as newlyweds when we unpacked our dishes, bedding and skis, and shifted the couch here, there, back again. Good times. Another spring.

"I don't suppose my grandson has visited."

I look over my shoulder and see my great-great-grandmother Clementine limping behind. She's in a long black dress and a white bonnet tied at the throat, the only outfit I've ever seen her in. She looks concerned and—from what I've just learned about disappearing ancestors—has every reason to be.

I wait for her to catch up. "No, sorry. But I'm sure Ebenezer will be all right. So stop worrying."

This is the first time I've ever given her advice.

She shakes her head but says nothing.

We walk for a couple more minutes.

Clementine says, "I'm pleased you're doing the proper thing, young man."

"What proper thing?" I ask.

"Visiting your wife and pleading with her to take you back."

I shake my head. "This is a B and E."

"What's a B and E?"

"Breaking and entering."

Clementine slows down. "Oh, my."

"Except I have a key, so it's simply entering."

"Oh, my."

We pass a building site where an idling concrete truck sits out front, its red-and-orange hopper slowly turning. The smell of fresh concrete takes me back to the summer between my sophomore and junior years at college when I drove a truck like this for the same outfit, Netterfield Construction. Uncle Sid got me the job. Later I learned that the company was secretly owned by Jack Ramsey, Hank and Freddie's gangster father.

Life would be a lot simpler if I still drove a concrete truck. Just not for the mob.

Clementine limps along beside me. "What you really need, young man, is a regular family to make up for the one you never had. I can picture you, Adele and your six children living a normal life in a nice little cottage next to a stream somewhere out in the country."

I would in fact like kids. Not sure about six, though. When we reach the condo, I slide the key into the lock. "Adele told me the week after we were married that she didn't want children."

"Oh, my."

I swing the door open for Clementine to enter first, even though she can walk through walls.

She folds her arms across her ample chest. "I am certainly *not* setting foot in there, young man. I want *nothing* to do with an illegal activity. Laws are—"

"'God's word on Earth.' Yeah, I know."

"No, you don't know. If you did, you wouldn't—"

I close the door, leaving her outside, muttering to herself.

I step into the condo and look around. Where would Adele have hidden the memory cards? That is, if she had lied about the burglary, which I'm pretty certain she did.

The place was originally a posh four-story brick residence, connected shoulder-to-shoulder with similar homes. Now it's two posh condos. Ours—Adele's now, I guess—occupies the first and second stories. I start at the ground-floor study, opening desk drawers, turning up the corner of the oriental rug, lifting pictures off the wall. Nothing. Although no one is home, I play the burglar and make as little noise as possible. I tiptoe into the living room, again checking under carpets, under seat cushions, behind pictures. Same for the dining nook, the downstairs bathroom, the kitchen. Still nothing. So I start up the stairs.

The steps squeak. Adele once remarked that at least we'd never have to worry about a burglar sneaking up on us while we were in bed. That was her one and only attempt at humor during the years I've known her.

Halfway up, I hear a noise in the master bedroom. Or I think I hear a noise.

I stop and listen—street traffic, an airliner passing high overhead, my breathing. But nothing else.

I ease my way to the top of the stairs.

"Who's there?" Adele says. Her voice shakes.

Shit!

I hesitate. "It's me."

"Jeff? You're not supposed to be here!"

Now there's anger in her voice.

"Neither are you. I was told you were at an off-site with Beckworth."

I step through the bedroom door.

Holy shit!

I squeeze my eyes closed, hold them shut, open them. But nothing has changed. Adele is still there in bed, naked. Beckworth lies on his back, asleep, smiling, naked. His chest is a tangle of curly black hair. So is his crotch. His limp pecker points to the left.

I look away.

I want to run away.

But my legs won't move.

Is this real?

Again I close my eyes, squeeze them shut, pause, open them. Nothing has changed. This didn't work after I shot my stepfather, and it doesn't work now.

Adele rises from the bed. She has beautiful firm breasts, beautiful long legs. Things I miss.

She says, "This isn't what it looks like."

"Then what is it?"

She says nothing.

I want to shout at her. I want to pound my fists into Beckworth's face. I want to rip out his ugly little black goatee.

I do nothing.

Hiram shouts, "Strangle both of them!"

He's standing next to me, eyeing Adele up and down, licking his lips, making obscene little clucking sounds.

I shake my head.

"Save your honor," he says.

I spot the iron poker leaning against the fireplace.

Hiram follows my eyes. "Do it! Do it!"

I can feel the poker in my hand, just as I can still feel the heavy gun in my hands before I shot my stepfather.

Adele bends over, picks up a pink blanket and wraps it around her. "You have to leave," she says, her voice quivering. She has a sharp nose, a thin face and shiny black hair, and she's a lot less pretty than I remembered.

I say, "We promised each other we wouldn't see anyone else until things were settled."

Adele says nothing.

Hiram says, "Slap her around until she's red in the face and tie the hairy guy's pecker in a knot!"

"No!" I say. "No, I won't!"

Adele jerks her head back. "You won't what?"

I shake my head.

Beckworth rolls onto his side and begins to snore. The bastard can sleep through anything.

I turn my back on the scene.

"You're a lily-livered coward!" Hiram says. "You're a disgrace to our family!"

I stumble down the stairs before I do anything stupid. I fly out the door and plop down on the bottom step. I no longer hear Hiram.

It's a sunny, warm day. A couple my age strolls past, arm-in-arm, all smiles and laughter. I want to shout that I just caught my wife in bed with another man. I want them to be as miserable as I am.

I put my head into my hands and close my eyes.

Fuck! Fuck! Fuck!

A game-changer. A turning point.

Melody would tell me it's an opportunity for a new start.

Hiram would tell me it's an opportunity for bloody vengeance.

Clementine would tell me it's an opportunity to learn to forgive.

I open my eyes to see Hiram sitting to my right and Clementine to my left, massaging her knee where it joins her peg leg.

Hiram leans around in front of me, turns his thumb my direction and says to Clementine, "I'm ashamed to be related to this guy. He caught his wife bare-assed in bed with a hairy fatso, but didn't lay a hand on either one of them."

Clementine clicks her tongue. "Oh my." She rests her hand on my shoulder as best she can. "You did the right thing, Jeff. You turned the other cheek. But now you must show forgiveness. Yes, you are hurt, and yes, you have a good reason to feel hurt, but in time you will recognize that Our Lord puts obstacles in front of us so that we will—"

"Cut the guy's nut sack off!" Hiram shouts.

Clementine says, "God wants you to—"

"Chop off his pecker and stuff it into his—"

"Stop talking, both of you!"

They do.

Part of me wants to march back upstairs, scream insults at Adele and punch Beckworth's sparkling white teeth down his throat, and part of me wants to jump up and run away. Instead I just sit there and do nothing. Dazed.

Clementine says, "I have learned to forgive sins of a similar nature, and I'm a better person for it. I'm referring of course to my own marriage, to its many humiliations and betrayals. And yet, I have found it in my soul to forgive my errant partner."

Hiram isn't listening. He rarely listens to his wife. He says, "There was this sheep farmer I knew—a fricking sheep farmer, for cripes sake—who stole my girl away at a dance and—"

"Shut the fuck up!"

"Language, language," Clementine says.

"And so I sneaked onto his ranch one night," Hiram says with a chuckle, "and I shoveled a big wagon load of steaming sheep droppings into his brand new carriage, right to the top. I've never laughed so hard in my whole life."

"I don't want to hear this," I say.

"Well, you should. You shouldn't let that hairy claim-jumper get away scot-free," Hiram says. "But you are. You just sit there and feel sorry for yourself. Are you a man or a mouse?"

Good question.

"Well?" Hiram says.

I get up and walk over to Beckworth's brand new BMW convertible parked in front of the building. The top is down, and I can smell the leather seats. I take a deep breath, pull my right foot back and kick the driver's door. *Thump!* I leave a small dent. I kick again. Another thump, another miniscule dent.

"That's it?" Hiram says. "That's it? You're a mouse. You should go back upstairs and kick the gonads off the guy who's just made whoopee with your woman!"

"Stop that, Jeff!" Clementine shouts. "Stop that right now!"

I kick the car again. My sneaker flies off.

Humiliated, I hop over, pick up the shoe, sit on the sidewalk and tug the sneaker back on.

Hiram says, "Mouse."

I say, "Fuck you!"

Clementine says, "Language!"

Again I see Adele's perky breasts, her flat tummy, her tanned long legs, her fuzzy black pubic hair, and I see Beckworth lying asleep on his back, his pecker limp, smiling the smile of the recently fucked.

I remember Hiram's tale of a carriage brimming with fresh sheep shit. It's not something he did, of course, but borrowed from one of his novels. Hiram created powerful visuals in his writings, I have to admit. The only reason to read him.

The sun glints off the hood of Beckworth's blue BMW, pristine except for three miserable little scuffs in the driver's side. A car like that costs a couple hundred times as much as a broken-down, shithouse-hauling pickup with an orthographic defect.

Now what? More kicking?

Scratch the paint?

Take a dump on the driver's seat?

No, I can do a hell of a lot better than that.

Chapter 11

SCORPIO Oct. 23 – Nov. 21

Accept with cheer the help of friends. Everyone is a performer on life's stage. When spurned, take concrete steps.

I walk fast, Hiram and Clementine floating along beside me. "I don't need you two here."

"Running away, are we?" Hiram says. He slips around in front of me and makes chicken wings. *"Puck! Puck! Puck!"*

"Hush!" Clementine says. "Jeff is doing the intelligent thing."

"No," I say. "I am sure as hell *not* doing the intelligent thing. And I'm not running away, either. Now leave me alone, both of you."

Of course they don't.

The mixer truck is still where I saw it before, a newer model of the one I drove that summer in college. The engine is running, the hopper rotating. Workmen sit in a circle under the tree across the street, laughing, drinking coffee, eating donuts, not looking my direction.

I ease into the driver's seat. Clementine vacillates, then slips through the passenger door and sits beside me. Hiram follows. He says, "I've got a good idea of what's coming, and this is going to be a whale of a lot of fun."

Clementine says, "Do you have permission to drive this vehicle, young man?"

I back the truck up. It emits a series of sharp beeps. I glance at the men across the street. One of them waves, assuming I'm on the crew. I wave back. So does Hiram, both hands.

Clementine says, "Oh, my."

I put the truck in gear, and we pull away.

Hiram is fascinated by the controls—What does that lever do? What's that button for? What's this thingy?

"You ask too many questions."

For once I get to say that back to him.

I ease between the cars parked close on both side.

Again the image of Adele naked in bed with Beckworth pops into my head. Ugly, ugly, ugly.

I pull up in front of the condo and back the truck up close to the front bumper of the open convertible. I climb out of the cab, add an extension to the chute and position it over the driver's seat. I flip a switch on the control panel, and concrete starts to rumble down the chute.

Clementine says, "Oh, my."

"Hot diggity!" Hiram says. He jumps up and down and waves his arms overhead. "Hot diggity!"

The concrete oozes and flows across the carpeted floor mats, then rises to the shift lever, the leather seats, the dash, the top of the doors. The car sinks lower and lower, squeaking and groaning. Welding points pop. The windshield bursts free and flops forward. Lumpy gray concrete slathers across the hood.

The tires explode one by one: *Bang! Bang! Bang! Bang!*

Hiram high-fives me, his hand passing through mine. He shouts, "Did you see how the windshield split right down the middle!"

"I sure as hell did!"

The driver's side door bursts open and spills a pyramid of concrete onto the street. Then the other passenger door breaks open with a loud *Whack!*"

Hiram says, "Beautiful!"

Clementine says, "Oh, my."

The axles break, the wheels bow inward, the frame slams to the pavement.

Hiram says, "Yahoo!" and we do another airy high-five.

Across the street, a middle-aged man and woman tumble out of their home, stand on the sidewalk and stare, open mouthed.

I shout, "It's performance art!"

The man wears a ghastly green shirt hanging halfway out. The woman cradles a fat yellow cat. He takes out his phone and starts tapping keys. No mystery who he's calling.

Now the BMW is a wet gray mound, with only the front bumper visible. The air smells of wet concrete. I climb into the cab, shut off the engine, and rejoin Hiram and Clementine. A dozen people are now standing across the street, chattering to each other. I pick out the words, 'Performance artist.'

"Young man," Clementine says in her schoolmarm voice, "you have made it much harder to ever win Adele back."

"Win her back?" I whisper. "I just caught her fucking her boss!"

"Language!"

"Okay, I caught the two of them making the beast with two backs."

Clementine—a lover of Shakespeare—smiles faintly at the reference. She turns to Hiram, lifts her chin, looks down her nose at him and says in the same sharp voice that she no doubt once used to rouse sleepy students, "You get married, and you stay married, even if your partner is a lying, scheming lout."

Hiram ignores her and continues tapping, or trying to tap, his toe against the mound of concrete.

I hear footsteps. I swing around to see Adele thumping down the steps. Her slacks are red, her misbuttoned blouse a mismatching pink, one shoe blue, the other black. She's wearing a pair of small, rectangular, black-rimmed glasses that give her a pinched look.

She points at the heap of concrete. "Is that…?"

"Yup."

Stunned, Adele settles slowly onto the bottom step. "It's only a month old."

"Even better."

I see her rising from her bed, naked and beautiful. I see Beckworth, his mouth open, his pecker limp.

"Slap her silly!" Hiram shouts.

I shake my head, bend over and grab the potted geranium sitting at the foot of the steps. I bounce the flowerpot in my hand. Should I smash it against the side of the building? Or toss it through the living room window? Either would be satisfying.

I glance down at Adele. She'd love to see me lose control, love to see me break something, love to lecture me afterward. I don't want to give her the satisfaction. I set the pot down.

Neither of us looks directly at the other. It's been that way since the separation.

"Give her hell," Hiram says. "Then hop on your bronco and ride out of town before the sheriff's posse gets here."

"Nope."

"What?" Adele says.

I turn my back to her and face the crowd gathered across the street. "Were you banging Beckworth even before we separated?"

No response.

"You used to make fun of the guy," I say. "His phony British accent, his ugly black goatee, his snobbishness, his zero sense of humor. Was that all a show to keep me from catching on?"

Again, no response.

I should have guessed—the late nights at work, the offsite meetings, the unresponsive sex.

I feel fury building in me again. I turn back to Adele. She playing it cool now. She's good at that. The ice queen.

She redoes her blouse so the buttons line up. "You should leave. The neighbors have probably phoned the police."

I shrug.

She looks up at me for the first time. "Just what do you think you were doing sneaking around in my home like that?"

"Searching for my recorder's memory cards. I know damn well you lied about the burglary."

"I didn't lie," Adele says.

That's her high-pitched voice when she's lying.

I say, "It would be easy for me to check the police logs and contact the insurance company. So why don't you save time and hand the cards over?"

Long silence, then "Because they're gone."

"Gone?"

She looks away. "I was so angry with you that I threw them in the trash."

"You did what?"

"I threw them away."

"Why?"

Adele folds her hands on her lap. "I told you, it was because I was so angry at you. See, you never listen to me."

Unbelievable!

Why would Adele do that to me? Why?

I turn in a complete circle, look skyward, wait for an answer.

Then it comes like a bolt out of the blue.

Oh, shit!

I should have guessed!

I bend down and shout in Adele's face, "It was that slimy bastard Beckworth who paid off the trial witnesses, wasn't it? He was jealous that I got the Pulitzer, and he was jealous that you were married to me!"

Adele keeps her head turned away.

"Well?" I say.

Adele shrugs, still not looking at me.

I take her chin in my hand, turn her toward me and lean down until our faces are inches apart. "Were you part of this?"

Adele closes her eyes. "No."

"But you knew."

"Not until after Beckworth insisted I give him the memory chips."
Adele opens her eyes. "I told him I didn't know where they were. He
kept asking, but I stuck to my story. After a while I got suspicious and
listened to the recorded interviews. That's when I found out about the
witnesses who lied. I concluded that Beckworth was the culprit, not
the contractor who operated the shelters."

"Why in hell didn't you tell me when you found this out?"

No response.

"And why didn't you destroy the chips when you had first found
them?"

"I wanted something to hold over Beckworth. I didn't quite trust
him."

"But you kept on fucking him anyway, didn't you?"

She keeps her eyes turned away.

I straighten up. "I'm waiting."

My pulse pounds. I'm breathing in bursts.

I grab the flowerpot and hurl it against the building.

Pow!

Dirt, geraniums and shards of pottery fly in all directions.

Adele pretends not to notice. Now she looks up at me, her
expression hard. "I want a divorce."

"Not as much as I do!"

I step back and let my arms drop.

It hurt hearing myself say that. Other people get divorces. Willy
got a divorce. Sherwood got a divorce. But not me. I always assumed
it would never happen to me.

Now it has.

The guy in the awful green shirt waddles across the street and stops
a few feet in front of me. "I must complain about—"

"Fuck off!"

"What?"

"Fuck off!" I step forward until we're inches apart. He's about a foot shorter than I am. I point across the street. "Get your fat ass over there right now, or I'll back the truck up to your living room and fill it with concrete!"

He stumbles backward, turns around, hustles across the street.

Adele says calmly, "I've been wanting to say something like that to him since the first day we moved in."

The first day we moved in, a long time ago, her a different person, me a different person.

Adele says, "You'd better get away before the police arrive."

Her voice is cool, odd, distant, like a stranger's. Was I ever married to this woman?

Hiram says, "Slap her around. If you don't have the *cajones* for that, at least tell her what a witch she is."

Clementine says, "Forgive her. Control your anger."

Anger? Yeah, I'm angry.

But shouldn't I be angrier? Shouldn't I be boiling mad, trembling all over, shouting and screaming and smashing more geranium pots against the side of the building?

But I don't feel that way. It's all over, all decided. Everything that I once felt for this woman has slipped away. Did I ever really love her, this woman seated near me, this stranger with a stranger's voice? She doesn't even look the same. I don't remember that her nose was so pointy, her eyes so small, her mouth so tight. Who is this woman in the red slacks and ugly pink blouse?

My mind drifts toward Melody. I see her smiling at me across the newsroom, tapping her watch to remind me of a deadline, walking over and tapping me in the head. I smell lilac perfume. Melody.

"There's a woman at the magazine who keeps asking me out," I say. "I've of course been turning her down because I'm married."

That's not quite true. No, it's an outright lie. It's always been so easy to lie to Adele, and for Adele to lie to me.

She doesn't change expression.

I say, "She's funny and smart and exotically beautiful—a real femme fatale."

Still no response. Adele gets to her feet, calm and collected, back to her normal cool composure. "Beckworth loved that car. He'll bring charges, you know."

"No, he won't."

"No?"

"If he does," I say, "I'll tell his puritanical boss at the *Globe* that I caught him porking a subordinate. There goes his job. Tell him that."

Adele gives this some thought. "At least he'll try to make you pay for the damage."

"Let him."

We hear sirens.

She says, "You'd better get moving."

"That's what a lawbreaker would do."

"What are you?"

"A performance artist."

Chapter 12

A hint of a smile from Adele, then she stands up. "I'm going back upstairs to break the news to Beckworth."

A squad car squeals up, its siren dies down, and two policemen step out. The driver saunters over to the BMW, crouches down and examines the front bumper. "Is that your car under there?"

"Nope. It belongs to my wife's lover. I just caught him upstairs banging her."

The cop tips his hat back. "Well played."

"I figured."

"But I've got to take you in."

"I figured."

Another squad car pulls up. The first two cops walk over and explain the situation to the driver. He laughs, looks my direction and gives me the thumbs up.

Then they cuff me, drive me to the station, remove my handcuffs and sit me at a desk where an avuncular cop with gray sideburns types up a report. He lets me call Uncle Sid on my cell.

When he answers, I say, "I might not be in at work for a while."

"You finally got some smarts and got the hell out of town?"

"More like the Back Bay police station."

"A police station? What'd you do?"

"To begin with, I stole a concrete truck from Netterfield Construction site, and then I—"

"Netterfield? Damn it, Jeff! Hank Ramsey owns the company! You know that, don't you?"

"Yup, and… uh… hold on, the cop at the front desk is waving me over. I'll get back to you."

The cop hands me the desk phone. "It's your lawyer."

Lawyer? I haven't called a lawyer. "Yes?" I say into the phone.

"That car was brand new, you bastard!"

"Fuck you, Beckworth!"

The cop raises an eyebrow.

"No, Jeffrey, you're the one who's fucked if you don't accept my terms. I won't press charges, but only if you promise to keep your fat mouth shut about the… uh… little scene you witnessed earlier."

His terms? They were mine, relayed through Adele. The narcissistic peckerhead always has to pretend he's in charge. "I don't know," I say, dragging my words out. "It seems like your boss should find out that—"

"Do you want to go to prison?"

"It'll give me a chance to work through my stack of old *New Yorkers*."

"Then do you want the courts to sell your house to reimburse me for my destroyed BMW?"

I pause as if I were thinking this over. Which I'm not. "Okay, I guess, but only because I don't want to see Adele's reputation damaged."

"Give the phone back to the cop."

I hand it to him.

He listens, nods, hangs up and gives me a curious look. "You lucked out. For some reason, the guy's not pressing charges, but we've still got you on stealing the…" He looks over my shoulder. "Uh, oh."

I turn around. Hank and Freddie are ambling my direction. Uncle Sid must have called them and pleaded my case. Hank wears a dark blue suit, Freddie a sleeveless black shirt. Hank spreads his arms and smiles. "Hey Bill, how's life treating you?"

The cop behind the desk shrugs. "Doing okay."

A sergeant steps out from a back office.

Hank pumps his hand. "Hey, Max, how're the wife and kids? You got three boys now, right?"

He holds up four fingers.

Hank slaps him on the back. "Keeping yourself busy."

Max gestures toward me. "That's the guy who stole your truck."

"This is all a big misunderstanding," Hank says. "The jerk works for me." Hank grabs me by the elbow. "Give me a minute to talk to this dickhead."

He walks me to a corner. "That's my truck you stole, asshole!"

"Just one more of life's little coincidences. Your truck was the closest one around."

"What the hell were you thinking?" he asks.

"I wasn't thinking. I had just caught my wife boinking her boss."

Hank takes this in. "So you took it out on the guy's Beemer?"

"Yup."

"Next time shoot him in the balls and leave my trucks out of it."

Hank leads me back to the sergeant, pats me on the shoulder and says in a chuckly loud voice, "I love this doofus even though he got his brains in his ass. I tell him to drive a load of concrete to a BMW dealer across town, and what does the dumb shit do? He drives six blocks away and fills up some guy's BMW with concrete? Can you believe that?"

Neither cop appears to believe that, but they say nothing.

Hank reaches up and smacks my cheek. "Stupidest guy I got working for me."

The desk sergeant says, "What about that pile of concrete? It can't stay there."

"I'll send my guys over before it hardens."

The sergeant nods, then says to me, "You're free to go. Just stay away from concrete trucks."

A touch of police station levity.

I step outside. Hank and Freddie follow.

Hank says, "Okay, the little woman's getting something on the side. So what? It happens all the time. Most guys don't go around stealing trucks and destroying expensive cars. But you do. What the hell got into your head?"

"I don't know."

"You don't know? You don't fucking know?"

"No."

But I do know. As hard as I tried, I had let Hiram get into my head. Again.

• • •

I start walking toward the closest subway station, but get only two blocks before a gray Buick pulls over to the curb. It's Sid. He motions me inside. I get in and tell him about Adele and Beckworth.

"It hurts now, but in the long run you're better off without her," Uncle Sid says.

"Maybe."

He glances over at me. "Why steal a cement truck?"

"So I could fill Beckworth's new BMW with concrete."

"Say you're joking."

"Nope."

Uncle Sid smiles. "To the top?"

"Over the top."

"You've got style," Uncle Sid says and pats my knee. "Where's your pickup?"

"I'll give you directions."

He pulls away. "You out on bail?"

"I'm free and clear. I have enough leverage on the guy to keep him from pressing charges, and Hank said I didn't steal the truck because I work for him."

"The cops believed that?"

"Not for a minute."

Sid guns the engine, cuts off a taxi and ignores the honking. He still drives as if he were behind the wheel of a getaway car. He says, "Sometimes I can't figure out why you do what you do. You were like that as a kid. Remember the time you barricaded the principal in his office? What in hell made you do that?"

That was Hiram's idea.

"Then there was that day you and Willy stole all the ice cream from the school lunch freezer and sold cones during recess."

That was Ebenezer's idea.

Sid reaches over and pats my knee. "Still, you were basically a good kid. Willy, too. How's he doing?"

"Okay. He's fixing up my house until he finds a job."

"Good to hear."

Willy idolized Uncle Sid, partly because of his mob connections, but mostly because Uncle Sid was so kind to him. Once, after Willy had taken an especially bad beating from his dad, I reported it to Uncle Sid, and he got a Ramsey soldier out to rough up Willy's dad. Willy never got hit again, and his life got easier. Somewhat easier, anyway.

Uncle Sid cruises through a red light. "I was sick when I found out Willy had gone to prison."

"He says he's never going back. He didn't particularly like the place."

"No one does. And you sure as hell wouldn't have, either. What in hell were you thinking when you destroyed that car?" Sid hits the horn and sends a teenager leaping back onto the curb. "You're lucky to be free. Did you think you'd be safe from Hank in prison?"

"Nope."

"Bet your ass," Uncle Sid says. He's silent for a moment. "You weren't trying to get yourself locked up to atone for... well, you know?"

I shake my head. Nothing will ever atone for that. "Nope."

Sid glances over at me, then back at the road. "Well, don't do something dumbass like that again. You want to stay out of prison. Take if from someone who knows."

Mom and I were late the day they released Uncle Sid. We trotted across the parking lot to the prison gate. Mom rushed up and threw her arms around an old man with gray hair and baggy brown pants. I just stood there. Has Mom made a mistake? Who is this guy? Then he reached around behind her, smiled and gave me thumbs-up. I started to bawl.

I say, "You gave up four years of your life for me."

Uncle Sid pats my knee. "Don't think of it that way. Hell, things weren't so bad in the can. The food was lousy, but I survived." He laughs. "Shit, I even had status there because everyone took me for a killer, not just a gofer who got sent out to pick up the boss's dry cleaning. I denied I'd killed anyone, but always in such a way that no one would believe me. Shit, guys stepped aside when I walked through the cell block. Even old man Ramsey was impressed. He sent me pastries, cold cuts, expensive cheeses, cigarettes and pot, and once even smuggled a hooker inside."

Uncle Sid stops the car across from the lot where my pickup is parked. He turns toward me. "I still have a reputation with guys in the North End, guys with connections. They nod when they see me on the street." Uncle Sid shuts off the engine. "Hell, a few years back, I was even approached in a bar by a heavy from a Baltimore outfit who wanted me to whack his boss."

"No kidding?"

"No kidding."

"What did you do?"

"What do you think I did? I turned him down, of course. But I took my time. I pulled out my phone and pretended to study the calendar, then I told the guy I was booked up through the next year."

We both lean our heads back and laugh.

We've always been able to make each other laugh.

"So," Uncle Sid says, "I got something out of my time away."

That's what he always calls it—his 'time away.' What he mostly got out of it was gray hair, a hacking cough that's never left him, a stoop, and a tinge of gloom. I say, "Thanks for what you did for me. I'm sorry."

"You keep saying that. Don't."

I start to get out of the car, but Uncle Sid grabs my arm and pulls me back.

He taps his chest. "It's all in here."

"What is?"

"What I did. For once I got something right." Uncle Sid's voice is gravely and shaky. "You didn't have to grow up with anyone ever knowing about the… incident. Think of how kids would have treated you at school? They'd have called you names. You wouldn't have had any friends, your teachers would have treated you like shit, and no girl would have dated you. You'd have been branded for life."

"But you—"

"Let me enjoy it." Uncle Sid says, again tapping his chest. "Four years, yeah, to be perfectly honest, they mostly sucked. But I've had a couple decades since then to feel good about myself. I haven't done much to be proud of in my life. I broke the law a bunch of times, I disgraced my family, but here's this one time I got something right." Uncle Sid's voice cracks. "I'll carry it to my grave."

I lay my hand on his shoulder. I want to say something, but don't know what it would be. Thanks would be appropriate, but Uncle Sid doesn't want to hear that.

We sit for a couple minutes, both looking straight ahead. Eventually the big lump in my throat goes down. Uncle Sid stops sniffling.

"So," I say, "you were asked to whack some guy, but you couldn't fit it into your busy schedule?"

Uncle Sid laughs. "Yup."

"That's great—'The Overbooked Hitman.' That's my next article."

He punches my shoulder. "Like hell it is."

Chapter 13

SCORPIO Oct. 23 – Nov. 21

To win someone's love, find out what they love.
Vinegar does a fine job of removing concrete stains.

I call in sick the next morning, which in a way I am. I sleep late, drink beer, jog, try to read but can't concentrate, sleep some more, lift weights, watch TV, swear at the news, drink more beer. I can't keep the image of a hairy, naked Beckworth from creeping into my head. In the evening I sit Willy down and relate my troubles. Since he's had a wife dump him, I ask how he handled things.

"I said to myself 'Screw it' and moved on."

"Did it work?" I ask.

"Seems so. Anyway, maybe this is the best thing that could have happened to you."

Willy and Adele loathed each other.

Willy knows me better than anyone except Uncle Sid. "You might be right," I say.

"I'm always right."

The next day I arrive at work two hours late, take off my sneakers, set them on my desk and use a wooden ruler to chip at the dried concrete. I pile the pieces next to the toy fire engine. Sweet souvenirs.

I look up to see Sherwood standing nearby, coffee cup in hand.

He watches me work for a minute, then says, "You look like the guy who let a grounder roll through his legs and cost his team the World Series. What's going on?"

"Nothing, really."

"Nothing? Instead of writing, you're stabbing at your shoes with a ruler, your hair is a mess, your eyes are bloodshot, and your breath smells like the dumpster behind a butcher shop. So, talk to me."

I glance across the newsroom. Janet is talking into her phone, and Melody is squinting at her screen. "I caught Adele in bed with her asshole boss."

Sherwood takes a step back. Coffee spills. He spreads the puddle around with the tip of his shoe. "Oh."

"Yeah, oh."

"That's tough, Jeff. What are you going to do about it?"

I pull on my left sneaker. "I've already taken concrete steps."

Sherwood nods. "After I found out my wife was cheating, I pretended I didn't know about it and did nothing. I always take the easy way out." Sherwood sighs. "I go from comfort zone to comfort zone."

"We all do."

"But I'm better at it," Sherwood says and shuffles back to his desk. I watch him go. The man I don't want to become.

I open my word processor to a new file and type:

Yum, Yum!

Which successful TV late-night host bakes his own scrumptious fruit cakes? The answer will surprise you because...

I stop typing.

Again I see Beckworth's slimy shrunken dick pasted against his woolly groin. Again I see Adele rising from bed, her nipples erect. Again I smell sex.

I bang my fist on my desk. The cement pile crumbles. The Spirit of St. Louis rolls onto the floor and bends a wing.

I pick the plane up and set it back on the desk.

Janet looks up from her work. "Anything I can do for you, Jeff?"

"Would you beat the shit out of some guy for me?"

"I'll be glad to, dear," she says and turns to her monitor. "Just let me finish up here."

I close my eyes and take three deep breaths as Clementine advises me to at moments like this. I picture the stream that runs near the Concord house. It's autumn. Red-and-yellow leaves float past. I see a great blue heron standing on its long legs at water's edge. Now it's winter, and I'm on skis atop a high and sunny slope in Vermont, anticipating the run, powdery fresh snow below me, a refreshing breeze on my cheeks.

And Adele is beside me, smiling. We loved to ski. The best times we had together.

I open my eyes. Melody is watching from across the newsroom. She cocks her head, twists her mouth into a funny angle, flutters her eyes, then smiles. In spite of my crappy mood, I smile back. We lock eyes, then she smiles again, and I'm no longer angry.

But I want to be angry, furious, thunderously ripped. So I picture Adele stepping out of bed, walking toward me, naked, her dark muff glistening. I see Beckworth again, his mouth half open. I hear him snoring.

I take three more deep breathes. Just say 'Screw it' and move on. Listen to the wisdom of Willy the Philosopher.

I pick up the Spirit of Saint Louis and straighten the bent wing. In politics Lindbergh sucked, but the guy had guts. He flew a fragile and overloaded single-engine plane across the Atlantic. Free as a bird.

I hold the plane up and spin the propeller, just as I used to do when I was a little kid sitting on the faded red oriental rug in the middle of the living room. I was free back then, before the shooting. Free as a bird.

I set the plane back on my desk and replay the movie of Beckworth's BMW sinking under concrete, the doors bursting open and the windshield shattering, and I hear the tires explode one by one—*pop, pop, pop, pop*—and I hear the axles snap. Beautiful, absolutely beautiful. The work of a great performance artist.

Melody sidles over. "It's good to see you smiling again. When you got into work, I was afraid to come over because you looked ready to bite someone's head off. What's wrong?"

"Nothing's wrong, okay?"

Melody steps back.

"Sorry," I say. "Sorry, Melody." I reach out and touch her wrist.

"Want to talk about it?"

Not really, but Melody will eventually find out because Sherwood is the company gossip. "I caught Adele in bed with her boss."

Melody jerks her head back. Her jaw drops.

"We're getting a divorce," I say.

"Well, I should hope so!" She screws up her mouth. "Did you actually—"

"Catch them in the act? Not quite. But right afterward."

"Sorry." She half closes her eyes and studies me. "You didn't do something stupid, did you?"

"Would I do that?"

"You would do that."

"Nothing that harmed anyone."

Melody nods, darts her eyes about. She's trying to come up with something else to say.

So am I. I watch Sherwood standing at Janet's desk, whispering, now and then glancing in my direction. The word is already getting around.

I point at the sheet of paper in Melody's hand. "What do you have for me?"

"Oh, this," Melody says, looking at it as if for the first time. "It's just a summary of what I found out about terrorist prisons on U.S.

soil. We can talk about this later. You have more important things on your mind."

"Which I'd like to forget." I take the paper and skim through it. "Looks as if you weren't able to find anything on the subject."

"Which is something."

Sherwood's right. Melody does find excuses for talking to me. A nice thought. I point at a comma. "Is that necessary?"

She glances at the page. "Serial commas are optional. Certainly you know that."

Certainly I know that. And Melody knows that I know that. My way of getting her to hang around a little longer. And she knows that, too. "Melody, if you can find the time, I'll like you to keep working on this and get back to me regularly, several times a day, even just to update me that you're not getting anything. Also, please find out what you can about recently built federal buildings that are like prisons but are actually not prisons."

"I don't know what that means."

"Neither do I. That's why I need your help."

"Then I can bring you anything, and you won't know the difference."

She pinches my cheek and smiles. Melody is a pincher, a toucher, a smiler. She's buoyant, sweet, sometimes ditzy, and probably the smartest person I've ever met. If not that, the nicest, which is all that matters.

Also there are those curves.

Today she's wearing tight black jeans and a gray cardigan, partly unbuttoned, with a faint tan dribble down the front of her white blouse. She often arrives at work with wet spots from where she's scrubbed at food stains. Her four-year-old is a messy eater.

She shifts from foot to foot.

I try to think up something to say to keep her around longer, something to make her laugh. But I'm not in much of a laugh-making mood. Maybe something to make her think? What did I

read about porpoises in today's newspaper? They communicate by...
what? Slapping their tails? Vocalizations? Can't remember.

What the hell—why don't I just come out and ask her out on a
date? I'm no longer quite a married man. Still, I know she'll turn me
down again.

Then I recall the horoscope Janet wrote for me today: 'To win
someone's love, find out what they love.'

I say, "I'll bet Dawn loves the merry-go-round on the Boston
Greenway."

Melody shakes her head. "I've never taken her."

"Never?"

"Never."

"She would love it," I say.

"I'm sure she would."

"Would you let me take her?"

Melody cocks her head to the side. "I suppose—"

"You're invited, too."

Melody shifts from one foot to the other, opens her mouth to say
something, closes it, blushes.

"Sunday afternoon?" I say.

Melody looks at her hands. "Sure. Dawn would love it."

I search for something else to talk about, but nothing comes. I'm
the high school freshman who's asked the cheerleader at the next
desk out on a date, and to his surprise she's said yes.

Porpoises? Should I try to talk about porpoises? Just make
something up about how they communicate? Then I remember
something I read this morning. "I saw in the sports section that a
speedy wide receiver's just been signed."

"Maybe they'll get to the World Series this year."

"Wide receivers play football," I say with a satisfied smile. "You
don't know how comforting it is to find out that there's something
you don't know. In fact—"

Melody is grinning.

"You did know," I say. "You were jerking my chain." My desk phone rings. I check the caller. "Sorry, but I have to take this."

I watch Melody walk back to her desk. Yes, she's definitely wearing tighter jeans to work.

I pick up the receiver. "Yes."

"You are a flaming asshole!"

"It's always nice hearing from you, Drucker."

"You stole a truck and destroyed some guy's ragtop. What in hell was that all about?"

"It wasn't just some guy, it was the slimebucket I'd just caught porking my wife."

Silence, then, "Oh."

"Yeah, oh."

"But you're still in a shitload of trouble."

"Nope. The car's owner isn't pressing charges, and Hank Ramsey got me off for stealing his truck."

"Hank Ramsey? You stole Hank Ramsey's truck? Why in hell did you do that?"

"I got some bad advice."

"Bad advice?" Drucker says. "Who in hell thought it was a good advice to steal a cement truck from a mob-owned construction company and destroy a brand new BMW?

"A giver of bad advice."

"If you knew that, then why in hell did you listen?"

Good question. Why in hell did I listen? Why in hell have I ever listened to Hiram? Or Clementine? Or Ebenezer or Colette? "Maybe this time the advice wasn't so bad after all."

"What do you mean?"

"It helped me cement my relationship with Hank."

Drucker groans and hangs up.

Chapter 14

SCORPIO Oct. 23 – Nov. 21

Fear is only in your head, where it grows and grows. Dwelling on your own troubles makes you miss those of others. Romance flourishes when sprinkled with surprise.

I park my truck, walk to Boston Harbor and find an open bench near the disputed Christopher Columbus statue that gazes out over the harbor. My watch reads 12:50. Melody and her daughter are due in ten minutes. Melody's always on time. No surprise there. Adele was never on time. No surprise there, either.

I stand up, yawn, stretch, and try to look nonchalant while I turn in a slow circle to check out the neighborhood. I don't see Hank, Freddie, Drucker, or any suspicious-looking characters crouched behind the trash cans. Driving in from Concord, I doubled back several times and did the same once I got to Boston. The last thing I want is to bring attention to Melody and Dawn.

Although I don't spot mobsters or mischief-makers, I do see the air shimmering about a couple hundred feet off to my left, right next to a teenage juggler who keeps dropping his pins. Hiram? I sure as hell hope not. I don't want his warped advice on wooing a woman. Clementine? Not so good either. She'd lecture me about my marriage.

The ancestors turns solid long enough to tell it's a man. Is that Grandpa Ebenezer? It sure looks like him—same big belly, same curled mustache. Then he falls down.

Falls down? That's something new. And poof—he's gone.

What the hell was that all about?

The next time I see Clementine or Hiram, I'll report that Ebenezer hasn't gone Back There yet. Worrisome.

A taxi pulls up, and Melody and Dawn step out. One o'clock on the dot.

Dawn has chubby cheeks, big eyes like her mother and the same wavy red hair. She's in jeans and a pink shirt covered in bunnies. She clutches a round Quaker Oats box with red crayon scribbles on the side.

Melody has on a sleeveless white blouse and tight tan slacks.

When they reach me, Melody says, "Dawn, this is Jeff, the friend I told you about."

Dawn slips behind Melody, peers around from behind her and stares at me.

Melody shifts to her other foot and lowers her voice. "Let's begin with a few ground rules. This isn't a date. I don't date married—"

"I'm getting a divorce."

"You've already told me that. But technically you're still married."

"I guess so." I point at Dawn's shoe. "May I retie it?"

She nods.

I kneel down and tie the laces. "Is the pretty lady your little sister?"

Dawn giggles. "You're silly."

Melody says, "Jeff is indeed silly."

I point at the box that Dawn is clutching. "What's in there? A puppy?"

"You're silly."

Melody releases her mother's hand, shyly opens the box and shows me the inside.

I see three pebbles, four pennies, a dried oak leaf, an empty gum wrapper, a tiny brown bear, and a lump of something that I don't want to know about.

I say, "You like to collect things?"

Dawn nods.

Melody bends down and inspects the oatmeal box. "I once found a dead finch in there." Melody says and straightens up. "Checks out okay today, though."

I dig into my jacket pocket, take out a marble-sized blue globe on a short metal chain and show it to Dawn. "I gave ten dollars at that Save-the-Earth booth over there, and they handed me this. Would you like it?"

Dawn snatches the globe, dumps it into the box and closes the lid.

"What do we say," Melody asks.

"Thank you."

"You're welcome." I stand up. "Now let's go for a walk, and later you and your baby sister can take me on the merry-go-round."

"You're silly."

We walk, Melody on the left, me on the right, Dawn in the middle. To my surprise, she reaches up and takes my hand. It's tiny, soft, warm and sticky, and it feels just right.

We stroll along the Greenway, the stretch of grassy pathways, small trees, shrubs and flowers that a few years back replaced the awkward elevated road that ran along the harbor. We pass vendor stands selling brightly color prints of Venice, cutting boards, silver earrings and tie-dye shirts.

"Do people still wear tie-die shirts?" I ask.

"Ironically, I believe," Melody says.

There's also honey, hats, homemade soap and jars of beard oil.

"What's beard oil for?" I ask.

"Beards, I should think."

Traffic slips by on both sides, an occasional airliner passes high overhead, and someone in a speeding red Civic plays rock music loud enough to break windows, but for now I'm in a green space, safe from the outside world. I try to forget about Adele, OASIS, Drucker, Hank, the murderous Freddie, the errant Grandfather Ebenezer and how a whole line of my family could disappear without a trace.

We pass a tall man in kilts who's playing a wheezing bagpipe. Dawn points at his knees. "He's silly."

We come upon an open-air children's theater. Six actors cavort in dragon costumes. Kids squeal, laugh, clap their hands.

Dawn pushes her face into her mother's leg. "I'm scared."

"Me, too," I say.

Dawn looks up at me.

I bend down. "Want to know what I do when I'm frightened?"

Dawn shakes her head.

"I say magic words to make me safe. Do you know any magic words?"

She shakes her head again.

I hold out my hands. "May I pick you up?"

Dawn nods.

I lift her up, sit her on my shoulder and say, "Goobly, doobly, hoop."

Dawn giggles. "Goppity, gop, gop."

I say, "Hoopity, doopity, poopity."

Dawn says, "Poopity, poop, poop!"

Melody says, "Good grief."

Dawn says, "Poop, doop, poop!"

I say, "Poop, ploop, poop!"

Melody says, "Okay, children, that's enough." She tugs my elbow. "Time for the merry-go-round."

I carry Dawn to the merry-go-round and sit her on the butterfly she's pointed out. Melody holds her around the waist. I climb onto a pensive black-and-white skunk. Dawn points at me and giggles.

We ride three times to Joni Mitchell's 'Circle Game.' Dawn wants to go again, but Melody lifts her off the butterfly. "Let's find someplace to sit. I'm pooped."

"Poop!" Dawn shouts. "Mommy said 'Poop'!"

We find a play yard and turn Dawn loose. Melody and I sit side-by-side, watching Dawn go up and down the slide, over and over, squealing each trip down.

Melody sets the oatmeal box next to her foot. "You like kids."

"Nope. I'm just trying to impress you."

"I think you like kids."

"I'm just trying to impress you."

Dawn reminds me of Willy's younger sister—same chubby cheeks, same string of questions, same need for attention. Whenever Willy's parents went on a bender and disappeared, sometimes for days, I'd come over and help Willy take care of Jeannie. When she was eight, she went to live with an aunt in California. We both missed her.

Dawn waves from the top of the slide. We wave back.

A baseball rolls up to our feet. Two teenagers are playing catch nearby. Before I can reach for the ball, Melody snatches it up, goes into a windup and hurls it at the guy with the catcher's mitt.

Whack!

The boy examines the ball in his mitt. "A perfect slider!" he shouts. "Can you pitch for our team?"

"Can't," Melody says, sitting back down. "I'm under contract to the Red Sox."

"Where'd you learn to throw a ball like that?" I ask.

"From my three older brothers. They let me play baseball with them, climb rocks, explore caves, that sort of thing."

"You liked that?"

"Not always, but I refused to let them see me frightened. Sometimes they'd dare me to do stuff they were scared of. I was the only one not afraid to bungee jump, for example." Melody touches her finger against a front tooth. "I chipped this one when I tried to skateboard down some library steps. Also, I once broke my arm skiing off trail and fractured three ribs when I fell from a pine tree."

"Now I'm afraid of you."

"You'd better be," Melody says, punching my shoulder.

Again we exchange waves with Dawn atop the slide.

After a minute Melody says, "I'm still digging for information on OASIS, but not getting very far. I did find out that Congress scheduled a hearing two years ago on OASIS's activities, then canceled it, no reason given. I'll keep digging." Melody lays her hand on my forearm. "I assume you're writing an article exposing OASIS?"

"Maybe."

"Do you intend to sell it to a national newspaper?"

"Maybe."

"That's what you say when you mean 'No.' Melody studies me for a long moment. "Are you in some kind of trouble?"

"No, of course not."

"Then why are you acting so mysterious?"

I wave at Dawn at the top of the slide. "Okay, I probably shouldn't tell you this, but Sid has me working on a special project for a mutual acquaintance. Nothing important. That's all I can say."

"Oh."

I can't tell whether Melody believes me or not. I hate lying to her, this woman who probably never fibbed even as a child. Marriage with Adele was a string of lies—some were mine, most were hers. So much deviousness. So much tension. Lying to Melody about OASIS is for her own good, I keep telling myself, so it's justified. But I know that's how small lies turn into big lies.

At least I can come clean about something else. I turn to Melody, her warm hand still resting on my arm. "I wasn't honest the other day when I said I hadn't done something stupid after I caught Adele in bed with her boss."

"I figured you were fibbing." She pulls her hand back. "Okay, buster, tell me what you did."

"Uh... well, I broke into Adele's home, stole a truck, filled her boyfriend's $70,000 convertible with concrete and got hauled off to a police station."

Melody opens her mouth, closes it.

I fill in the details, leaving out the part about Hank Ramsey.

Still Melody says nothing.

Dawn races over to show us a faint red mark on her elbow. Melody kisses it. "All better."

"All better," Dawn says and scampers back to the slide.

Melody says, "You must have been deeply hurt after you witnessed the… uh… incident with Adele."

"I sure as hell was."

"And extremely stupid."

"That, too."

"But I understand," Melody said, her voice going small. "I know from experience what a hurt can do to a person." She squeezes my arm. "You just have to dust yourself off and move on."

"That's what Willy keeps telling me, only in more colorful terms."

I want to reach over and touch Melody's hand, her arm, her shoulder. I want to kiss the side of her neck. But I don't. "You said that you 'know from experience.' Want to talk about it?"

Melody looks off to her left. "Five years ago this month, my ex-husband followed me home from the newspaper where I was an editor, pushed his way into my apartment and…" Melody closes her mouth and turns to watch Dawn atop the slide, who's waving both arms to get our attention.

I say, "Dawn…?"

"Yes."

Neither of us speaks for a minute.

I say, "You never thought to…?"

"No."

"Does your ex-husband know?"

"His cousin called three weeks after the attack and said my ex had been killed in a motorcycle accident." After a long silence, Melody says, "It was a relief, to tell the awful truth. But I was still traumatized by what he'd done to me. I stopped going into work and went into a deep funk. I had no family within a thousand miles, no money, no life. I drew the shades, ate fudge ripple ice cream all day long and watched 24/7 news. Then Dawn started kicking, and—and just like that—I got my life back. I told myself I was never going to feel sorry for myself again, or be unhappy, or make the people around me unhappy."

I want to pull Melody into my arms. Instead I say, "That works?"

"Most of the time."

"How did you end up here?"

"I moved from Providence to Boston, got a job at the *Tattler* and rented a tiny apartment. My landlady's a sweet woman who has three Siamese cats, plays the harmonica and—small world—dated your Uncle Sid years ago."

"No kidding?"

Melody takes a tissue from her handbag, dabs her eyes and smiles, happy to have moved on to a new subject. "No, I'm not kidding. They dated for years. My landlady wanted to get married, but Sid didn't. It seems he was still pining for an old flame."

"The romantic old goat."

"Who'd have guessed?"

I cringe when I see Dawn ride down the slide on her stomach, but she lands with a thump and a smile. "You're always so bubbly and good-natured," I say. "I'd never have guessed you had a care in the world."

"Everyone has a scar that won't heal," Melody says and stuffs the tissue back into her bag. "Including you. Maybe especially you. Want to talk about it?"

"Not a chance."

"Because you're a man?"

"Because I'm a man."

Melody rolls her eyes.

Again the air wobbles off to my left. A figure appears, falls, disappears. What the hell?

Dawn starts wailing and runs over to us. She says a mean boy pushed ahead of her in line. Melody scoops her up and sets her on her lap. "I think someone is overtired and cranky."

"When I get overtired," I say, "I get cranky, too."

Melody stands up, still holding Dawn. "Then we'd better get both of you home before there's a major meltdown."

We start toward my pickup.

Dawn rests her head on her mother's shoulder and stares at me, no longer crying. She's already forgotten about the line-jumping meanie. "Mommy says you don't wear shoes and you play with a toy airplane."

"I do."

"Grownups don't play with toys."

"I do."

"That's silly," Dawn says.

"I am silly."

"Mommy says you're funny and cute and you—"

"Rest your head on my shoulder," Melody says, pushing Dawn down. "Time for beddy-bye."

I offer to take us somewhere to eat, but Melody wants to get Dawn home. When we get close to my pickup, Melody stops in her tracks.

I say, "Uh… when I offered to give you a ride home, I guess I wasn't thinking about how grungy my truck looks." I hold up my phone. "Let me call a taxi."

She pulls my hand down. "Nope."

"You're sure?"

"I'm sure. But it *is* shocking."

"Shocking?"

"Yes, shocking."

Melody hands Dawn to me. She rests her head on my shoulder. Her hair is warm and damp, and she smells of soap and perspiration.

Melody opens her purse, takes out a box of crayons, selects the red, walks over to the door on the driver's side and adds the missing 'l' in 'Instalation.'

She steps back, hands on hips. "There, all better. Is the other side equally flawed?"

"Yup."

Melody goes around to the other door, comes back a moment later and drops the crayon into her purse. She takes Dawn from me, hooks her into the car seat I bought the day before, and we drive away.

Melody pats the dash. "My uncle had a 1995 Chevy just like this. Does it have the 4.3 liter V6, the 5.0 liter V8, or the 5.7 liter V8?"

"Uh…"

"From the way it accelerates," Melody says, "I'd guess it's the 5.7."

"How do you know so much about trucks?"

"My dad owned an auto repair shop. As a kid I used to like to hang around and help out, especially with the stock car. When I got to be a teenager, he'd let me drive it around the track as fast as I liked, and even let me race, but only a few times. That was too bad because I was a much better driver than the guy he'd hired. He never won. I won twice. By the way, your front end needs aligning. That's why it shimmies."

"Is there anything you don't know?"

Melody reaches around Dawn and punches me lightly on the shoulder. "Nope."

I pull over in front of her apartment. Dawn wakes up, and I carry her to the door and set her on her feet. Melody takes out her key.

I say, "Is a kiss permitted?"

"Uh…"

"Just a small one?"

"Well."

I hold my thumb and forefinger a half inch apart. "Just the tiniest?"

Melody shifts from one foot to the other, glances down at Dawn, back at me. "I suppose so." She drags out her words.

I lean forward.

Melody goes up on tiptoes and leans forward.

I bend over, scoop up Dawn, kiss her on the top of the head and set her back down.

Melody leans back, blinks twice, then gives me a wry smile.

I shake her hand, tell her that I had a really swell time, walk away, and don't look back.

Romance flourishes when sprinkled with surprise.

When I get back to my pickup, I'm shocked to find Grandpa Ebenezer inside, slumped in the seat, his hair a tangle, his tie undone, his eyes rolling in their sockets. Usually he's neat, natty, composed.

"What's wrong, Grandpa?"

Ebenezer blinks, shakes his head, says nothing.

I start the engine and pull away. "Your Grandmother Clementine is worried sick about you. Where have you been all this time? Shouldn't you be Back There?"

Ebenezer lifts his hand, drops it onto his knee, lowers his head and falls asleep.

Chapter 15

SCORPIO Oct. 23 - Nov. 21

Never be afraid to ask questions, even if you fear the answer. The world we occupy is strange and wonderful. For easy wallpaper removal, use a diluted mixture of vinegar and water.

Grandpa Ebenezer snores all the way to Concord. I leave him asleep in the pickup and go inside the house. I didn't smell alcohol on his breath. Then again, does he even have a breath? And have I ever seen an ancestor sleep?

Ebenezer hasn't been by in a year and a half, so his appearance today is a surprise. He's my dad's father, a jolly, heavy-bellied womanizer.

I find Willy scraping wallpaper in the living room. Clear plastic sheets cover the furniture and floor, and shreds of flowered green paper stick to his elbows. He waves his scraper. "I've been expecting you for a while."

"Sorry, but things ran late."

"No problem." Willy points at the scraper lying on a chair. "Join in the fun."

I grab a chicken leg from the bucket of KFC and start working on a patch of dampened wallpaper, scraping with my right hand and holding the chicken in my left. "I was on a date with Melody, my editor. Well, sort of a date."

"How did it go?"

"There was a goodbye kiss at the door."

"That's a start."

We work for half an hour, saying nothing until Willy tosses his scraper on a chair. "I'm hanging it up. The game's starting."

"I'll be along in a few minutes."

But it takes me an hour to grind through four layers of paper before I reach the plaster underneath. A trip back through time. I wonder who chose each layer of wallpaper and whether they were happy with it afterward.

"Your grandmother picked out the blue with the yellow flowers."

I turn around. It's Grandpa Ebenezer. His suit is wrinkled, his pointy black shoes are scuffed, his hair flies in all directions.

"What's happened to you?" I ask.

"They caught me and put me in a cell."

"Who caught you? What cell?"

Ebenezer shakes his head and settles silently onto a desk chair covered in plastic. "There were flashing lights, and it was a terrible place."

"What are you talking about?"

Ebenezer points a shaky finger at the spot on the wall where I'd painted a test swatch. "Tan's all wrong," he says and closes his eyes. "They ran electricity through my head. I begged them to stop but they wouldn't."

"You could talk to them? Who were they? Relatives?"

"No. It wasn't exactly talking, but they seemed to know what I was thinking. Maybe it had something to do with the electricity. Or the bright lights. They kept flashing and the room was ugly. I hated the room. It was gray. I hate gray."

"You're not making much sense," I say, turning back to scrape the wall. "I hadn't expected drinking to be such a problem where you… uh… live. I was picturing angels with harps."

Ebenezer gets up and stands beside me. "I was in Boston, heading to your magazine to give you advise on how to keep Adele from taking you to the cleaners, when a flash of light knocked me off my feet. I woke up in a cell."

"A cell?"

"It hurt," Ebenezer says and spreads his arms. "And I'm still hurting all over. And I'm exhausted. That's something new. Nothing's ever given me pain before when I was visiting. But this time—God Almighty—it hurt like the dickens. I passed out whenever they shot electricity through my head. I tried to escape but couldn't get through the walls."

"But you're here now."

"The lights went out last night during the big thunderstorm, and I got away. A couple others, too, but they got snatched back up right away. They were still mobile since they were late arrivals like me."

"What do you mean by 'still mobile' and 'late arrivals'?"

Ebenezer's eyes roll upward. "I don't like gray or tan, and you've never told me what idiot nailed the sitting room door shut."

"Uh… I'm not exactly sure who it was."

"I slipped inside once and saw dried blood on the carpet. You should pull the nails and open the door." Ebenezer scratches his scalp with both hands. "My head is still buzzing on account of the electricity."

I slip the scraper under a big strip of paper, pull it free and drop it into the trash can. "You'd better stay away from your Grandmother Clementine until you sober up. And you need to get Back There right now. You'd better get moving."

"I've got lots of time yet," Ebenezer says. "And I'm not drunk." He peers around the room. "I built this house."

"I know."

"Before I went to prison and lost all my money."

"I know."

"Tan's a terrible color."

"You've already said that." I grab the last drumstick. "I think you're having a drunken flashback to your time in prison."

"Blue would be a better color. My walls were gray—or did I say that already? Because they were lined in lead."

Lead? I stop working. "What walls?"

"My cell walls. I told you that already. Or I think I did. I'm having trouble remembering." Ebenezer rubs his temples.

"You're sure the walls were lead?"

"Ugly as hell. The whole place was ugly. The guards were ugly, too."

The roar of the TV reaches us. "Fuck!" Willy hollers. "Goddamn it! Son of a bitch!"

A Yankee home run.

"Your friend has a foul mouth," Ebenezer says. "Like Cedric."

"Cedric?"

"One of my guards. He swore a lot, too."

"Uh-huh."

"But Quincy was gentlemanly."

Cedric? Quincy?

I drop the scraper to the floor.

Cedric and Quincy were the two guards who caught Willy and me at the OASIS site.

I turn around and face Ebenezer. "You're sure they were Quincy and Cedric?"

"That's right. Quincy was tall and didn't talk much, and Cedric was pudgy and dumb as a biscuit." Ebenezer drops onto the couch, loosens his tie and stretches out full-length. "Instead of paint, you should put up wallpaper. It's classier. As for Adele's getting all your money, here's my advice: Tell your lawyer to—"

"Are you sure that's their names?"

"No need to shout. Would you forget the scoundrels who sent electricity squirting through your noggin?"

I can't believe what I'm hearing. Lead walls? Quincy? Cedric? Has Ebenezer been to the OASIS site?

"Grandpa, I want you to meet my buddy. Don't go anywhere."

He spreads his arms. "I have all of eternity."

I rush into the television room. Willy is slumped in front of the TV, a beer bottle in one hand, the other reaching into a bag of potato chips balanced on his stomach. "Willy, do you remember the names of the two guards from that day we checked out the OASIS site?"

"Quincy was the tall one, and the little prick was... um... Cedric. What's up?"

"My Grandpa Ebenezer says he's seen them. I want you to meet him. Or is that too weird?"

"I like weird," Willy says, sitting up and setting the beer and chips on the coffee table. "Beats the goat rodeo I'm watching—top of the fifth and the Yankees are up four runs."

Willy gets up and follows me, then stops. "He's not going to have rotting gray skin hanging off him like strips of wallpaper, is he?"

"No, he's not a corpse. Besides, you won't be able to see him."

"Right." Willy starts walking again. "Is he an angel?"

"Far from it. Just a normal, middle-aged man with a pot belly and a police record. I once pointed out his picture to you on the Ancestor Wall."

"Spooky."

Grandpa Ebenezer is sprawled on his back on the couch, his eyes closed, his fingers laced across his belly.

"Grandpa, this is my best buddy Willy."

Ebenezer opens one eye.

Willy grins. "Hi, there." He extends his hand, then pulls it back. "Can he hear me?"

"Yes, but you won't be able to hear him, so I'll act as the go-between." I turn back to Ebenezer. "Willy worked construction on a building that you may know something about. I want to ask both of you a few questions."

Ebenezer sits up and yawns. "Keep it short. I'm exhausted."

"Willy, what color were the cell walls?"

"Gray, because they were lined in lead." Willy sits on the couch.

"Uh... not there," I say.

"What?"

"You're on top of my Grandfather."

Willy jumps up, swats at the seat of his pants with both hands and stands close to me. "Sorry, buddy."

I say, "Ebenezer, did your room—"

"Cell."

"Did your cell have a window, a sink and toilet?"

"No."

I turn to Willy. "He says not."

"This is all freaky fun, Jeff, but what's this all about?"

"Just wait," I say. "Grandpa, was there a big room filled with electrical cables?"

"I don't know. They didn't let me out much."

"He doesn't know," I say to Willy.

I turn back to Ebenezer. "What about a cafeteria?"

"It's a tiny room where the guards and other workers ate."

I relay this to Willy.

"Grandpa, what were your guard's names?"

"Quincy and Cedric—I told you that already."

I repeat this to Willy.

He shakes his head. "Holy shit. Lead-lined cells without plumbing, guards named Quincy and Cedric. Hell, man, it sounds like your grandpa's been to the site."

"It seems so."

Ebenezer says, "The people running the place wanted me to spy."

"Spy?" I say. "They wanted you to *spy*?"

"That's what I said."

"Spy on who?"

"They never said."

"Did you ever hear anyone talk about a company called OASIS?" I ask.

Ebenezer lies back down and rolls over to face the wall. "Let me get some rest. My head is buzzing."

Willy and I stand there for a while longer, then go back to the TV room. We slump down on the couch and watch without comment as the Red Sox rally to a three-run lead, then blow it at the bottom of the ninth. Willy's so deep in thought that he doesn't throw anything at the screen.

He aims the remote at the TV, turns it off, leans back and shakes his head. "This whole thing is definitely on the weird side, old buddy."

"Welcome to my world."

Chapter 16

SCORPIO Oct. 23 – Nov. 21

Recognize that not all battles can be won. Make the best of the worst situations. Surprises make life worth living. Salt air clears the sinuses.

Willy goes to bed, but I remain slumped on the couch, half aware of the mindless post-game chatter, and trying to make sense of Ebenezer's story.

Why did OASIS abduct him, and how did they pull it off? They must also be holding other ancestors because Ebenezer mentioned late comers. How many? Will OASIS try to grab Ebenezer again?

I rush into the office to warn him, but he's already gone. To Back There, I hope.

I head for the kitchen, grab a slice of cold pepperoni pizza from the box on the counter and sit at the table. I take one bite, chew, swallow, push the rest away.

Willy comes downstairs. His hairy calves show beneath the red-and-blue Superman robe his girlfriend gave him for his birthday. He grabs a beer from the fridge, the last piece of pizza from the box, and sits across from me.

"Couldn't sleep," he says.

Willy once slept through a tornado.

He says. "What do you make of what your grandpa had to say?"

"Still processing."

"Think it's true?"

"Seems so," I say.

"Why in hell is OASIS scooping up ghosts?"

"For spying, Ebenezer claimed, but he also said a lot of other crazy stuff. Maybe OASIS wants a window into the past. Maybe it's a way to finally put a bunch of conspiracy theories to bed. Was Napoleon poisoned? Were there multiple shooters in Dallas? That sort of thing. Historians would love it."

"You think that's what OASIS is up to?" Willy asks.

I reflect on this, then shake my head.

Willy waves his bottle. "The Department of Defense funds OASIS, right?"

"So does the CIA."

"Neither outfit is much interested in history. You should ask Drucker what the hell's going on."

"Fat chance he'll give me a straight answer," I say.

"Of course he won't give you a straight answer, but you're a journalist, remember? Ask enough indirect questions and eventually you'll find out the truth. Know who told me that?"

I shake my head.

Willy grins. "You did."

"Then it has to be true." I glance at the clock over the kitchen sink. "I can't call now—it's the middle of the night."

Willy raises a forefinger. "The very best time to interview a reluctant subject is when their guard is down."

"I said that, too?"

Willy lobs his bottle into the recycle bin and gets to his feet. "Nope. I made it up."

I watch him go. His robe has a large yellow 'S' on the back. I wish the real Superman would show up about now. I could use his help.

Maybe Willy's right. If not, I'll at least have the pleasure of waking

Drucker from one of his dreams of mischief and mayhem. I pick up my phone.

A groggy Drucker answers. "Who in hell is this?"

"Hi, Drucker. Say, I didn't catch you asleep, did I?"

"What in hell do you think? It's one in the morning."

I hear a woman's voice. Probably Drucker's FBI girlfriend.

"We need to talk," I say.

"Not now."

"Yes, now."

"Tomorrow," Drucker says. "And what you got to say better be good. Meet me in Salem, one o'clock at the House of the Seven Gables parking lot."

"Why Salem?" I ask.

"I'm staying here a couple nights with my little friend."

"Why not meet someplace halfway in between?"

"See you tomorrow," Drucker says.

• • •

I steer my pickup into the parking lot of the House of the Seven Gables, shut off the engine, lean back and close my eyes. I haven't been here since the fourth grade, the year after I'd started talking again and Mom had stopped homeschooling me.

Someone slaps the pickup's roof. "Hey buddy, my septic tank is all backed up, and I need you to deliver a shithouse!"

I open my eyes, open the door and step outside. Drucker is wearing an expensive gray suit, a maroon tie and a cranky expression. He steps back, lights a cigar and checks his watch, this one gold. "My time's valuable. Talk."

I describe in detail the layout of the cells at the OASIS site, the gray walls lined in lead, the guards' lunch room, the design of the hallway light fixtures and the dearth of toilets.

A gray-haired woman leads a cluster of grade-schoolers past. She glares at Drucker and his cigar. He expels a big cloud of smoke. "Have a nice day, mam."

He turns to me and points his cigar at The House of the Seven Gables. "You know, I've never been inside the place. Have you?"

"Goddamn it, Drucker, didn't you hear what I just said?"

He flicks cigar ashes onto a bed of yellow tulips. "I read your story about people who get ancestor visits."

"You're changing the subject."

"Great prose. You're a skilled writer. Maybe someday you'll win a Pulitzer. Oops, I guess I forgot and said 'Pulitzer' when I'd promised never to say 'Pulitzer' again."

"Fuck you, Drucker. But I'm glad to hear you've become a regular reader of our fine magazine."

Drucker shakes his head. "I have an app that scans the Web for stories like that."

"Why?"

"Because I do."

"Do you get ancestor—"

"Of course not," Drucker says, and motions me to follow him. He shuffles toward the visitor entrance and settles down on the low stone wall across from it. "Sit," he says.

I don't. "What are you and OASIS up to?"

"Your dumbass housemate, one William Henry Morse, worked at the OASIS site before he got sent to the pokey for stealing a backhoe."

Uh, oh. "I know what you're thinking,' I say, "but Willy's not my source. I got my information from—"

"Him. You got your information from him. Admit it."

"No, it was an anonymous tip."

"That's bullshit," Drucker says, and stubs his cigar out on the stone wall and flips the butt into the bushes. "Or it's half bullshit, if you can visualize such a thing. Some of the stuff you told me about the site probably did come from Willy, but not all because he was incarcerated before the inside of the building was finished. He wouldn't know about the light fixtures, for example. So who's your other source?"

I hold up my hands in surrender. "Okay, I guess I'll have to come clean." I sit on the wall. "A while back, I sneaked into the OASIS building."

"That's more bullpucky. You didn't get inside, or even close. We got you and Willy on surveillance tapes." Drucker watches a pretty brunette drift past. "But it's time for me to come clean—I already know where you got the rest of your information."

"No, you don't."

Again that grin.

Drucker lights another cigar.

I step clear of the smoke.

Drucker yawns and says, "How's your grandfather Ebenezer doing these days?"

Ebenezer? *Ebenezer!*

"What are you talking about?" I say. "He's been dead for thirty years."

Drucker rolls his cigar to the other side of his mouth. "Spare me. We know all about him, and we know all about you. We learned about the connection between you and your grandfather when we tapped his brain waves. He was on his way to see you when we snatched him."

I'm stunned.

I look away. Noisy teens pile out of a school bus, laughing and pushing. Enjoying life.

Deny everything? No, I'd be wasting my breath. "Drucker, you're a bastard. My grandfather's in terrible shape—exhausted, disoriented, fearful. You had no right to do that to him."

Drucker shrugs. "Dead people are dead. Period. They don't suffer."

"Ebenezer did, and you know it. Even dead people have rights."

Drucker snorts. "You gotta be kidding."

"I sure as hell am not. In fact—"

"Before you wrote that article about ancestral visits, did you think you were the only person getting them?"

I say nothing.

"We've known about them for years," Drucker says. "One of our highly unhygienic geniuses at OASIS used to claim that his great-grandfather kept visiting him with all sorts of shitty advice. We ignored the guy, but he wrote a grant proposal, and—surprise!—the Department of Defense okayed it. Big bucks. And once we got into researching the subject, it turns out that our odorous whiz kid wasn't nuts after all. That's how Project Spook got rolling."

"*Project Spook?* What in hell is Project Spook?"

"Glad you asked," Drucker says. He stands up and presses his hands against his lower back. "My left ass cheek has fallen asleep, so let's walk. What I have to say is going to take some time."

We head toward the harbor. The House of the Seven Gables sits to our right. It's an imposing building with the requisite seven peaks, its siding an ominous black, the windows small and creepy. It's a place of mystery, ghosts, witches, betrayal.

Drucker says, "What I've told you and what I'm going to tell you is *uber*-secret, so if you leak one word of it I will—as they say—have to kill you."

"Then don't tell me."

"Got to," Drucker says.

"Why?"

"Just shut up and listen. I'll start with the technical stuff—which I admit I don't understand all that well—then operational matters, which I do understand because I'm the chief architect. OASIS employs about a hundred-and-fifty experts in disparate fields, but all have several things in common: They're brilliant, hardworking, believe in the paranormal, and have lost jobs because they're so squirrelly. They've done work on telekinesis, teleporting, stuff like that."

"Which I read about on the Web."

"Good for you. Now shut up and pay attention. We built the OASIS site to look like a self-storage facility, although I don't think it would fool anyone who got up close. By the way, I came up with the name for the building—'Spirit Storage'—pretty clever, huh?"

I ignore this. "How did you capture my grandfather?"

"Something to do with ultraviolet light, I'm told, but I don't understand the science and don't give a rat's ass anyway. We've developed a special beam gun—sounds like bad science fiction, doesn't it?—that fits in a van along with a device that detects any ancestor who might be floating around nearby. We're working on a portable version that combines both units, which I'll get to later because it involves you."

"How?"

"Just listen, okay? We didn't actually interrogate your grandfather and the others, but extracted their through brain waves. We can't hear our ghostly guests in the normal fashion, and they can't hear us, but we can implant ideas into their heads. We can also see them and even shift them from place to place as long as they stay bathed in ultraviolet light. The fact that people like you can see and communicate with your ancestors is critical for our operation."

"What operation?"

"You'll find out," Drucker says with a grin. He pokes me in the chest. "All this talk about ray guns and brain waves must sound like one of your unhinged stories."

"They make more sense."

We sit on a low stone bench facing the harbor. A skinny long pier stretches off to our left, another one to the right, with a squat, square lighthouse resting at its end. Dozens of sailboats bob at their moorings, their bows turned upwind. Two others are underway, heeling far over, their sails flapping loudly.

I turn to Drucker. "Why don't your captives simply walk through the walls and escape?"

"The interior's coated in lead. Low currents of electricity flow through the walls, ceilings and floors. It's not enough for humans to feel, but enough to keep our spooks from slipping away."

"Then how did Ebenezer escape?"

Drucker pulls his mouth to the side. "The fucking electricity went out for a few minutes. A couple others got away, too, but we scooped them up."

"How many are you holding?"

"That sure as hell won't happen again because we've installed a big mother of a backup generator."

"I asked a question."

"Which," Drucker says, "I didn't answer."

"Why in hell are you capturing ancestors?"

"My butt's falling asleep again," Drucker says. He stands up, leans both elbows on the railing and looks out over the harbor.

I stand beside him. "Again, why are you snatching ghosts?"

Drucker turns toward me. "What's the most useful thing a spy could do?"

"I have no goddamn idea."

Drucker grins and raises his forefinger. "Turn invisible."

I take a step back.

Grandpa Ebenezer had babbled about spying.

"I don't believe it!"

"Believe it," Drucker says. "If you were going to design a spy, what traits would you want them to have?"

"I'm not in the business of—"

"You'd want your person to be able to slip unnoticed into the enemy's war room, their missile centers, their president's office, and bedroom. Maybe especially the bedroom. Even if our see-through secret agent somehow got caught, hell, the guy's dead already. Logistically, they're a dream. They don't eat, they don't piss and moan about not getting paid enough, they don't fall in love, catch the clap or get into barroom brawls. They can fly first class anywhere in the world without buying a ticket. They can even sit on the pilot's lap and pretend to fly the plane if they want. Like I said, the perfect spy. Better than reconnaissance drones or satellite spies or even James Bond, who is a real pain in the ass to his handlers."

"James Bond can plant explosives, steal secret documents and shoot bad guys. Ghosts can't."

"Ordinary agents can handle that sort of thing," Drucker says. "Now listen up. We're planning to set up three-person teams: the ancestor, a techie, and the ghost's minder, who'll be a descendant and—"

"A descendant?"

"That's what I said."

"Like me?"

'Stop interrupting," Drucker says. "Like I was saying, we need a minder/relative along on a mission because we need a line of communication between our transparent spy and the people running the mission. That's the minder's job. The techie on the team will carry the portable version of our super-duper ray gun just in case our ghostly agent tries to bug out."

"Why would the ancestor cooperate?"

"We have our ways."

I think of Grandpa Ebenezer and the torture he endured. "You're a bastard."

"That's why I'm so good at my job."

"Why would a minder cooperate?"

"Because they'll be doing a great service for their country."

"And?" I ask.

"And we'll blackmail them, or offer a ton of money, or threaten the safety of their family," Drucker says with a shrug. "The usual stuff."

"In your world."

Drucker grins. "It's your world now."

I let this sink in.

Someone's hammering in the boatyard to our left. The breeze

brings the scent of the sea, and a sailboat comes hard about and points toward open water. I imagine myself stealing a boat like that and sailing away to parts unknown.

Drucker gives me his awful grin. "I'm shacked up with a lady from the FBI who's itching to send your Uncle Sid to prison for money laundering."

"You told me that before."

"I'm repeating it so you won't forget."

I picture my uncle standing in front of the prison the day Mom and I picked him up, skinny and gray, sad and lonely. No, I haven't forgotten.

Drucker says, "Our snazzy mobile ray gun will be operational in a couple of weeks. Your team will be all ready to go by then. It seems there's this retired army general who's been meeting in secret with a Russian diplomat at the U.N. We've tried to catch the two on listening devices, but they're too careful. So our plan is to send a ghost agent to their next meeting. The two of you will have a ball in New York—eat at great restaurants, see the sights, take in a show or two. Your ancestor won't even have to buy a ticket. Sounds good, doesn't it?"

"No, it sure as hell doesn't. Do you plan on snatching Ebenezer again?"

"Probably not. We kind of wore him out last time."

"Then which other ancestor?"

Drucker yawns. "Have you read *The House of The Seven Gables?* I started it a couple times but gave up. Too dark."

"You didn't answer my question."

Drucker lights another cigar.

I'll have to warn Hiram, Clementine and Colette. Ebenezer, too, just in case Drucker is lying about not wanting him back. "You know what happens if an ancestor stays here too long, don't you?"

Drucker shakes out the match. "I have some idea."

"*Some idea?* You sure as hell know more than that. You know damn well that if they disappear, they take all their descendants with them."

Drucker shrugs.

"That's the real hold you have over the minders, isn't it?"

Drucker grins and puffs on his cigar.

"So how long do you plan on keeping the ancestors captive?"

"As long as it takes for them to do their job. We'll try to get them back on time, of course, but if one of them is on a particularly important mission, we might let them slip past their... uh... expiration date." Drucker chuckles. "I like that—'expiration date.'"

I snatch his cigar from his mouth and toss it into the water. "Drucker, you're a bastard!"

"Hey! Goddamn it!"

I grab the front of his jacket with both hands, shake him hard, pull him close and scream into his face, "You don't give a shit, do you? You could end up killing thousands of people. It's murder, goddamn it!"

Drucker jerks free. "What the fuck!" He steps back, opens his jacket and lays his hand on his pistol. "Touch me again, and you'll join your goddamn ancestors."

"Then I won't be available to work for you, will I?"

"I'll find some other shmuck," Drucker says. He closes his jacket and lights another cigar, eyeing me all the time. He shakes out the match. "You tossed out the word 'murder' a minute ago. But technically it's not. Anyone who disappears will simply never have been born. And consider this: Only the tiniest fraction of eggs ever get fertilized, which means lots of potential people are never born anyway. You and me, we beat incredible odds. End of story."

Dad, Uncle Sid, Ebenezer and Hiram, plus all the relatives I've never heard of—all in danger of disappearing without a trace.

And me with them.

Chapter 17

SCORPIO Oct. 23 - Nov. 21

Today is a day to plan. Show kindness to others in time of need, even to those who annoy you. Vinegar makes an inexpensive and highly effective insect repellent.

I drive home in a cloud of disbelief, wandering over the centerline, getting honked at, shouted at, shown the finger. A few miles from Concord, I pull off the road, rest my forehead on the steering wheel and close my eyes.

I've been doing that a lot lately, closing my eyes. It's a habit I started right after I shot my stepfather. I closed my eyes then, hoping things would get better, opened them again, but things weren't better. It's never worked. But I keep trying.

Drucker wants to make spies of the dead.

Unbelievable.

So are visits from dead ancestors, of course, but that's something I've gotten used to.

A rap on my window. I open my eyes. It's a Concord cop whose name I can't remember.

"Sleeping it off, Jeff?"

I roll down my window. "Just resting my eyes."

"Better get moving."

I pull away.

For a while the cop took an interest in Mom, but couldn't deal with her problems. During the short time he was seeing her, he pulled Uncle Sid over for speeding one time, ignored the unboxed television sets stacked in the back seat, didn't issue a ticket, and drove away. A favor to Mom.

Fencing stolen TVs is one thing, money-laundering another. Is Uncle Sid out of that business? I'd like to think so, but I doubt it. When Hank Ramsey gets his hooks into you, you stay hooked. Surprisingly, money doesn't matter much to Uncle Sid, but family does, and that's no doubt where Hank was able to apply the pressure. Another reason I owe so much to my uncle.

I find Willy on the rear deck looking out over the marsh. His laptop is streaming a documentary about the French Revolution. He gets most of his information from documentaries and twenty-four-hour news. Reading has always been hard for him. I know because I tutored him through high school. He's probably dyslexic, but never got tested and refuses to now. He's intelligent but tries to hide it behind a who-gives-a-fuck attitude.

When he sees me, he reaches into the cooler next to his feet, pulls out a can of beer and tosses it to me.

I set the beer on the table. "I need to talk. It's important."

"Sure."

"Let's walk."

Willy sets his laptop next to my beer and follows me into the marsh.

We swish through shoulder-high reeds until we're a hundred yards from the house. "This is far enough," I say.

Willy tilts his beer can back and eyes me. "You're being mysterious enough."

"Listening devices."

"In the house?"

"And maybe my truck," I say, "And even your Mustang."

"That sure don't sound one bit paranoid."

"Wait until you hear my story."

I have a hard time starting.

"I'm waiting," Willy says.

I rehearse my lines in my head. They sound crazy to me and will no doubt sound even crazier to Willy. "When we were kids, and I told you that my dead ancestors visited, what did you think?"

"I thought, well, okay, my best buddy sees ghosts."

"Didn't you think I was nuts?"

Willy finishes his beer and crushes the can. "Nope."

"Do you think I'm crazy now?"

"No more than the other guys I hang out with."

"When we were talking with Ebenezer, did you think I was making everything up?"

Willy shakes his head. "The whole situation was definitely weird, I got to admit, but you couldn't have known so much about the OASIS site on your own. Someone was there feeding you info."

We move farther into the marsh. The ground is squishy and smells of rotting vegetation. As we walk, I tell Willy about Drucker and OASIS, about Ebenezer's capture and escape, about the abducted ancestors, their role as spies, my role as a handler, and how the ancestors and their progeny are in danger of disappearing.

Willy says, "Holy shit," and slaps a mosquito.

I wait for a response. "That's it? That's all you have to say?"

Willy whacks another mosquito. "Knowing you, you've already worked out some over-complicated plan for rescuing the ancestors and putting OASIS out of business."

"Not quite yet."

Willy lights a cigarette. "Do you think this spying shit could really work?"

I give this some thought. "Yes."

"Which means if we mess things up for OASIS, we're tinkering with national security. But if we don't, a shitload of people will never have been born, including you."

"Exactly. Except it's not 'we' but me who has to do the job."

Willy shakes his head. "You gotta let me help."

"You have a criminal record and too much to lose if we get caught."

"Doesn't matter. I'm in. End of argument."

He turns his back and takes a piss. "Let's torch the OASIS building."

"That might hurt the ancestors," I say. "Ebenezer felt real pain when he was a captive, which means that, when the ancestors are being held, they've more or less returned to a human state."

Willy looks over his shoulder. "Okay, then let's snatch Drucker and scare the shit out of him. Maybe slap him around some."

"No violence. No threats. And I don't think that would work anyway."

Willy zips up. "So what do we do?"

A fox darts past. We both jump.

"I don't know yet," I say.

I spot movement. Another fox? No, it's Hiram, drifting toward us through the reeds.

I wave my arms. "You're in danger! So are Clementine and Colette and Ebenezer! Go Back There right now!"

Willy says, "I'm guessing you've spotted an ancestor."

"My great-great-grandfather."

Hiram glides closer and hovers in front of me. His eyes are red, and tears fill the leathery wrinkles in his cheeks. His shirt is misbuttoned, and his cowboy hat sits on backward. "She's an angel."

"Who?"

"My Clementine. I'll never say an unkind word to her again, never cheat on her again, never—"

"Right, we'll talk about that later. Didn't you hear me just now? You're at risk. You have to be careful or you'll—"

"I'm a big phony," Hiram says in a shaky voice. "I can barely stay on a horse and have never been west of Chicago. Clementine's the hero, not me. We tell everyone she lost her leg in a train accident, but it happened during a holdup when she stepped in front of me and got shot in the leg." Hiram wipes his eyes on his shirtsleeve. "She took a bullet for me, and I'll never, ever treat her with anything but the respect she deserves. In fact, I'll start—"

"Was she abducted?"

Hiram blinks at me. "How did you know?"

"Did a man open the back door of a van and point a strange-looking gun at her?"

"That's right," Hiram says. "How did you know?"

"That's what happened to Ebenezer."

Hiram sniffles. "There was this flash of light, and poof, she disappeared. Then they drove off. I lost my Clementine, my loving Clementine."

Hiram shoulders begin to shake. He covers his face with his big red handkerchief and bawls.

I'm guessing OASIS didn't also take Hiram because they knew what he was like.

I rest my hand on his shoulder as best I can, then turn to Willy. "OASIS abducted my great-great-grandmother."

"I figured some shit like that had gone down."

Hiram blows his nose. "Without Clementine at my side, I can't go on living."

I feel sorry for him, drowning in misery. I think of Mom sitting in her rocker, eyes fixed on my father's photo on the Ancestor Wall, weeping and hugging herself. I would do somersaults, make funny faces and bring her cookies and glasses of milk. Sometimes she smiled and told me I was a good boy. Sometimes she looked right through me.

I air-pat Hiram's shoulder. "Don't worry, we'll get her back. Willy and I will fix everything. We're already working on a plan."

Hiram lowers his handkerchief and looks up at me. "I'll help."

"Of course you will. We can't do this without you."

"I'm great at planning because I'm a novelist. No one plans things out better than novelists. Remember how in *Yucca Gulch* the sheriff had to come up with a scheme for defeating the Thompson gang and at the same time keep the railroad company from—"

"Later," I say, giving his shoulder another air pat. "We'll talk about that later."

Chapter 18

SCORPIO Oct. 23 - Nov. 21

Know when to listen to others and when not to.
Today is the day to take charge of the rest of your life.
Fight for what you believe is right, no matter the
odds. Either fish or cut bait.

Willy and I rest our poles and tackle boxes on the bed of my pickup, climb into the cab and pull away.

Willy says, "We haven't gone fishing in years."

"Except we aren't exactly fishing."

"Just saying."

Willy and I used to catch bass and perch from the Concord River, back when they were safe to eat. Or at least when everyone thought they were safe to eat. I would give my catch to Willy because his family needed food more than we did.

I cruise through Concord center and turn toward the Revolutionary War battle site.

Willy rolls down his window. "Are Hiram, Ebenezer and Colette going to be there?"

Hiram and Ebenezer chuckle.

"Colette can't make it, but Hiram and Ebenezer are already here," I say. "Hiram's sitting on your left knee, Ebenezer on your right."

Willy grimaces and pulls his legs back. "Uh… sorry guys."

"No damage. They can hover."

"I should have guessed."

I park in the lot near the battle site. Willy and I grab our poles, gear, and the beer cooler, and we follow the wide dirt path leading to the old North Bridge. On each side are knee-high stone fences backed by maples and towering oaks. Off to the left stands the Old Manse, a comfortable gray house with a shingle roof, home to Ralph Waldo Emerson and later Nathaniel Hawthorne.

The famous footbridge is humped and wooden. Visitors lean over the railing to snap pictures of canoers passing underneath. A rolling field lies just beyond, bucolic today, once the site of a bloody battle.

We follow the stream to our old fishing hole, a place of warm memories and—more importantly—a spot where OASIS can't drive their van up close enough to snatch Hiram or Ebenezer.

We cast our lines, secure our poles under rocks, and retreat to a sun-warmed boulder a few feet back from the stream. It's about fifty feet wide here, thick with twigs and slow-moving leaves. Birds sing, turtles sun themselves on logs, and insects buzz past my ears. It's a good day for fishing but not so good for planning an attack on a government installation. Then again, what's a good day for that?

I take two beers from the cooler and hand one to Willy. "As I see it, we have four main goals. Specifically, they are—"

"Horse apples," Hiram says. He's seated on the rock to our right, his cowboy hat tilted down to shade his eyes from the sun. Hiram says, "You're sitting backward on the saddle. Just buy a gun, shoot Drucker, then Hank, then his dimwit brother. That's what the hero did in *Blood Canyon*, which if you remember—"

"I'm not shooting anyone."

"But you could—"

"I don't want to hear it."

Hiram shrugs and goes silent.

Ebenezer is sitting at the edge of the stream and soaking his feet. He lifts his left foot out of the water and scratches between the toes. They aren't wet because water can't stick, but he seems to be enjoying the experience. He half turns and shouts over his shoulder, "You should put me in charge, Jeff. Your caper is really nothing more than an elaborate swindle, and who'd be better than me at organizing one? Face it, you're no con artist. You couldn't hoodwink a baby out of a teething ring, much less deceive Drucker or Hank or the Federal government. I made over a million dollars with my little scheme, and I—"

"Got caught and went to prison," I say.

Ebenezer is quiet for a moment. "True, that is true. But until then I had a glorious life—an unending celebration of wine, women and song. And let me add, young man, that some of the money I made went into building the house you grew up in."

He's always throwing that back at me.

"I'm not putting you in charge, Grandpa. Your advice is as dicey as Hiram's."

Hiram says, "That's an insult!"

"It was meant as one," I say.

Ebenezer shakes his head and puts his feet back in the water.

A chattering couple paddles past in an orange kayak, trailing an expanding V that dissolves at the shoreline. Mom and I once rented a dented aluminum canoe here, but we only got a few feet from shore before she started to whimper, so I paddled us back.

"Before Hiram felt the need to chime in," I say, "I was listing my four goals: free the ancestors, destroy the site, prevent any resurrection of the project, and get Drucker and Hank off my back."

Willy traces a circle in the dirt with the toe of his boot. "How?"

"I've come up with a few ideas, but I'm hoping you three have more."

"I do," Hiram says. "Buy the biggest shooting iron they make and—"

"You've said that already. I'm not killing anyone."

Ebenezer shouts over his shoulder, "Then hire a hitman."

"Not a chance."

Willy says, "Maybe we can bribe an OASIS employee to release the captives."

"A possibility, I suppose. But I wouldn't know the right person to approach, and if it's the wrong one, they'd turn me in."

"Snatch an employee's kid." Hiram says. "Force them to cooperate. That's what happened in—"

"*Double Dealing,*" *I say,* "Except it was the bad guys who kidnapped a child, and the sheriff ended up wounding the boy in a shootout. And I'm not abducting anyone. Besides, there are better solutions."

"I haven't heard one yet," Hiram says.

"Then shut up and listen!" I shout.

Two women in matching yellow kayaks hear me, stare at me, at each other, paddle faster.

Willy grins, opens his mouth, sees my expression, closes his mouth.

I lower my voice. "Our first concern is the electricity. Ebenezer escaped because the power failed, which means we need to knock it out the day of the caper. A small, remotely controlled explosive attached to the incoming line should do the job. According to Drucker there's now a backup generator. So a few days ahead of time, I'll disguise myself as a repairman, talk my way into the building and sabotage the generator. As for rescuing the captives, we still have a lot more planning."

"After we kill the power," Willy says. "Can't the ghosts simply walk through the walls?"

Hiram snorts. "Don't call us ghosts."

I shake my head. "Ebenezer and a couple others were able to slip out of the OASIS building because they were recent abductees, but the ancestors captured earlier were weaker and could barely move. They'll have to be carried out, and then it'll take them several hours to recover enough to return Back There."

Hiram says, "We'll have to search the whole dang building for them. That'll take forever."

"We'll use the rough sketches Willy made of the site."

"Rough sketches?" Ebenezer says. "Not good enough. When I was developing my plans, the most important step was to obtain precise information. I never could get enough. In fact—"

"In fact," Hiram says, "you never did get enough, or you wouldn't have ended up in the hoosegow."

"A disgruntled lady friend betrayed me."

"You know that's a lie, Ebenezer. You screwed up, but you won't admit—"

"Stop arguing and listen to me!" I shout. "I'm in charge now. I'll entertain serious suggestions, but not the ones I've already rejected. Otherwise, keep your advice to yourself."

Hiram says, "You can't our reverse roles like that. Not after all these years."

"No? Just watch," I say. "The mission is critical, and there's no room for bad advice. So from now on, you listen to me. Got it?"

Silence.

Hiram opens his mouth but no words come out. He wobbles, fades, disappears. Ebenezer does the same. Just like that.

Not something I've seen before.

So what in hell just happened?

Chapter 19

SCORPIO Oct. 23 - Nov. 21

Fear clogs the soul, but confession cleanses it. Never believe that you alone have all the answers. Use a high-number sunblock even on cloudy days.

I go for an early morning run to clear my head. We've had two more planning sessions in the past two days. We've debated, shouted, lost our tempers, said things to each other we shouldn't have said, and accomplished nothing. The biggest problem is the lack of precise information about the layout of the OASIS site—for once Ebenezer is right, and he won't shut up about it. He continues to insist he should be the boss. So does Hiram. What a clusterfuck.

When Ebenezer isn't calling Hiram a bogus cowboy, and Hiram isn't calling Ebenezer a failed confidence man, they turn on Willy. They call him uncouth, unschooled, lower class. He can't hear them, of course, and I don't relay what they have said. I do pass their dreadful suggestions on to Willy, which gets a laugh and makes Hiram and Ebenezer say even worse things about him.

Willy insists we need a drone. I tell him we have no way of getting one inside either the OASIS site or the construction trailer and that it would be spotted if we did. I tell him he just wants a drone to play with. Then we also argue, which is rare for us.

I get back home after my run just as Uncle Sid calls and asks me to come into the office for a day. He says the temp he hired to replace me is a dud and had to be let go, and there's a midnight deadline. I say yes because I'm glad to take a break from planning. Also, I miss Melody. I call or email her several times a day on some pretext, always ending up by my suggesting we get together after hours, always her turning me down. Desperate, I chatter on about how cute Dawn is. All kids are cute, Melody tells me.

I drive to work, park my pickup in the mob-operated lot that gives us a deep discount, walk to the magazine office, climb the stairs and go directly to Uncle's Sid's office.

He rushes around his desk and gives me a clumsy hug. He smells of aftershave and cigarettes. He sits back down and motions toward the chair across the desk. "Why are you taking time off, Jeff?"

I sit down. "I told you—Willy's on my case to help him fix up the house."

Uncle Sid eyes me for a long moment. He can always tell when I'm lying. "Are you in trouble with Hank and Freddie?"

I wish it were that simple. "Some," I say.

"And?"

"And you don't want to know."

"Yes, I do."

"No, you don't."

Sid makes a face, opens the top desk drawer, pulls out a letter opener and starts cleaning his nails. "You were always like that as a kid. You kept everything to yourself. It's better not to."

"I know."

"Good. So tell me what's going on."

I shake my head. "As I said, you're better off not knowing."

"Why do you always think you have to protect me?"

"Because I owe you—four-and-a-half years of your life, to be precise."

"You don't owe me anything, Jeff. You're my closest relative. In fact, you're my only relative."

I want to say something but can't get it out. No need to. Uncle Sid knows how I feel about him.

We sit for a while without looking at each other without speaking.

Finally, Uncle Sid tosses the letter opener back in the drawer, slams the drawer and clears his throat. "Sherwood keeps asking about you. Janet does, too. She's obsessed about your well-being. And Melody keeps finding an excuse to drop by and steer the conversation in your direction. What kind of a kid were you? Did you have a pet? What were your hobbies? That sort of stuff."

"She's curious about everything."

"She's got a thing for you."

I shake my head. "I keep asking her out, and she turns me down."

"Eventually she'll come around. You just watch—when she gets into work today and sees you're back, she'll get even more perky than usual." Uncle Sid makes shooing motions with his hand. "Now get the hell out of here and earn your pay."

I return to my desk, switch on my computer and sort through dozens of emails. I glance up every minute or two for Melody to step through the door. Finally she arrives. I wave. She lifts her chin, doesn't smile, doesn't come over. She holds up four fingers: She needs four articles.

What's gotten into her? Something I did? Something I said?

I close my email and open my word processor.

Space Aliens Not Mentally Superior!

A top-secret government study of the caged aliens in Area 51 reveals that they are in fact incredibly stupid. It seems that neighboring planets gather up their most dimwitted and disagreeable citizens and rocket them to the Arizona desert. Before their trip, these unwanted beings are given Earthling shapes, false memories, driver's licenses, Macy's credit cards and...

I crack off 765 words, lean back and notice with relief that for the past few minutes I haven't thought about Drucker, Hank, Clementine, Adele, planning a dangerous caper or disappearing forever. Mostly disappearing forever.

I start another story:

Cold Fusion Works!

Despite what the public has been told, the discredited process of cold fusion, in which a nuclear reaction can take place at room temperature, is in fact possible! But don't expect to see the benefits of this miracle process anytime soon! A consortium of international oil companies has bought the invention for $1 billion from the developer! Reached at his home in the South of France where he lives with his wife and three Swedish mistresses, the developer refused...

That took an hour and a quarter because I lost time on the Web researching cold fusion. I sprinkled the text with exclamation points to drive Melody up the wall—payback for her snippy behavior. Now for the third story, a fluffy, feel-good piece:

Therapy Weasels Bring Joy to Teenagers!

An anonymous Silicon Valley billionaire has funded a program to provide trained therapy weasels to hundreds of California boys and girls in the hope that they will not have to suffer through high school the way he did. The first pack of these frisky critters went to boys who didn't make the first team in lacrosse, girls reduced to attending the prom with the chess club president, and...

Then the fourth story:

Queen Elizabeth Uses a Stand-in!

The Queen of England lives a quiet existence in a secluded chateau 110 kilometers south of Paris while a lookalike third cousin from Auckland fulfills her courtly duties! Tracked down this past week by our European correspondent, the Queen, after a lengthy series of denials, snuffed out her cigarette and admitted in her high-pitched voice that she "just couldn't put up any longer with all that parading around and nodding and having to smile at fools. And the hats! The hats!" She said she'd finally found contentment, although admitted to a touch of jealousy over her stand-in's soaring popularity and the her choice of gaudy headgear that makes her look like she just stepped out of a...

I reread the story, then lean back. What if a lookalike really had replaced the Queen? What if one of the sixteen bombs the Luftwaffe dropped on Buckingham Palace during the Second World War had killed her? Or what if a visiting royal ghost had stayed too long and the entire Windsor line had disappeared?

And what if I disappear?

Something I'd like to forget but know I never will.

I forward the four articles to Melody. That should put her in a better mood.

It doesn't. Twenty minutes later she stomps over to my desk, her face tight. She waves the printout. "The first article doesn't move me because I'm sick of aliens. The second has a million ugly exclamation marks, and the one about the British Queen is just simply tasteless, even by our standards. Finally, the cold fusion article is a rehash of one you wrote last April about a vinegar-soaked Ukrainian limestone that produces limitless electricity." Melody slumps her shoulders and blows out her breath. "But we're under such a tight deadline that I've been forced to go with this dreck anyway." She flaps the printout back and forth, fanning herself.

Melody's the sweetest and least threatening editor I've ever worked with. Except for today. "What's gotten into you?" I ask.

She tosses the sheets on my desk, puts her hands on her hips and glares down at me. "What's gotten into me? Well, what's gotten into *you?* You've become an impossible grumpy-pants lately. Every time I try to have a serious conversation, you get jokey and change the subject." She folds her hands across her chest, looks around the newsroom, turns back to me and says, "Actually, I know perfectly well what's got you into such a tizzy."

I think of Drucker and Hank, of Clementine and Hiram, of my dad and the generations of people who will disappear without a trace if I don't do something about it. "You couldn't possibly know."

"Well, you're wrong." Melody says with a sniff. "Let me help you."

"I don't need…"

She looks ready to cry, so I stop talking, stand up and put my hand on her shoulder. It's trembling. She looks at her feet.

"My stories are written and edited," I say. "So let's go for a long walk."

She nods without looking up. "Is the Public Gardens too far?"

"Nope."

"Take me for a ride on the swan boats," Melody says, lifting her head and giving me a weak smile. "I've never gone because Dawn is afraid of them."

"I am too. So you'll have to hug me."

We tell Uncle Sid that the articles are ready to go, which makes him grin, and that we'll be gone for a couple hours, which makes him grin even wider. Sid the Matchmaker.

We head out. I take her hand when we cross busy Congress Street, and I continue to hang on. She makes no effort to pull away.

"Yum," Hiram says.

I glance over my shoulder. Hiram is staring at Melody's tight white skirt. I want to shout at him but can only make a face. I turn back to Melody. "What did you mean when you said you know what's bugging me?"

Melody says nothing.

I give her hand a squeeze. "Well?"

She looks up at me, eyes half closed. "Who's Hiram?"

I drop her hand, stumble. "Who?"

"Hiram."

"I don't know anyone named Hiram."

"Yes, you do," Hiram says, "I'm right back here."

Melody puts her hand on my elbow. "No? Then what about Ebenezer?"

Am I really hearing this?

I shake my head. "Ebenezer? Hiram? What are you talking about?"

She tightens her grip on my elbow. "Last Tuesday I slipped down to the alley for some air and saw you there. You didn't see me because you were too busy waving your arms and arguing with an invisible person you called Ebenezer and another named Hiram, whom you referred to as an ersatz cowboy."

"Calumny!" Hiram shouts.

My heart starts to thump. "I think you dreamed that."

"My dreams are more interesting," Melody says, tugging my arm. "Is Ebenezer your grandfather?"

I open my mouth, close it, open it again, close it again.

We walk on.

Neither of us speaks.

I'm lightheaded and dazed, out of my body, looking on.

Next thing I know, I'm handing two tickets to a skinny teenage boy, who takes Melody by the hand and helps her into a swan boat. How did I get here? We sit in back, with only a grandmother and a squirmy three-year-old girl in the front row.

Hiram crowds up against Melody.

She squeezes my hand. "My Aunt Theresa used to insist she got visits from her ancestors. Like the rest of the family, Mom thought her sister was crazy, but never said so. Mom would sit patiently with Aunt Theresa at the kitchen table, drink cup after cup of coffee and let her carry on about how their great-grandmother would visit. I would listen from the next room. To me, everything my aunt said seemed to make sense, but I was just a kid. As I got older, I felt differently and started feeling sorry for her. Then I read your article about ancestor visits, and it knocked my socks off. What you wrote corresponded exactly to what Aunt Theresa had told us."

My jaw drops.

Melody says, "Let's talk."

I shake my head.

The little girl drops her pink sun hat in the water and starts to wail. The boy circles the boat back around so that the grandmother can retrieve the hat. The girl puts it on wet, drips running down her face. The grandmother snatches the hat off and wrings it out over the side.

Melody says, "You'll feel better if you open up to me."

I swallow twice, close my eyes, open them, clear my throat. "My ancestors visit me."

A long silence.

Melody says, "That took a lot of courage."

I don't know what to say. I don't know what to think.

Did I actually tell Melody that I talk to dead ancestors? Does she believe me?

Neither of us speaks. Melody continues to hold my hand. The boy steers us under a small iron bridge. Tourists lean over the railing and snap pictures. We circle a small island and return to the landing.

Melody says, "I want to go again."

"So do I," Hiram says.

I get out, buy two tickets, get back in, all in a fog.

Melody massages my shoulder. "Tell me about the visits."

Yes? No?

Yes. I've gone this far.

So I tell her about Hiram and Ebenezer, Clementine with her peg leg and my Great-Grandmother Colette who danced on the Paris stage. I tell her about how the four tend to show up when they think I need advice, about how it's usually bad (Hiram shouts "No, it's not!") but on occasion is good. I tell Melody that I should never have started taking their advice, and that over the years I've wanted to stop, tried to stop, but only in recent days have been able to push back. I tap the side of my head. "Now do you think I'm—"

"No, of course not."

"Just wait." I then tell her about Ebenezer's abduction and escape, Clementine's disappearance, Drucker and his cockamamie plan to use dead ancestors as spies and force people like me to act as their minders.

Melody takes a deep breath and lets it out with a long, slow whistle.

I ask, "Is this starting to sound like one of my *Tattler* articles?"

Melody shakes her head. "They aren't this good."

"Now do you think I'm crazy?"

"You asked me that already. And no, I don't. Nor was my Aunt Theresa. She was a smart and funny and loving person. But do you think you're crazy?"

"Sometimes. Less so since I got feedback from readers who get their own ancestral visits."

The boy pulls us away from the dock. The grandmother and the girl wearing the wet hat wave from the bridge. Melody waves back. Hiram sticks out his tongue.

Melody says, "There's nothing wrong with you."

"Most people wouldn't say that if they knew."

Melody rests her hand on my shoulder. "I'm not most people, and I'm glad you told me everything, Jeff."

Not everything. Not about the shooting. No, not about the shooting. Will the day come when I tell her? Maybe. Maybe not.

Probably not.

And I'm not ready to tell her that one of these days I could disappear without a trace. There's no reason to worry her since there's nothing she could do about the situation. If I pull off the caper and rescue Clementine, then life will go on as usual. If not, Melody will have never known me, and her life will follow a different path.

A dizzying thought.

We climb out of the boat and stroll around the pond, not looking at each other, each lost in our own thoughts.

Did I actually tell Melody my secret? Did she actually accept it? Incredible.

My feet are light, my head clear. It's a relief to share my secret. Especially with Melody. Sweet Melody.

She takes my hand and swings my arm back and forth. "You started to tell me how you're trying to save the captured ancestors."

I take a deep breath, pledge Melody to secrecy and tell her everything. I tell her about the OASIS site in the western part of the state and about Drucker and Hank. I tell her about the meetings, the disputes, the dead ends. "It all comes down to a lack of information and an excess of worthless suggestions. Willy wants to buy a drone, which would be useless. Hiram wants me to buy a pistol, dress up as a plumber, sneak into Hank's headquarters and start shooting, which is another one of his dumb ideas and would get me shot, and..."

"It is *not* a dumb idea," Hiram says. "In *The Sagebrush Massacre*, the hero—"

"...and Ebenezer has dreamed up a complicated Ponzi scheme that makes no sense whatsoever. I've kept him and Hiram on the team only because they know things about visiting ancestors that I don't know."

Hiram grumbles under his breath.

We make a complete circle of the pond in silence until Melody says, "As for getting the Ramseys off you back, I don't think you'll have enough hard evidence to get them hauled into court or even scared into leaving town."

"I don't either, but I can't come up with anything. Any ideas?"

Melody shakes her head. "Keep working on it. You'll think of something. You always do."

"I have to."

Melody stops under a low-hanging willow, reaches up and plucks a leaf. "One of your big problems is not knowing where to plant the explosives. For that, you'd need to get inside the construction trailer at the OASIS site, right?"

"Right, but that's impossible because the trailer's also the guardhouse."

"Also, if you could slip into Hank's Boston headquarters and Drucker's suburban office, you'd find out what those two scoundrels are up to."

"Right. And in the process get myself shot."

Melody kneels down, lays the leaf on the water and watches it drift away. "And just why is OASIS abducting ancestors?"

"I told you. It's because they're invisible and would make perfect spies."

Melody looks up at me and smiles.

"Oh," I say, taking a step back. "Oh."

Chapter 20

SCORPIO Oct. 23 – Nov. 21

Things are never quite what they seem. If leaders lead, others will follow. Cherish the good memories and forget the bad. Take a spoonful of vinegar each morning to neutralize those embarrassing bouts of gas.

I'm still a couple miles from the motel when my phone rings. It's Melody. I spot her a hundred feet back in my rearview mirror. She says, "How much farther?"

"Ten minutes, max. Are you still up for our special nooner?"

"Yes, except that's not what it is," Melody says.

"In any case, I appreciate what you're doing."

"You'd better, buster."

The line goes dead.

Colette is sitting beside me, with Ebenezer crowded up next to her. Hiram is jammed against the window.

Ebenezer just got through telling Colette that she had lovely eyes and beautiful black curls. Before that he'd made oblique and gentlemanly references to how she's kept herself in such good shape. He says, "Do you have plans for tonight?"

Colette touches the back of her head. "I'm seeing my hair dresser."

"Tomorrow night?"

"Bowling."

"The next night?" he asks.

"The repairman's coming to fix my cable TV."

Ebenezer slumps in his seat.

I turn to Colette. "Do you have hair dressers Back There? Bowling? Cable TV?"

She laughs. "Of course."

"But it's only candlepin bowling," Ebenezer says.

Now both of them laugh.

"Seriously," I say. "What's it really like—"

"The boy asks a lot of questions," Colette says.

"He always has," Ebenezer says.

I drive on.

It's drizzling by the time I pull into the Sunny Valley Motor Lodge twenty miles west of Concord, park the pickup and walk to the office. Willy has already rented the room, but for the sake of our charade, I have to kill a few minutes inside the office. I ask the rates, chat up the pretty redhead behind the desk, then grab a brochure for the Pic-It-Yourself Apple Orchard ("Fresh off the trees!!! A great experience for young and old!!! Bring a picnic lunch!!!").

I'm tempted to take the brochure to Melody and watch her go ballistic over the exclamation marks, but instead I slip it back into the rack and drive around behind the building. With dozens of high-tech companies a half hour away, this isolated motel is a handy spot for daytime hookups. That's what Hank, Drucker or their goons will have in mind if they've trailed me.

Melody sits in her Toyota at the far end of the lot, ducked down to give the impression she doesn't want to be seen.

I put my hand on the doorknob, look left, right, left, trying to appear nervous, then push the door open, hop inside and close the door behind me.

Willy gets up from a faded brown easy chair. "Finally," he says. "I'm bored out of my skull—two hours with no one to talk to, a dripping bathroom faucet, and a TV that only gets basic cable. Also, I think the place has mice."

"Any other complaints?"

Willy sits back down and picks up a bottle of Heineken. Two empties and a half-eaten pepperoni pizza rest atop the coffee table. "Yup. I've got no way to know if any of your ancestors are lurking about, which means I can't scratch my ass or fart out loud. Oops!"

Melody has just stepped through the door.

Willy gets to his feet. "Uh, sorry."

Melody extends her hand. "I'm Melody, and I grew up with three thunderously flatulent older brothers."

Willy shakes her hand and blushes. He smiles and Melody smiles back. Willy and Adele couldn't stand to be in the same room.

"Hiram, Ebenezer and Colette rode here with me," I say, then, as best I can I introduce them to Melody.

She says, "Hi," but doesn't know where to look.

Willy opens a bottle of beer and holds it out to Melody. She takes it and points at the pizza. Willy holds up the box, and she grabs a piece.

"What's a woman doing here?" Hiram asks.

Colette puts her hands on her hips. "*Imbécile*, haven't you noticed that I am a woman? What's the matter? Do women scare you? I'll bet Clementine does. I'll bet she—"

"Shut up!" Hiram shouts. "Don't you ever say anything bad about my Clementine. She's—"

"No, you shut up!" Ebenezer says, shaking his finger in Hiram's face. "Don't ever shout at this fine woman again, or I'll—"

"Okay, okay everyone!" I yell. "Settle down!"

"Hearing half a conversation," Melody says between bites of pizza, "is most peculiar."

"You'll get used to it," Willy says. "Almost."

I point at the left corner of the room. "Hiram, go stand there. Colette over by the dresser. Ebenezer stand in the other corner. And all of you stay there and be quiet unless I call on you."

Hiram glares at me. "Who put you in charge?"

"I put myself in charge, so get moving."

Everyone grumbles but obeys.

Melody and I sit side-by-side on the bed. Willy sinks farther into the easy chair.

I say, "Melody came up with a brilliant solution to one of our problems. Tell them."

She stands up, wrings her hands, looks at me. "They'll hear me okay?"

"Right, but I'll have to repeat what they say."

Melody wrings her hands again. "Jeff needs the building plans for the OASIS site to know where to plant the explosives, but he can't get into the OASIS construction trailer because it's also the guards' headquarter. In addition, it's critical that someone get inside the Ramsey headquarters and Drucker's second office outside Boston. We need to find out what each of those two parties is thinking. But this is of course impossible for Jeff, Willy and myself." Melody glances around the room. "But not Hiram, Ebenezer and Colette."

Melody sits back on the bed.

Her presentation was forceful, clear and to the point. And probably rehearsed. I'd expect nothing less of Melody.

No one talks. Cars roar past. Something scratches inside the walls—the mice Willy complained about?

I reach over with a napkin and wipe tomato sauce off Melody's chin.

Willy sets his beer down and says, "Brilliant." He holds out the pizza box. Melody takes a second piece.

Colette says, "I like it."

Ebenezer says, "Sounds good to me."

"The plan just might work," Hiram says, "but now that the lady's said her piece, tell her she's free to leave."

"Melody stays," I say.

Melody bites off the tip off her pizza. "What's that all about?"

"Hiram's afraid you'll go, but I made it clear that from now on you're a critical part of the planning team."

"That's not what I—"

"Good," Melody says. "What's my role on the big day?"

"I'm still working on it."

In fact, I'm not working on it. There is no role, not for a single mother with a young child. I can't let Melody get caught or worse. She'll raise hell when she discovers she's been left out, but I'll have to live with that.

I change the subject. "Willy's sketches are a help, but they don't tell us where to cut off the electricity or plant the explosives. Willy's seen the site plans on the walls inside the construction trailer, which means Colette can slip inside and—"

Hiram steps forward. "Why? Why not send me?"

"Because Colette was a Resistance leader and an explosives expert, that's why." I shoo Hiram back into his corner. "But I'll have a job for you, too."

"Something more important, I hope."

"*Merde,*" Colette says.

"Hussy!" Hiram shouts. "You're nothing but—"

Ebenezer shouts, "Don't you use that word with—"

"Shut up, everyone!"

"Weird," Melody says. "This is weird beyond belief."

Willy leans forward and taps his bottle against hers. "But kind of fun, don't you think?"

"Beats sitting at my desk all day and checking for dangling participles."

I say, "Ebenezer will slip into Drucker's office, and Hiram will infiltrate the Ramsey's headquarters. We'll incorporate what you've learned into our next planning session."

"More planning?" Hiram says. "Why don't we just—"

"As I said before, a few days before we blow up the OASIS building,

I'll go inside disguised as a repairman and sabotage the backup generator. As soon as we get the site plans, Willy, Colette and I will rig up the explosives. We'll destroy the building on a Sunday when the OASIS site is nearly empty. We'll call in a bomb threat ahead of time, of course, then set off a harmless explosive to make sure we've been taken seriously."

Willy rips the last piece of pizza in two and hands half to Melody. "Sounds like fun."

I turn to Ebenezer. "After you escaped, you said you couldn't walk for two hours, right?"

"More like three."

"From Willy's sketches, I estimate that there are thirty cells, which means at a maximum of thirty inmates. Ebenezer, how long will it take to get everyone out?"

"A couple hours, I'd guess."

"That's longer than I'd like, but we have no choice. While Ebenezer and Hiram are carrying people out, Colette will search the building for any ancestors who might be out of their cells. Any questions?"

Willy says, "Since there's no windows, the building will be pitch black after the generator stops."

Hiram rolls his eyes. "We can see in the dark."

I repeat this to Willy.

He says, "I should have guessed."

I look around the room. "Other questions? Suggestions?"

Hiram tips his cowboy hat back. "As I said, your plan is too complicated." He forms a gun with his thumb and forefinger. "*Bang! Bang! Bang!* Problem solved."

"I don't shoot people."

Hiram grins wickedly. "That's not how I remember things."

"Give it a rest, goddamn it!"

Melody tilts her head to the side and gives me a curious look.

"The meeting's over," I say.

Willy heads out the door. Hiram, Ebenezer and Colette slip

through the wall. Only Melody remains. She studies me for a while, then puts her hand on my shoulder. "You look like you've just seen a ghost."

"I have. Three."

"You know what I mean. Are you all right?"

"I'm fine."

But I'm not fine. When Hiram mentioned the shooting, I started to drift back.

The gun jumps in my hands. Blood splashes on the wallpaper. Mike slides to the floor, his back against the wall, blood pouring from the hole in his forehead. He looks surprised but says nothing. I keep the gun pointed at him.

Mom screams and jumps to her feet, wobbles, falls, gets back up. She touches her bleeding nose, then reaches out to me. "Give me the gun."

I don't. I keep it aimed at my stepfather. He just sits there, his eyes wide open. He's looking at me but not seeing me. Mom asks for the gun again, and I say no again.

I stand there, not moving, the pistol heavy in my hands, maybe for ten minutes, maybe for an hour, wondering if Mike will get back up and try to hurt Mom again.

I hear the front door open. Uncle Sid hurries into the house, takes the gun from me and lays it on the floor. He puts his hand on my back and guides me gently into the next room. "It'll be all right, Jeff. Everyone makes mistakes. I'll fix everything. Go upstairs to your room."

I don't. I peek from around the corner. Uncle Sid reaches inside his jacket, pulls out a gun, wipes it with his handkerchief, puts the gun in Mike's hand and squeezes the trigger. A bullet hits high up on the wall. I jump. Uncle Sid picks the other gun up off the floor, wipes it with his handkerchief and shoots Mike twice in the belly.

Bang! Bang!

Mike bounces twice and lies still.

Warm pee runs down my right leg.

Mom screams.

Uncle Sid rips the front of her blouse, musses her hair and puts his arm around her shoulder. "It's time to call the police."

Then I see Hiram standing next to me.

Chapter 21

SCORPIO Oct. 23 – Nov. 21

We can disguise our look but not our heart. Today's news will test your courage. Art is enjoyed most when shared with a friend.

The next morning, Ebenezer and I drive out of Concord and head toward Boston. I'm wearing a fake mustache, oversized reflective sunglasses and a floppy green gardening hat

Ebenezer looks over at me and smirks.

"What?" I ask.

Ebenezer chuckles.

"It's a disguise," I say. "Disguises are supposed to look funny."

"If you say so."

I pull into the parking lot at the Route 128 train station on the Boston/New York line. I'm driving a rented gray Chevy, much less an attention-grabber than my porta-potty pickup. Yesterday, I trailed Drucker to the office building facing this lot.

I turn off the engine. "Check back every hour."

Ebenezer yawns. "I'm already bored."

"You've said that twice already."

He slips through the door and glides toward a soulless and gray one-story concrete building with vertical slit windows, the New England satellite of OASIS. A sign out front lists the tenants, among them "Phantom Enterprises." Drucker's twisted sense of humor.

I slump down, insert my ear buds, get the music going and take a sip of coffee. It'll be a long day. I too am already bored.

Well-dressed men and women with briefcases hurry importantly onto the eastbound toward Boston. Others catch the train in the other direction to New York City—attorneys, high-tech executives, civil servants—normal people with normal jobs that have nothing to do with ghosts and gangsters.

Bored, I eat my turkey sandwich, then a bag of chips, then an apple. Lunch at midmorning.

An hour later, Ebenezer emerges through the side of the building, glides my direction, slips through the door and settles down beside me. "Phantom Enterprises is nothing more than one room and one desk."

"Not surprising. Drucker probably uses this office to meet with people who aren't supposed to know about the main Boston OASIS office and labs."

"My guess too." Ebenezer says, yawning and stretching.

"What's Drucker been up to?"

Ebenezer yawns again. His teeth are yellow from decades of chewing tobacco. "He checked the news and weather online, opened the Red Sox site for a couple of minutes, then had a long, lovey-dovey phone chat with his girlfriend from the FBI."

"That's it?"

"That's it."

"Weren't there any papers lying around that you could have read? Didn't Drucker write emails or make other phone calls?"

Ebenezer shrugs. "No documents, no emails. Just one call from an OASIS engineer. He's stopping by later."

"Why didn't you say that right away?"

Ebenezer scratches his left ear, then yawns. "It didn't seem important."

"Well it is. You'll sit in on the meeting."

Ebenezer shakes his head. "There's this woman I'm supposed to meet."

"Back to work."

Ebenezer grumbles and lumbers off.

I soon fall asleep.

Ebenezer drifts back sometime later and wakes me. "Drucker's eating powdered donuts and searching through sites listing overseas property."

"Where?"

"South Africa, Thailand, the Middle East."

"That doesn't sound like someone looking for a vacation rental."

"My thoughts too," Ebenezer says. "What do you think he's up to?"

"You never know with Drucker. Anything else to report?"

"He ordered out for sushi," Ebenezer says through a yawn. "Am I through for the day?"

"Nope. Get back inside. Drucker's meeting that engineer, remember?"

Ebenezer leaves.

I drift off to sleep again and wake up to a tapping on my window. It's a railroad employee in a blue shirt with a red name tag that reads, 'Mel.'

I roll down my window.

Mel points at an overhead surveillance camera. "You've been sitting out here all alone for hours. I saw you talking to yourself. You okay?"

I scrunch up my face. "Uh... no, I'm not okay. Cindy rushed away right after breakfast and said she was going to New York City on business, but didn't take her briefcase, and I think she went there with a man for a day on the town. So I'm waiting here to catch them when they come back together."

People in my line of work always have a story ready.

"Is it okay if I stay?" I ask.

Mel scratches the back of his neck. "You're not breaking any law... unless you got plans to—"

"Nope," I say, raising my hands in surrender. "Just a lot of shouting."

Mel lowers his eyes. "I had a wife that cheated on me."

"Sorry."

Mel slaps the roof of my car. "Shit happens." He takes a few steps, stops, looks back and says, "Then I found someone better."

Someone better.

I smell Melody's perfume, feel the touch of her hand, picture how she fills out her jeans.

Did Beckworth do me a favor? Maybe. Probably. But given a chance, I'd still load his BMW with concrete.

Ebenezer slips into the truck. "Drucker is one weird fellow."

"That I knew."

"He's up to something illegal, maybe a swindle of some kind. I know because I was in the trade and one of the best. My Ponzi scheme ran for three-and-a-half years before my arrest and would have gone on forever if a woman hadn't betrayed me. I knew she wasn't all that trustworthy, but I never expected her to —"

"You were telling me that Drucker's weird."

"Right. Get this: His desk drawers are stuffed with $100 bills, maybe a couple hundred thousand dollars. I know because I watched him take out the bundles and count them, twice, all the time humming "Sgt. Pepper's Lonely Hearts Club Band."

I lean back. "You're kidding."

"Nope. Do you think it's OASIS money?"

I shake my head. "If it were theirs, they'd have made him keep it in a safe. When he worked for the CIA, he was accused of embezzlement, but the charges were eventually dropped."

"Why doesn't he keep it at home?"

"He's dating an FBI agent. She might find it."

"Right," Ebenezer says. "Why not a safety deposit box?"

"I don't know—maybe he's afraid OASIS would find out. Drucker's paranoid." Off in the distance, Mel stops sweeping the platform and waves at me. I wave back. "Did the engineer stop by?"

"Oh, yeah. A half hour ago. He brought along the new, portable version of the bigger machine that they used when they snatched me."

"Why didn't you tell me right away?" I say, sitting up and starting the engine. "We've got to get you the hell out of here!" I back up and squeal out of the parking lot. "Sorry I put you in danger."

"No danger," Ebenezer says, spreading his hands. "The engineer didn't turn the damn thing on. If he had, well, I wouldn't be here."

My stomach drops. I could have lost Ebenezer. I don't want to think about it.

He adjusts his tie in the side mirror. "The techie said the device will be operational in ten days."

I lift my foot off the gas pedal. "Just ten days?"

"That's what he said."

"Then I have to move the caper up to nine days from today. Go Back There, contact Hiram, and tell him to get back down here right away. It's his turn to play spy."

"He'll piss and moan."

"So what's new?"

• • •

The next morning, I head for a café down the street from Hank's headquarters in Boston's North End, again in my ridiculous mustache, sunglasses, and drooping gardening hat. I've sent Hiram inside the headquarters.

He comes back an hour later, but says he has nothing of value because Hank doesn't do business on the phone, doesn't speak about anything of importance with Freddie and the other goons, and doesn't write anything down. Hiram says he thinks that Hank's afraid his place is bugged. I agree.

Hiram complains about his mission. I send him back inside.

A text arrives:

> No, you cannot interview me! And if you ever try to contact
> me again, I'll get my lawyer after you!
>
> Jennie K.

This a delayed reply from one of the women who'd lied at the shelter director's trial. I didn't think she's cooperate, just as the others hadn't, but I had to try.

Ask again? Beg? Offer money?

Probably nothing would work. Does it even matter any longer? A journalism prize doesn't seem all that important to someone who might disappear forever.

Hiram drifts back a few minutes later. "Hank's getting ready to meet someone."

"Who?"

"Don't know, but I heard the guy shouting on the other end, and he sounded like Hank has scared the horse apples out of him."

"Hank has that effect on people."

A couple minutes later, Hiram and I spot Hank leaving his headquarters. Hiram leaves the café and falls in behind him, and I follow far enough back so Hank and his two bodyguards won't notice me. Hank turns into a tiny park that runs between Hanover Street and the Old North Church. He settles onto a bench next to a mousy man with darting eyes.

Hiram glides over and stands behind the two, makes faces, sticks out his tongue, and pretends to put his fingers in Hank's ears. Hiram's idea of fun.

I ease into the middle of a cluster of German tourists, their guide dressed up as Benjamin Franklin. He starts reciting Longfellow's poem:

Listen my children and you shall hear
Of the midnight ride of...

A beefy young man is leaning against an iron fence twenty feet behind Hank, gazing into the open guidebook in his hands. Off to my right, another man of similar bulk slouches against the statue of Paul Revere on horseback. Hank's bodyguards.

The German tourists shuffle their feet and whisper back and forth, unable to decode the Boston accent.

Then he climbed the tower of the Old North Church,
By the wooden stairs, with stealthy...

Hiram stops clowning, leans forward and concentrates on what Hank and the other man are saying.

Tourists snap smartphone pictures of the church, the statue, the man dressed up as Ben.

After a couple minutes, Hank stands up, drops his cigarette butt, and takes off in the direction of his office. His bodyguards fall in twenty paces behind. The man Hank had met scurries in the other direction, passing by just a few feet in front of me. His nose makes mousy little twitches. The meeting did not go well.

I ease away from the crowd, the docent's voice trailing off:

And so through the night went his cry of alarm
To every Middlesex village and...

Hiram joins me.

"Who's the man Hank talked to?" I ask.

"That's the owner on paper of Hank's construction company, the one that built the OASIS site. Hank's as angry as a coyote with his paw in a trap because the guy hasn't found out Drucker's identity yet."

"That's all they talked about?" I ask.

Hiram turns to watch a mother holding up her toddler to get a better look at Paul Revere on his horse.

"Well?" I say.

Hiram tugs at his mustache. "Hank told the guy that you're useful now but will have to be taken care of later."

"Taken care of later?"

"That's his expression."

I think of Melody, Dawn and Uncle Sid. I think of eating pizza and watching baseball on TV with Willy. I think of my house and my job, Janet and Sherwood.

But I shouldn't be surprised. I know too much.

Hiram says, "So now you gotta bushwhack Hank and Freddie. Also the mousy guy while you're at it. Save yourself. Save Clementine. Save the other ancestors."

"No. We're doing things my way."

"Your plan is a barrel of rotten apples. Mine's simple and straightforward. You should listen to me the way you used to."

The way I used to.

When Hiram showed up for the first time, I said, "Who are you?" and he said, "You know who I am."

Together we watched two men in white coats lay a sheet over Mike, lift him onto a gurney and wheel him off, his right arm dangling.

My life was never the same after that.

•   •   •

Drucker points at a portrait of Samuel Adams. "That guy looks like he's trying to hold back a fart."

"You're a fun guy to visit a museum with."

We're standing in the new wing of the Museum of Fine Arts in Boston. Meeting here was Drucker's idea. Zero chances that the Ramseys would show up at a place like this, Drucker said. I'd tried to tell my story over the phone, but Drucker said we had to meet face to face. He's gotten especially paranoid lately. My doing, I hope. What I have to tell him today should push him over the edge.

Drucker says, "When's the last time you talked with Hank?"

"Yesterday," I say, then for verisimilitude add, "late last night, actually. When he called, I was watching a rerun of *The Big Sleep*, right at the part where Humphrey Bogart—"

"Yeah, yeah. What did the guy want?"

"To meet with me today."

"And?" Drucker says.

"And I'm meeting with you instead. That shows how I have my priorities straight and—"

"Hank still doesn't know my identity?"

"Nope," I say.

For once I'm telling Drucker the truth.

"If he ever finds out," Drucker says, shaking his head, "the bastard will try to whack me."

It's fun watching Drucker squirm.

"There is that possibility," I say brightly.

Drucker studies me for a moment. "So what's the big news you have for me? It'd better be pretty damn good to drag me all the way down here."

"I've made a contact inside the Ramsey gang, just as you suggested. It was a clever idea, by the way."

He raises an eyebrow. "A contact? No shit?"

"No shit. I followed the guy from Hank's headquarters to a bar in the North End, sat on the stool beside him, complained about the Red Sox bullpen, Congress, the rainy weather and the delays on the subway, then I bought the guy a half dozen beers and got him to talking. As he got drunker and drunker, it slowly came out that he was 'displeased with his current employer'—his words, only slurred—and he wanted out. I told him I could help, that I had the right connections."

Precise details make even the biggest of lies believable.

Drucker lifts an eyebrow, studies me, then says, "What's his name?"

Uh, oh. I should have thought of that before. I fumble for a name. Make it something common, something Drucker can't trace through the internet. Sam Jones? Tom Smith? No, don't give a name. Keep things simple. "My guy wouldn't tell me."

"You didn't ask? That was a dickhead move."

"Of course I asked. He said he'd give out his name as soon as he sees a written guarantee getting him into the Federal Witness Protection Program. Then we'll set up a meeting, just him, you and me. But no wires, no watchers, no FBI."

"Of course," Drucker says, lifting his hands in surrender. "I can be trusted."

Sure, you can.

"Hank's sending him to Miami on some nefarious mission," I say. "But he'll get back on the fourteenth."

Which with luck is two days after we rescue the ancestors and turn the OASIS site into rubble.

"Okay," Drucker says. "So you've made a contact. Maybe you're not as worthless as I thought. What else have you got?"

Two teenage boys move in close. One says, "Is that the Samuel Adams who makes the beer that Tommie drinks?"

Drucker and I shift to the next room. A tour group stands in a half circle in front of a massive painting of George Washington on horseback. George gives me a severe look for all the lies I'm telling, he whom it's claimed never told a lie. I lower my voice to a whisper. "My contact says Hank and Freddie plan on blowing up the OASIS site."

Drucker's head snaps back. "You're shitting me!"

The tour group swings around as a unit and stares.

Drucker and I step farther away.

"You're sure?" Drucker says, his voice lowered.

"My guy says Hank's ripped about losing those contracts."

"He must be royally pissed to try something like that. Only an idiot would blow up a federal building."

I give that some thought. "I'm sure you're right. Only an idiot."

"When's it happening?"

"In a couple months," I say with a shrug and a reassuring smile. "But Hank might just be talking big. You know how mobsters are. So you shouldn't really worry."

"I shouldn't really worry! Of course I should worry! *Fuck!*"

Again the tour group stares. Drucker and I move to the back of the gallery.

Drucker pokes his tongue around in his mouth, massages the back of his neck, tugs his earlobe. "I'll contact the FBI about cutting a deal with your guy," Drucker says. He looks around the gallery, then shakes his head. "But I still can't believe Hank would pull shit like that."

"Maybe he's just bluffing," I say in a sprightly voice. "Mobsters have that tendency."

Drucker grunts and shifts to his other foot.

It's fun watching him fidget.

He half closes his eyes. "You're having fun, aren't you?"

"I always have fun when we're together. Maybe we can meet here again sometime, you know, not to talk business, but just to enjoy the exhibits. Museums are a lot more fun when you go with a pal."

Chapter 22

SCORPIO Oct. 23 – Nov. 21

One's greatest happiness is to bring happiness to others. It's good for the soul to be a little naughty from time to time. Soak that germ-laden kitchen sponge in vinegar.

I go home, grab a beer from the fridge and carry my laptop to the rear deck overlooking the marsh. I figure I deserve some downtime, so for the next few hours I'm going to forget all about the caper, Drucker, a Ramsey bullet through the brain or disappearing without a trace.

I email Kevin in Norman, Oklahoma.

> Kevin,
>
> In your email to the Tattler, you stated that you receive visits from your ancestors. Could we discuss this? Nothing will appear in print, of course.
>
> Jeff Beekle

I lean back and wait for a reply. Red-winged blackbirds sway atop cattails, a young rabbit hops across the back lawn, a dog barks in the distance.

I get an immediate response:

Sure, anytime.

Kevin

I type:

Thanks.

How often do you receive ancestor visits, and what is your state of mind when you get them? Are you upset? Scared? In trouble? Also, you mentioned in your email that you were traumatized as a child. Could you be specific?

Jeff

I hear Willy walk into the kitchen, the refrigerator door open and close, a chair scrape across the floor.

Kevin replies:

I don't keep track of how often. It's pretty irregular. They seem to show up when something's bugging me but not always. You said, 'state of mind.' Do you think I'm crazy? Sometimes I do.

Yes, something horrible happened when I was a kid, but I don't want to talk about it.

Kevin

My reply:

My apologies, Kevin. I in no way questioned your mental stability. Remember, many others have had the same experience.

Do your ancestors give you advice? Is it sound? Do you follow it? If so, do you ever think you should not have listened?

Jeff

Reply:

My Grandpa Leonard mentors me on almost everything.
His ideas are great, so yeah I do follow his advice.

Well, maybe what he tells me isn't always so great. But I
usually go ahead anyway and do what he wants.
To tell the truth, I've got self-confidence issues. My wife
left me on account of them. Sometimes I tell myself I
shouldn't listen to Grandpa Leonard, but I do anyway.
I gotta go now because the plumber's here to fix the sink.

Kevin

Harold K. from Fayetteville, NC included a telephone number in
his email and said I could call. I do.

"Yes?" the voice says.

"Harold?"

"Yup."

"I'm Jeff Beekle from the *Boston Tattler*. You responded to the
article I wrote about people who get visits from their ancestors.
Would you be willing to answer a few questions? I promise that
what you say will not appear in print."

Long hesitation. "Okay, I guess."

Harold has a shy voice, distant, as if he's holding the phone far
away.

I say, "Could you tell me about the trauma you said you experienced
as a boy?"

Another long hesitation. "I was out playing with my little brother
and was supposed to watch him, but he chased a ball into the street
and a truck was coming and…" Harold stops talking.

"I'm sorry," I say. "Let's talk about something else. Do your
ancestors give you advice? If so, do you follow it?"

Harold sniffles, blows his nose, sniffles again. "Yeah," they're always
telling me to do this or do that. They're pretty bossy. They started

showing up right away afterward, you know, after it happened. Danny was only three years old and..."

Again Harold closes down.

"I'm sorry to be putting you though this," I say.

"Mom never blamed me, but I kind of wish that she would have because then I'd feel..."

His voice trails off again. More sniffling.

"I guess I don't want to talk no more," he says. "Please don't call back."

The line goes dead.

Poor guy. I'm sorry I called him. I lay the phone down. It immediately chimes. The caller's number is blocked. "Yes," I say.

"Reggie?"

"He's out."

"I'll call back later," Hank says.

I go inside the house, get the burner phone, return to the deck and tap in Hank's number.

"You're not answering my calls," Hank says.

"I've been busy. I have a real job that pays me real money."

"Tell it to someone who gives a rat's ass. When I call, you jump to attention, got it? When I say we meet, you drop everything and meet me, got it?"

"I'll try to remember."

"You'd fucking better. Your uncle never jerks me around like this. By the way, he's not been looking so good lately. I hope he's not got something serious."

Uncle Sid looks as healthy as a horse. But I get what Hank's saying. Drucker's a bluffer, Hank isn't.

"Are you trying to scare me?" I say.

"Would I do that?"

"You're a scary guy."

Hank snorts.

He's flattered. I meant him to be.

I say, "I made a contact inside OASIS."

"No shit?"

"I checked on the finances of the OASIS employees as you suggested, but haven't had any luck finding out who's come into a lot of money. But I did find someone who's drowning in debt. I set up a meeting with him at that new Starbucks on Quincy Street. You know it? No? You don't? Anyway, he's desperate. He sank all his money into his wife's hair-braiding salon, but after just three-and-a-half months, she cleaned out the till and ran off with a guy who operates a highly profitable mink ranch in upstate—"

"Yeah, yeah, yeah. Get to the point. What'll this jerk cost me?"

"Twenty big ones."

Long wait, then, "You'd better be giving me this straight because, well, you can use your imagination."

My imagination pictures a shallow grave at the foot of some mountain in New Hampshire. "He's out of town right now, but I've got a sit-down set up for the thirteenth."

One day after we blow up the site.

"You choose the hour and place," I say.

I hear a match strike. Hank says. "I'll get back to you."

"By the way," I add, "my contact says the FBI is following you."

"Shit, I knew that."

Of course Hank knew that. I'd said that to get on his good side.

"And," Hank adds, "you knew that I knew that. I'm not stupid."

The line goes dead.

No, Hank's not stupid. Something I should never forget.

· · ·

The next afternoon, I drive into Boston to meet Eleanor Peterson, the teacher who contacted me about her ancestral visits. On the way I call Uncle Sid and leave one more message advising him to get out of town. It probably won't do any good, but I have to keep trying.

I park in the underground lot beneath Boston Common and jog across the street to the Public Garden. I'm thirty-five minutes late because I got caught in traffic. Has Eleanor given up on me and left? After how badly I upset Harold, that might not be such a bad thing.

No, there she is, wearing the broad blue sun hat that she said would identify her. She's sits on a park bench and clutches a large black handbag. She has a round face, gray hair and wears rimless glasses.

"Sorry I'm late," I say.

Eleanor beams, jumps up and hugs me. She barely comes up to my chest.

I hug her back, then try to step away.

She clings to me. A teenage girl smiles at us. So does a guy in a gray hoodie. So does a cop on horseback.

Finally, she releases me, sits down and taps the seat beside her.

I sit down. "I'm late because I had—"

"Oh don't apologize, young man. Your wonderful article changed my life. I hope you're proud of yourself."

It's been a long time since I've been proud of myself. "Well I was just doing what—"

"I love these tulips and flowering trees," Eleanor says with a sweep of her hand. "And especially those willows dipping the tips of their branches in the water. The swan boats are magical, right out of Wagner. Have you ever ridden on them?"

"In fact, the other day—"

"I'm sorry to have dragged you out here like this," Eleanor says, "but I wanted to meet you face to face. Phones and emails are so impersonal, don't you think?" She taps my knee. "Now why don't you ask those questions you said you had for me."

"Well, what I especially want to know is if, when you were a child, did you ever experience—"

"It was my stepfather," Eleanor says, her voice sinking, her eyes going unfocused. "I put up with it from when I was twelve until I was sixteen, then ran away from home."

She bites her lower lip.

Uh, oh. Not wanting to make her cry the way Harold did when he talked about his little brother, I change the subject. "Do your ancestors give you advice? Is it good advice, and—"

"Not always," Eleanor says, her eyes coming back into focus. "But I've always followed it, and I suspect I always will. I'm too old to change, too full of doubts about my ability to make decisions. Do you understand?"

I nod. "I know what it's like to be traumatized at a young age and to lose all confidence in ever making the right decision."

For once she doesn't interrupt me.

Eleanor studies me. "I think that you, too, get visits from your ancestors."

I watch the mounted policeman stop his horse to let a girl reach up and pat its nose. A nice image.

I turn back to Eleanor.

"Yes," I say, just above a whisper. Then louder: "Yes. Ever since I was six years old."

She leans in and hugs me. I hug back. She's warm, soft, heavily perfumed.

She releases me and looks at her watch. Her eyes are wet. "I can only stay a few more minutes, I'm afraid, because I have to catch the bus back to Albany."

"You came all the way from Albany just to—"

"Don't worry about it," Eleanor says and pats my knee. "I love riding along and watching the countryside pass by. Besides, I have company."

I look around. "Company?"

"Granny, this is Jeff Beekle. Jeff, this is Anna Mikhailov."

The closest person to us is the cop on the horse. "Oh."

"When I told Granny who I was coming to see, she said she just had to come along. She's eager to meet you."

"Why?"

"She wouldn't say."

I look around. "Okay, but… Uh."

Eleanor points to her left. "She over there."

I turn and wave my fingers.

Now I know how Willy and Melody feel when my ancestors show up.

"We have a lot of fun together," Eleanor says with a giggle. "Sometimes at my bridge club, Granny slips around behind the other players and tells me the cards they're holding. Since we're not playing for money, it's not a sin." Eleanor giggles again. "It's kind of fun to be naughty once in a while isn't it?"

"It's good for the soul. Tell me, does your grandmother—"

"I don't understand," Eleanor says.

"I was asking if your grandmother—'"

Eleanor waves her hands. "Sorry, not you, Jeffrey. I meant I didn't understand what Granny was saying. Her Russian accent is rather thick."

Eleanor listens, then turns to me. "Granny says she's extremely proud to meet you. Back There, everyone's cheering for you to succeed in you upcoming endeavor. I keep asking Granny what it is and why it's so important, but she won't tell me. She says it's best I don't know."

Eleanor listens to her invisible grandmother, nods a couple times and says, "Granny's extremely worried. She says her mother, my great-grandmother Alyona, has gone missing from Back There."

Uh, oh. "Gone missing? For how long?"

Eleanor pauses, listens, then says, "For too long, it seems. I don't know what she means by too long, but Granny is quiet upset, which is unlike her." Eleanor is quiet for a moment, then adds, "In fact, I've never seen her cry."

My heart sinks. OASIS must have grabbed Eleanor's great-grandmother, probably for her Russian language skills. "I'm sorry," I say. "Can your grandmother be more specific as to—"

"I'm sorry to get all weepy like this," Eleanor says, dabbing a tissue at the corners of her eyes. "It's just that… hold on a second."

Eleanor listens, then turns to me. "Granny says not to give up no matter how difficult the situation is." Eleanor gives me a puzzled look. "Can you tell me what this is all about?"

Should I tell her that she'll disappear if my stupid caper fails? No, of course not. If she disappears, she disappears, and there's nothing anyone can do about it. So why worry her? "It's nothing important," I say. "Just—"

"Well, I'm certain that it is in fact something important," Eleanor says, a bit miffed. "But I won't pry." She checks her watch. "Well, Granny and I have to leave now if we're going to catch the Albany bus." She gives me a forgiving smile and squeezes me around the waist. "Granny says you're doing the right thing."

I hug Eleanor back. "I certainly hope so."

Chapter 23

SCORPIO Oct. 23 – Nov. 21

The human body is a thing of beauty. Today is a day to call upon your quick wit and courage. Vinegar is an excellent and inexpensive solvent.

I wake up to find my great-grandmother sitting on the window seat in my bedroom. Colette's dressed in her usual faded French Army trousers and a black, long-sleeve shirt. Colette is forever forty, a touch plump but still curvy and pretty, her head covered in wild black curls.

I'm in just my boxer shorts. My skin crawls. I pull the sheet up to my neck. "Have you been here all night?"

"Off and on. By the way, nice pecs, big guy."

"You're my great-grandmother, for God sake. You shouldn't notice things like that." I stand up, clutching the sheet around me. "Turn around. I have to get dressed."

"You're kidding."

"Do I sound like I'm kidding?"

"That's unbelievable. With all the problems you have, you're worried about me seeing you in your skivvies?" Colette squeezes the thumb of her left hand with the forefinger and thumb of her other hand. "One, there's the baggy-faced Drucker who threatens to send your Uncle Sid to prison for money-laundering." Colette pinches her

forefinger. "Two, a mobster plans on killing you. Three, blowing up a federal building could get you twenty years, minimum. Four, Adele has cleaned out your bank account and has probably destroyed those little thingies... uh..."

"Memory cards."

"Right," Colette says, shifting her grip to her pinky. "And OASIS has abducted your great-great-grandmother Clementine and might not release her in time for her to get Back There, which will doom the rest of her family line. That doesn't include your mother and me, I'm happy to report, because we're not Clementine's descendants, but does include you."

"Anything else?"

Colette switches hands and grabs her thumb. "And six, you don't own a bed."

"I prefer sleeping on a mattress on the floor."

"You can be weird at times."

"Blame my ancestors."

Colette makes a face and turns her back.

I hurry getting dressed. In the hallway, we run into Willy, who is barefoot, shirtless and wearing jeans.

He peers past me into my bedroom. "I heard you talking to someone." He drops his voice. "Do you have your cute editor in there?"

I introduce Colette.

She says, "He's yummy. He reminds me of the Norman farm boy I once went for a roll in the hay with."

I turn to Willy. "She says you're yummy and remind her of an ex-lover."

Willy takes a step back. "More than I can handle." He scampers to the bathroom and locks the door behind him.

We step out of the house and head toward my pickup.

Colette stops halfway and points at my pickup. "You're expecting me to ride all the way to the OASIS site in a truck that delivers poop shacks?"

"No one can see you except me."

"It's the idea," Colette says.

"Get over it."

She hesitates, shrugs, slips through the door and settles onto the passenger seat.

I lay my toolkit, hard hat and safety glasses in the bed of the pickup, along with the backpack holding my disguise.

I get into the driver's seat, start the engine, and we pull away.

Colette puts her feet up on the dash. She has on combat boots, all ready for a day of action. "One of my favorite gentlemen was a Polish count who owned oodles of castles," she says. "He liked to drive me in his Rolls-Royce convertible up and down the Champs-Élysées for all of Paris to see."

I turn west toward the OASIS site. "My Rolls is in the shop."

"I'll bet you tell that to all your girls."

Where does she learn expressions like that? Do they have TVs Back There? I would ask, but I know I wouldn't get a straight answer.

Neither of us speaks for several minutes. Finally, Colette says, "My count was a colonel in the Polish cavalry." Now her voice is small and far away. "The Germans killed him the very first day of the war."

"Sorry," I say, turning toward her. "Did you decide to join the Resistance on account of him?"

"Partly, and partly for the adventure, I have to admit. And for a while it was an adventure, blowing up buildings and Nazi supply trains and watching tanks and troops tumble into ravines. But later all that killing got to me. The German soldiers had mothers, fathers, siblings, kids, just like anyone else."

She unlaces her left boot, laces it again, tugging hard on the leather cords. "But today should be fun because no one gets hurt, and there's no chance I'll get caught."

The Nazis caught Colette in late 1944, executed her in early 1945. She left behind a seven-year-old daughter, who a dozen years later would marry a GI, move to the U.S. and give birth to my mother.

I say, "I'm not sure I'd be brave enough to do what you did."

"Sure, you would. It takes *cajones* to blow up a federal building."

"Maybe, but would I do it if I weren't also saving myself?"

"You would," Colette says. "Trust me. I've known you since you were six years old."

I want to believe her.

We ride the rest of the way in silence. Is Colette thinking about the day ahead? Her years in the Resistance? The daughter she didn't get to see grow up? The expressions on the faces of the soldiers in her firing squad the moment before they pulled the trigger?

I park a mile from the site and grab everything from the back of the pickup. I trudge up the hill that overlooks the old army base, with Colette floating ahead to point out where I should walk to avoid the surveillance cameras that caught Willy and me during our visit.

At the crest of the hill, I get down on my stomach and peer through my binoculars at the OASIS building a couple hundred feet below. It looks the same, a windowless, four-story brick heap with 'Spirit Storage' over the front door. The construction trailer hasn't been removed, apparently because it's been turned into the guardhouse.

I give Colette the thumbs-up. She pumps her fist overhead—where did she pick that up?—glides down the hill and disappears through the side of the trailer.

Sometimes my ancestors float, sometimes they walk, and sometimes it's a waltzing combination of both. I once asked Hiram why that was, and he said, "Because."

I slather on more mosquito repellent, drink half a bottle of water and eat all my trail mix.

A half hour later, Colette floats back up the hill. "The building plans are still thumbtacked to the wall of the trailer," she says. "I had to memorize everything because I forgot to bring invisible paper and pencil from Back There." She scratches her curls. "I'd never have made a mistake like that during my days in the Resistance."

I take my sketchpad from the backpack and draw a large square to represent the building.

Colette taps the top edge of the page. "There's a wide door right here behind the building. I'm guessing that's where they keep the van that captured Ebenezer and the others." She puts her finger on the middle of the square. "That's the computer room, and over here are the cells, and here..."

She talks for five minutes, with me sketching and flipping pages as fast as I can. Her memory is excellent, her instructions clear. Hiram or Ebenezer would have been useless at this, and we'd have ended up arguing. Finally, Colette says, "That's all I've got for now. I'll make more trips. I wish it were safe for me to go into the main building."

"Don't even think about it," I say, looking up at her. "You wouldn't get back out. By the way, was anyone in the trailer?"

Colette smirks. "Just a chubby little guard with 'Cedric' on his name tag and the face of an *imbécile*. He's eating powdered donuts and watching internet porn."

"Uh, oh. I hope he wasn't...?"

"Oh, he was."

"Sorry."

Colette laughs. "Not something I haven't seen a hundred times." I don't ask her to elaborate.

She returns a second time, a third, a fourth. I fill a couple dozen pages. During her final trip, she checks out a manhole a couple hundred feet to the right of the building. She returns with a smile and high-fives me (do they watch basketball Back There?). "I went down the manhole and followed the tunnel all the way. It's stuffed with pipes for water, sewer and the electrical lines, but there's enough room for you and Willy if you crawl. I've already scoped out where to put the explosives."

I draw the utility tunnel according to her instructions.

She says, "This reminds me of my days in the Resistance, only not so exciting."

"Wait until we blow up the building," I say, slipping my sketchpad into my tool kit. "Now turn around. I have to change."

Colette smirks.

"Turn," I say.

She does.

I dump my backpack on the ground, squirm out of my shirt and jeans and pull on a gray, one-piece uniform. I put on a silly black wig, a silly black mustache, yellow-tinted safety glasses and a silly orange hard hat. "You can turn around now."

Colette giggles.

"What?" I ask.

"You look nerdy."

"Where did you learn that word?"

She picks up a pebble and hands it to me. "Put this in your shoe to make you limp. People will pay more attention to your bodily movements than your face. They'll remember you as a big guy with a limp, not as a big guy with a dorky mustache."

I do what she says. On matters like this, I can count on her advice.

I hook the toolkit's canvas strap over my shoulder and start down the hill, following the route that Colette points to avoid the surveillance cameras. A gallon jug of chemicals sloshes in my backpack, a nasty concoction Melody brewed from something she'd researched on the internet.

I get three steps inside the building before a tall thin guard with a black unibrow rushes over. His tag reads 'Lionel.' He looks me up and down. "Who in hell are you?"

I set my toolkit down. "I'm here to do the regularly scheduled follow-up inspection on the new backup generator."

"Nobody told me you were coming."

"Do they tell you everything that happens here?"

Lionel doesn't know how to respond. He takes out his phone. "Stay right there,"

He steps a few feet away and talks into his phone, watching me all the time. He says a few things I can't hear, then slips the phone back into his pocket. "We don't know nothing about your coming."

"No? You should have, because I called ahead."

"Yeah, well we got no record of it."

That's because I in fact hadn't called. I didn't want to take the chance that someone at OASIS would decide to change the time for my arrival and call the company that installed the generator. I sling my toolkit over my shoulder. "What the hell, I'm overbooked today anyway, Lionel. But if the electricity goes out, the backup generator fails, and the place goes dark, well, don't blame me, Lionel. I just hope your boss won't come down too hard on you, Lionel."

I turn to go.

"Wait!" he says. "Come back here." He hesitates, then signals me to follow. I limp along behind him, down a set of stairs, along a narrow hallway and into a musty room with overhead pipes, a hulking gray backup generator up on concrete blocks, and a mouse that scurries behind a barrel.

I set my toolkit down, take out Willy's electrical meter and hook it up to a black wire leading to the generator. I do that gingerly, since I have no idea of what I'm doing. I check the reading, grunt, then move on to another wire, then another.

Lionel sits on a barrel and yawns hugely.

I slip the meter back into the toolkit and say, "The electrical connections look dandy."

Lionel nods and yawns again. He has wide teeth and a plump, pink tongue.

I take out a screwdriver and bang its handle against the pipe leading from the gas tank to the generator. "It's solid," I say. I rap my knuckles against the tank. It sounds full, probably a couple hundred gallons. Whoever filled it would have left enough room for heat expansion as well as a for a gallon of a powerful concoction of bleach, vinegar and whatever else Melody mixed together.

"Do you like working here?" I ask cheerfully.

Lionel grunts. He's sleepy and bored out of his skull, which is just how I want him to be.

"Now for the additive," I chirp. "This'll do a bang-up job of keeping the gasoline fresh for months."

Lionel gives me a 'what-the-hell-do-I-care' look.

I open the jug, go up on my toes, unscrew the cap to the tank and watch Melody's Magic Mixture glug-glug inside. When Willy and I tested the stuff on an old lawnmower, the engine seized up in under three minutes.

"That does it," I say brightly. "Now I've got to get moving. I have six more jobs today."

Another 'who-gives-a-shit' look from Lionel. He leads me to the front exit, grunts something and pulls the door open to let me out.

Where I run into Quincy and Cedric.

I take a couple steps, greatly exaggerating my limp.

Both glance down at my left foot.

I swing my toolkit up onto my right shoulder to block their view, hurry down the walkway, down the driveway and down the road to my pickup. Only then do I remove the pebble from my shoe. I pull my sketchbook from the toolkit, toss my stuff onto the bed of the pickup and get behind the wheel.

Colette is waiting on the front seat. "How did it go?"

"The job went fine, but I had a close call."

"It's always more exciting that way."

"Excitement is something I can do without." I start drawing what I saw of the inside of the building.

Colette says, "You should have left the sketchbook back here in the pickup. If you'd been caught, they'd have searched your toolbox."

She's right. I look up. "I'd have survived only two days in the Resistance."

"More like one."

Chapter 24

SCORPIO Oct. 23 - Nov. 21

Measure the moments of your life, not by the calendar, but by happy memories. Take time to reflect on your good deeds and the satisfaction they have brought you. Denim is never suitable for formal occasions.

I get home to find Uncle Sid slumped on a kitchen chair, clutching a cup in both hands and staring at the wall. I pour myself some coffee and sit across the table from him. "What's up?" I ask.

"Nothing much. What about you?"

"Just relaxing and enjoying my time off."

Uncle Sid glances around the kitchen. "I miss your Mom every day."

"So do I, but you didn't drive out here just to tell me that."

Uncle Sid turns back to me. "How come you took a vacation?"

"I've told you that already—I'm helping Willy fix up the house."

"You don't know which end of a hammer to grab onto."

"Willy's instructing me."

Uncle Sid leans forward on his elbows. "You're hiding something from me."

"What makes you say that?"

"I lived here with you for five years and can tell when something's bothering you. Has Hank Ramsey made you do something you don't—"

"How are things going at the magazine without me?" I ask.

"That almost sounds like you want to shift topics."

"Does it?"

Uncle Sid shakes his head, then takes a sip of coffee. He knows he'll get nothing more out of me.

He says, "We miss you at work, Melody especially. So do Janet and Sherwood. You hold the place together." Uncle Sid gets up and opens the refrigerator. "Do you have anything to feed your poor old uncle?"

I take out my phone. "I'll call for a pizza."

Uncle Sid sits down, waits for me to order, then says, "I meant it when I said you hold the place together. I've told you maybe five hundred times that I'm thinking of retiring to a warmer place, but I haven't told you this: When I do, I'm turning the management of the *Tattler* over to you."

"Me? Why me?"

"You're my only relative."

"I'm touched."

"Don't be. Just don't do something stupid and run the place into the ground."

I'd suspected that Uncle Sid would someday put me in control of the magazine. But do I see myself growing old at the *Tattler*? Do I see myself as Sherwood's boss? Melody's?

But Uncle Sid is deceiving himself. As long as Hank owns the magazine, there's not a chance in hell he'll let me run it because he knows I won't launder his dirty money. He'll put one of his halfwit goons in charge—many even Freddie. All that would change, of course, if Hank and Freddie should wind up in prison for destroying a federal building.

"But…" Uncle Sid says, not finishing his sentence.

"But what?"

"But it won't be easy. There's a certain financial complication."

By that he means the money laundering.

"I'm working on something that'll take care of the complication."

"How can you? You don't even know what it is," Uncle Sid says. "And what exactly are you talking about?"

"It's my secret."

"You were a secretive kid."

"A sign of genius."

"That's not how I'd put it." Uncle Sid lifts his coffee cup to his lips, pauses, sets it down. "Give it a lot of thought, though. You might not want to tie yourself down to a rag like the *Tattler*. Frankly, you've got way too much talent. Every major newspaper in the country will try to snatch you up once you get your Pulitzer back. How's that going, by the way?"

"It's not going. The memory chips have been lost, stolen, or destroyed."

"That sucks."

"Maybe, maybe not. I've pretty much made my peace with the situation."

"That's good to hear." Uncle Sid says. He reaches across the table, pats my hand, then glances up at the kitchen clock. "How long did they say the pizza would take?"

"Twenty minutes."

This is our routine: Uncle Sid drops by with some pretext for why he has to see me, and we chat at the kitchen table, drink coffee, talk about Mom, and I order a pizza. He likes coming out to the place. We had good times when he lived here with me. We rarely argued, rarely got in each other's way. Also, the place reminds him of Mom. Sometimes Uncle Sid stays until midnight and on occasion sleeps over in the bedroom he had as a kid. But not tonight. I have to hustle him out the door early. Willy, Colette and I have a big night ahead.

Uncle Sid points his cup at the clock. "I won that thing at a carnival your Mom and I went to, at a shooting gallery. Back before she married my brother, of course. Does it still lose five minutes a day?"

"Minimum."

A clown in a bright orange costume points his right arm at the hour, his left at the minute. The numerals are lavender, the background pink. It has to be the ugliest timepiece in all of New England. Each morning before I went to school, Mom would climb up on a chair and move the minute hand forward. After she got sick, I did the job. Following her death, I never bothered, so right now the clock is either eight hours and twenty minutes slow or three hours and forty minutes fast.

Uncle Sid grins. "Your mother loved goofy things like that clock. I once watched her explain to a neighbor that the thing was a great work of art, worth thousands of dollars, all with a straight face. The woman stood there nodding, not knowing what in hell to think. Your mom liked to put people on. She thought everyone took the world too seriously. That's why she put jack-o-lanterns across the road that time, and why she painted the garage with red-and-yellow stripes, and why she'd go shopping in town braless and barefoot. She never gave a damn about what anyone thought of her. She had a wicked sense of humor. She was a lot of fun."

"She certainly was."

We've had this conversation many times, and I know what's coming.

Uncle Sid says, "Then somewhere along the line, what was fun slipped into something else."

Well put.

He looks up from his cup. "You were always good to your mom. Without you taking care of her, she'd have ended up in an institution. It was my brother's death in that fire that did it. It kept eating at her until it just got to be too much."

That and watching her six-year-old son shoot her second husband through the forehead. Uncle Sid would never say that, however. Bringing up my father's death is his way of telling me not to blame myself for Mom's deterioration.

"Toward the end," I say, "I remember her standing in front of Dad's photo in his fireman's uniform and pleading for him not to go back into the burning building. She seemed to think she could reverse time."

"I wish she could have," Uncle Sid says, looking at his hands. "My brother was a hero, and I admired him, but to tell the truth, as kids we didn't get along all that well. We were always arguing and scrapping. What he had, I wanted, and what I had, he wanted. Things usually ended with a fight, one of us happy, the other pissed as hell. It wasn't much better after we grew up."

"That's the way brothers are."

"We were worse. Your mother always said…"

Uncle Sid doesn't finish his sentence.

We're silent for a minute, then he says, "Your Grandpa Ebenezer always took your father's side. No surprise there, since he was the good kid. Pop never beat me, but he shouted a lot. To tell the truth, I was a little relieved when Pop got sent to the pokey for that Ponzi swindle. When he got out, he went back to shouting at me. With reason, I guess. I was always a screw up."

"Maybe as a kid, but not after you got older," I say. "You took care of Mom and me. You brought us food every week, and slipped her cash when you thought I wasn't looking." I get up and refill uncle Sid's cup. "She needed kindness after how my stepfather treated her."

"I hated Mike, I mean really hated him. I warned your mother he was a mean drunk, but she didn't listen."

"She wasn't always the best listener."

"To tell the truth," Uncle Sid says, glancing around the room, "I thought about killing the bastard but didn't have the guts. I once went to Hank and got the name of a guy who could take care of the situation. That was how Hank put it: 'I know this guy who can take care of the situation.' I carried the phone number around for a year, then threw it away."

"I took care of the situation for you."

Uncle Sid jerks his head back in surprise.

I'm just as surprised for having blurted that out. We rarely mention the shooting, and we sure as hell never joke about it.

We stare at each other for a few seconds, then burst out laughing.

Chapter 25

SCORPIO Oct. 23 - Nov. 21

*Judge yourself not by what you do for yourself,
but what you do for others. Great pleasure can be
achieved by working as a team. No matter how well
it is treated, a caged animal is never content.*

As soon as the pizza is finished, I ease Uncle Sid out the door and climb into bed for a couple hours. I don't sleep, but lie on my back worrying about a plan that's too complicated, too dangerous and just plain stupid.

At 11:00 P.M. I knock on Willy's door, and we load up my pickup—a pinch bar for lifting the manhole cover, coils of electrical cable, and two backpacks stuffed with gloves, kneepads, hardhats, water, snacks and numerous small tools. We also load the blasting caps and eight-inch sticks of dynamite that Willy stole from a construction site.

It's a two-hour drive to the OASIS site. I'm pumping adrenalin all the way, and Willy is sleeping all the way. Doesn't anything bother the guy?

I park a mile from the site and shake Willy awake. He yawns, stretches, and says, "I was dreaming we were kids back stealing watermelons from the Johnson farm."

"I wish we were."

We put on gloves to avoid leaving fingerprints and grab our backpacks and the rest of the gear. This time we approach the OASIS site through the flat, wooded area to the right of the building.

Colette soon appears at my side, right on schedule. She's wearing boots, baggy army pants and a dented old U.S. Army helmet scrunched down over her black curls. She points at our backpacks. "Did you bring everything on my list?"

"Yes."

"Back in the day," Colette says, "we always carried duplicates of everything, at least when the Brits parachuted us enough supplies. Did you bring extras?"

"Of course," I say.

Colette is bossy as hell, but her advice on nitty-gritty matters like this is sound. Over the years, however, her guidance—mostly on matters of the heart—has been a train wreck. Throughout high school, she steered me away from the right girls and toward the wrong ones, did the same during college, and like Clementine, she noisily approved of Adele.

"No disguise tonight?" she asks.

"No disguise."

"Good. You looked dorky."

"Where do you learn words like 'dorky' and expressions like 'back in the day'?"

She shrugs, doesn't answer, then signals Willy and me to stop walking. "Lie down," she says, patting the air. "I'll go ahead and check for guards." She moves off.

I lie down. Willy glances at me and does the same.

Colette drifts back fifteen minutes later. "The only guards are a couple of slackers smoking against the front entrance. So let's get moving. I'll steer you past the security cameras."

We crawl through the tall grass until we reach the manhole to the right of the building. Willy pries up the cover, and together we slide it aside. I climb down a steel ladder, followed by Colette and Willy. He grunts, swears, and pulls the manhole cover back in place.

We turn on our hardhat lights. The tunnel is about three feet square. The smell of damp concrete takes me back to the gleeful destruction of Beckworth's BMW, the popping tires, the snapping springs. A steel pipe a half foot in diameter and three smaller ones run overhead. According to the building plans, the smallest pipe holds the main electrical line. Willy wires an explosive to it.

I take off my backpack, lay it in front of me, and push it forward as I crawl.

Willy follows, doing the same. Colette passes through us and takes the lead.

I unspool wire as we go, two for the warning charge and two for each of the main explosives. Redundancy.

Water rushes through an overhead pipe.

"Someone just took a dump," Willy reports.

"Thanks for pointing that out."

The going is tough—push the backpack ahead, crawl to it, bang your head on a pipe, curse, push the backpack ahead, bang your head again, curse again. Colette calls out how far we've gone and how far we have to go. Unnecessary information, but I pass it on to Willy anyway.

He says, "I need a break."

We stop to rest.

Colette looks back at me, "You've got Ebenezer and Hiram pissed off. Especially Hiram."

"Both want to be in charge of the operation. They hate taking orders from me. Even at his best, Hiram's a pain in the butt."

"That I can believe," Colette says. "But he's always bragging about you Back There."

"Hiram brags about me? You've got to be kidding."

Colette takes off her helmet and shakes her head. Curls fly. She scratches her scalp with both hands. "He talks about how you went to

Cornell and then to the Colombia School of Journalism, and he tells everyone about your Pulitzer."

"Which I got to keep for less than a month."

Colette pulls her helmet back on and fastens the chin strap. "That he never mentions."

We resume crawling.

I say, "I don't know how Clementine has put up with Hiram for all these years. He doesn't listen to her, showers her with insults, and leaves her alone for long stretches while he chases other women."

Colette chuckles. "She's found solace."

"I suppose you mean in the Bible."

Colette looks back at me and grins. "In the arms of a series of lovers."

I stop crawling. "You can't be serious."

"Oh, I am. Her latest is a Guatemalan, a life guard when he was alive, a hunky guy twenty years her junior."

"Does Hiram know?"

"Nope."

I start crawling again. "Who'd have guessed."

"Right. Who'd have guessed. The secrets we harbor."

Willy says, "I think I'm missing out on half of a very interesting conversation."

"I'll fill you in later."

Colette slips around behind us. "Here's something else I'll bet you didn't know. After Ebenezer got out of prison, he spent the rest of his life paying back every one of his Ponzi victims."

"That can't be true."

"It is."

"Why didn't he ever tell me?" I ask.

"It's not part of his image."

"The old goat—who'd have guessed?"

Willy says, "I gotta hear about that, too."

"Later," I say.

We keep crawling.

I try to digest what Colette just told me about Clementine, Hiram and Ebenezer. I'll never think of them the same way again.

"I just thought of something," Willy says. "Since Colette can zip right through solid objects, how come she doesn't just meet us at the end of the tunnel?"

Jeff passes this on to Colette.

Colette says, "Because it's more fun this way, Willy. Plus, from where I am back here, I get to watch your cute *derrière* while you squirm along in those tight jeans."

I tell Willy what she said about having fun but not about his jeans.

The tunnel splits when it reaches the building, with one wing continuing straight and the other turning left beneath the front foundation. That's the one we follow.

After we've crawled a couple dozen feet, Colette taps a vertical steel shaft. "That's a main support column."

I pass the word on to Willy.

He takes several sticks of dynamite from a sealed plastic bag, attaches a detonator to them, hooks up the primary wire and the backup, and duct-tapes the charges to the column.

We crawl on.

"Put the second one here," Colette says, patting as best she can a steel column.

I tell Willy what she said.

Willy attaches more dynamite.

We repeat the operation six more times.

Colette leads us farther into the tunnel. "Tell Willy to tape the warning explosive up against that pipe."

Willy does, and then we're through.

The tunnel is too narrow for us to turn around, so we have to crawl backward, dragging our backpacks behind us. It's hard going, so we stop every few minutes to catch our breath. Air in the tunnel is acrid, and my nervous sweat is toxic. I fight claustrophobia.

It takes an hour to reach the manhole. By then we're filthy, hot, tired and cranky.

Colette slips out first to check around. She hurries back, waving her hands. "There's a guard patrolling the woods with an automatic rifle. Stay here until I give you the all clear." She goes back outside.

We wait. A half hour. An hour. Forever.

The tunnel walls get tighter and tighter and the air more and more foul. My joints stiffen, and I long to stand up and move around. The darkness is total because we've switched off our helmet lights to save the batteries. Every fifteen minutes, I hear Willy taking a leak, his claustrophobia worse than mine. Finally, there's something that gets to him.

He says, "Let's get the hell out and take our chances."

"No, stay here."

Twenty minutes later, Colette drifts back down. "He's gone."

I scramble up the ladder and shoulder the manhole cover aside.

Fresh air rolls over me. Stars shine and night birds chirp. The tall weeds are damp with dew. I want pull off my boots and socks and run barefoot in circles, shout and wave my arms. Instead I slide out and lie on my stomach. So does Willy.

He crawls past me to the spot inside the tree line where he'll be stationed during the caper, trailing the wires behind him. I cut a groove in the soil with my hunting knife, bury the wires, close the damp soil back over them, then crawl a little ways forward and repeat the operation. Over and over. Willy works toward me, doing the same. Colette stands guard. We finish in twenty minutes, pack up our gear, grab our backpacks, jog to the pickup and take off.

Willy and Colette chatter in my right ear, both at the same time. Both are charged up. Both can hardly wait for the big day. Willy says the blast will be humongous. Colette says it will be *incroyable*.

Incroyable—'unbelievable.' Right.

It will be unbelievable if I can pull this off. Hiram's right, the plan is too complicated. But it's sure as hell better than anything he's proposed.

Or Ebenezer has. So everything rests on my shoulders. Clementine depends on me to get her Back There before she disappears forever without a trace, taking Ebenezer with her. And Dad.

And me.

Chapter 26

SCORPIO Oct. 23 – Nov. 21

Confession is good for the soul. Bad moments can lead to surprisingly good moments. Vinegar makes a fine mosquito repellent.

I push a spatula under the salmon and lift a corner—it's black underneath. I glance into the dining room. Melody is sipping wine at the table, editing one of Sherwood's articles on her laptop, and grumbling to herself about weak verbs.

"Melody, how do you like your salmon?"

"However you make it," she says.

"What about black on the bottom?" I ask.

"Sure, why not."

Adele would have been all over me for this.

Dawn's at a sleepover, and Willy's gone to a Red Sox game with his girlfriend and from there to his own sleepover, so I've invited Melody out to my house. She's been nagging me to see it. I thought that cooking a meal for her would make me look normal, domestic, steady, not the guy who goes barefoot in the office, consorts with ghosts, and is just two days away from blowing up a federal building.

The salmon is overdone, the asparagus mushy, the brown rice as crunchy as sand.

When I told Willy I was cooking a meal for Melody, he said, "I thought you liked her?"

I carry the two plates into the dining room, set one next to Melody, the other across the table for myself, and sit down.

Melody pushes her laptop aside, slides her plate in front of her and says, "Lovely. You remembered that I like to eat healthy."

"You haven't tasted it yet."

"I'm sure it's delicious," She says. She takes a big bite of salmon, swallows, swallows again. And again.

I stab a limp asparagus stalk. Halfway to my mouth, it slips off my fork and flops wetly onto the plate.

Melody takes another bite of salmon, chews, smiles weakly at me, chews some more.

"Listen," I say, "why don't I scramble some eggs? You look like you're—"

"Worried about Dawn? I sure am. I've never been away from her overnight. Dawn's too young for a sleepover, but my friend talked me into it."

Melody, the smoother of bad moments.

We pick at our food for a couple more minutes, making cheery small talk, then the doorbell rings. It's a gangly teenage boy with a starter goatee. He holds out three boxes. "One gorgonzola-and-pear pizza and two salads."

"I didn't order this."

"Isn't this 44 Clarke Lane?"

"It is, but how—"

"It's already paid for," The boy says, holding up the delivery slip to read. "By one Willy Morse."

I hand the boy a big tip and carry the boxes into the dining room.

Melody tries to hide her relief. "I'm certain Willy ordered the pizza for himself and forgot about it."

"Nice try."

"Or the pizza place made a mistake."

"Nice try again," I say. "Let's eat on the rear deck."

We sit side-by-side on white wooden rockers, trays on our laps. Adele visited the house only once—she'd refused to live here—and sat beside me on the same chair where Melody is sitting and watched the same sun go down. Adele scrambled inside after a mosquito landed on her wrist.

"It's beautiful out here," Melody says. "Do you own the marsh?"

"Some, but most is the town's conservation land. It's filled with fox, coyotes, deer, and all sorts of birds."

"I'll bet you spent a lot of time out there when you were a boy, you and Willy."

"We did."

And Mom, too. Sometimes we'd hike around in circles, hour after hour, me trailing behind, her not speaking. Sometimes she'd start grass fires that I had to stamp out. Sometimes she'd carry a spade, dig holes, then fill them in again. Sometimes she'd bring pillows and blankets and spend the night outside, her sleeping, me sitting up, shivering in a blanket, waving mosquitoes away from her face. I would lead her home in the morning.

I said, "Mom loved the marsh and the house. She lived here her entire adult life. Just before she died—that was about twenty years ago—she made me promise not to sell the place. So I haven't."

"You're a kind person."

"Maybe, maybe not," I say.

"You are. Live with it."

We dig into our food.

Mom was certainly kind. And eccentric. After I killed Mike, she started going barefoot, went months without a shower, wore her prematurely graying hair halfway down her back, and talked out loud to the photos and portraits on the Ancestor Wall. Her only real human contact beside me was Uncle Sid.

Mom had a wicked sense of humor, however, and a goofy sense of play. One Halloween, we stole two dozen pumpkins from a neighbor, stayed up most of the night carving them into grotesque jack-o'-lanterns, lit candles inside, and set them across the road out front. The policeman who showed up gave her a gentle warning and later paid for the pumpkins out of his own pocket. A year after Mike was out of the picture, he took Mom out to dinner a couple times but soon found her too much to handle.

Which she was. In her final years, she got even odder and thinner and more taciturn. I tried to get her to eat more and to see a doctor, but she refused. Her eyes sank into their sockets, and her shoulders narrowed. She spent most days in a rocking chair looking out the front window. She'd tell me she was waiting for Dad to come home. Other days she would talk about his death and about how he was never coming home.

Willy was the only kid who'd set foot inside the house. He loved Mom, and she loved him. Other classmates teased me about her. They said she was a witch, and they wouldn't trick or treat at our place because they said the house was haunted. Which in a way it was. I got into lots of fights on account of Mom, but I was the biggest kid in school and always won. Willy was about the smallest. I fought his fights too.

By the time I started junior high, I pretty much took over running the house. I'd heat up the frozen dinners Uncle Sid brought out each week, wash our clothes and more-or-less clean the place. A couple days could go by with Mom not talking to me but only to the portraits on the Ancestor Wall. Some days she would talk out loud to herself and say things I didn't want to hear.

Melody slaps a mosquito, then another. "You're not eating."

I pick up a slice of pizza. "I was thinking about the house and my mother."

"She'd be happy to see how you're fixing up the place."

"Willy's doing the real work. I'm useless at that sort of thing." I wave my piece of pizza. "My talents lie in wordsmithing but especially in the field of culinary arts."

Melody giggles. A nice sound.

I slap a mosquito. Melody slaps a mosquito.

I get up, hold out my hand and pull her to her feet. "Let's go inside while we still have some blood left."

We carry our trays to the dining room.

After we've finished eating, I take Melody on a tour. It's an odd feeling to be showing off the house where you've grown up, especially if you'd killed a man there. The place remains for me an odd combination of warm memories and horror. Every time I walk past the Shooting Room, I relive the moment. Maybe I'm doing penance by living here. Maybe that's the real reason I haven't sold the house.

I show Melody the upstairs and the downstairs and even take her to the basement with its clutter of bicycles, broken snow blowers, book boxes, rubber boots. On the way back upstairs, I explain about how Emerson once visited the house to borrow a cup of Ovaltine, of how Louisa May Alcott sketched the living room wallpaper for use in *Little Women,* and how George Washington twice stopped off here, climbed down from his horse and took a piss up against the front porch.

Again that sweet giggle. "Uh-huh," she says and links her arm with mine.

We climb back up to the first floor. Melody stops at the Shooting Room door and touches one of the nails holding it closed. "I'll bet that Jack the Ripper's ghost lives in there. Better, the room is filled with gold doubloons."

I try to tug her away.

She holds me back. "One last story, buster. The tour's not over yet. Tell me the tale of the mystery room with the door nailed shut."

"Willy sealed it up because of termites."

Melody tilts her head. She's not buying that.

"It's the truth," I say and pull my arm free.

She studies me for a while, then reaches up and touches my cheek. "What's the real story?"

"I just told you." I remove her hand. "Termites got into the room, so Willy nailed the door closed until the exterminator can get here. He's supposed to have come last week, but his grandmother got sick, and he had to fly to Albuquerque, but he'll..."

I stop talking.

Lies. For years I listened to the lies that Adele told me, and I listened to the lies that I told her. Lies, lies, lies.

I'm sick of lies.

And secrets. I never told Adele of the shooting because I knew she couldn't handle it. So it was always there between us, keeping us apart. But she sensed there was something inside me I wasn't letting out. She said I was haunted, that I was never quite there with her, that she often felt lonesome in my presence.

I tried to turn her concerns into jokes, and I told lies about how I was feeling.

I got good at lying.

No more lies. Not to Melody.

I lean my back against the wall and look at the ceiling. My cheeks are warm, my mouth dry. "It's not a pretty story," I say, not much above a whisper. "You won't like it, and you won't like me after your hear it."

"I don't see how—"

"Wait."

Melody bites her lower lip the way she does when she's worried.

I tell her about how my drunken stepfather would slap my mother around, about her screams in the night, about hearing her sobbing in the bathroom, and how in the morning I'd watch her hand him his lunch in a brown paper bag, smile and give him a peck on the cheek.

My voice comes out in a monotone that I don't recognize. As I speak, I'm not looking at Melody but at the door. Paint has peeled off it in long brown strips. I count the nails. Eighteen. They were hammered in by the man Uncle Sid hired from his jail cell a few days after the shooting, a half year before his sentencing, five years before I would see him again.

"When I was six years old, my stepfather came home blind drunk and mad as hell because he'd lost a bar fight. He punched Mom in the stomach, knocked her down and kicked her in the side while she was on the floor." I tap my knuckles against the door. "They were inside this room, and the door was open. I was watching from here, right about where you're standing."

Melody steps forward, arms out, ready to hug me. I shake my head. She lowers her arms.

"Whenever Mike came home drunk and Mom saw a beating coming, she would phone Uncle Sid, and he'd rush right out. But he had to drive all the way from Boston."

A lump closes my throat. I swallow, cough, swallow, start talking again in that odd faraway voice. "Mom was afraid of a lot of things, especially home invasions, so she kept a loaded pistol in her bedside table. The gun had been Dad's."

Melody's eyes widen.

"My Dad was a hero. He rushed back into a burning building to save another firefighter."

Again Melody tries to hug me. Again I shake my head.

"I ran upstairs and came back down with the gun."

Melody shakes her head and bites her lip.

I take a deep breath, pause, then say, "I shot my stepfather in the forehead."

Melody blinks several times. "Did he...?"

"Die? Yes."

My left eyelid starts to quiver.

Now I let Melody hug me.

"You were just a boy," she says, squeezing me tight. "You were protecting your mother. You were a hero like your father. I'll bet he would have been proud of you."

I shake my head. "Uncle Sid was the real hero."

"What does that mean?"

"You know he did time in prison, right?"

Melody nods. Tears have started.

"After Uncle Sid got here, he took the pistol from my hand and told me to go to my room. But I didn't. I watched from around the corner. He put his own gun in Mike's hand and fired it into the wall. Then he used his handkerchief to wipe my fingerprints off the gun I'd killed Mike with, and he fired it into Mike's body. I think that was to get traces of gunpowder on his own hand, or maybe it was just to made Uncle Sid feel better. He hated Mike as much as I did."

Melody opens her mouth to say something, but I shake my head.

"When the police came, Uncle Sid confessed, and they cuffed him and took him away. He pleaded self-defense and got off easy for the shooting but faced an illegal weapons charge. The judge gave him a stiff sentence because of his prison record and his association with the Ramseys. Uncle Sid gave up four-and-a-half years of his life for me."

"No wonder you love him so much. And he loves you."

"And he loved my mother. After her funeral, he and I stood out on the front lawn, both bawling our eyes out. He put his arm around me and said, 'I'll move out here and take care of you, like you were my own son.' I was fourteen at the time. Uncle Sid took care of me until I went to college."

"He's a good man. You're a good man."

I shake my head. "I'm a murderer."

"No, you're not, Jeff. Just the opposite. You're a hero. You protected your mother. You made the right decision. I understand exactly what went through you mind."

I shake my head again. "No, you don't. What was going through my mind when I pulled the trigger," I say, my voice slow and shaky, "was how much I wanted my stepfather dead. I was standing only a few feet away and could have shot him in the leg. In fact, I didn't have to shoot him at all. He had his hands raised and was backing away. He said, 'Don't.' That's the last thing the man ever said: 'Don't.' I pulled the trigger three times, and the last bullet hit him in the forehead."

Melody takes a couple steps back.

"I wanted him dead," I whisper. "I watched him sitting on the floor, his back against the wall, kicking and twitching, and I felt good. No, I felt great. I could have wounded him. Or done nothing. Instead, I murdered him."

Again I feel the gun in my hand. Again I hear the terrible noise it made. Again I see the blood splatter against the wallpaper, hear Mom gasp, see her look of horror.

Melody takes my face in both hands. Tears run down her cheeks. "You were only six years old, Jeff. You protected your mother. I'll bet she gave you a big hug and called you a hero like your father."

"She said I'd made a mistake, that I'd made a terrible mistake. Hiram showed up right away and also said I'd made a mistake. He told me that from now on he'd make all my decisions. I didn't talk for the next couple of years, except to my ancestors."

"What an awful, awful experience for a young boy. Of course you were traumatized by the… uh… event."

"By the shooting. Call it what it is. But more than the shooting, I felt guilty about how much I enjoyed killing my stepfather and…"

I stop talking.

Melody says nothing.

I steer her into the front hall. "I'll say goodnight from here."

"Here? Why?"

"Why? *Why?* Because I just confessed to murder, that's why."

Melody wipes her tears with the back of her hand, forces a smile and pokes me in the stomach. "You haven't fed me dessert yet, buster."

"Dessert?"

"Right. What's for dessert?"

"Uh… strawberry shortcake with whipped cream."

"My favorite—how did you know?"

"I asked Dawn."

Melody bites her lip at the mention of Dawn.

"You're worried about her, aren't you?" I say.

"She's too young for a sleepover," Melody says, her eyes wandering. Then she tilts her head to the side. "But I'm not."

Chapter 27

SCORPIO Oct. 23 – Nov. 21

Things left unsaid are often said the loudest. Stop beating yourself up for things you cannot change. Intimacy is like a tasty dessert.

I scoop Melody up in both arms, carry her upstairs and lay her on the mattress. "I'm afraid I don't own a bed."

Melody pats the mattress. "Who needs a bed?"

"This was my room when I was a boy."

She points at my dresser. "I guessed that from the Millennium Falcon decal."

"I was a nerdy kid."

Silence.

Okay, now what? It's been a while. Pull off my clothes? Pull off her clothes? Sing? Tap dance?

Melody gets to her feet. "Which way to the bathroom?"

"Down the hall and on the left."

I watch her go.

"You couldn't have handled that worse."

I swing around. It's Colette.

I clamp both hands over my trouser bulge. "What in hell are you doing here?"

"You need guidance. You bring a young lady to your bedroom, then stand there with your jaw hanging open. You're supposed to take charge, to woo her, make her laugh, show her that—"

"Go away!"

She puts her hands on her hips. "You should be thanking me. I'm here to—"

"Out!"

I hear the bathroom door open and close.

"Out! Right now! No more advice on how I lead my love life! Out!"

Colette sniffs, takes on a hurt look, wavers, shrinks.

Shrinks? Am I seeing things?

Then she disappears.

Melody steps into the room and looks around. "Were you talking to someone?"

"I stubbed my big toe on the dresser and swore at it."

Melody nods.

Now what do I do? What do I say? I shift from foot to foot. Colette's right. I am a klutz.

Melody opens the top button of her blouse. "I'm worried that you'll get caught destroying the OASIS building." She undoes the rest of the buttons and drops the blouse onto the floor. "I think I sent Dawn off without her toothbrush." Off comes the bra. "I love old houses."

I pull my shirt over my head, step out of my slacks, tug off my socks.

Melody unzips her skirt, lets it slide down around her ankles, kicks it away. "I still want that dessert you promised. Sid liked the articles you wrote yesterday. I'm worried about your little caper—or did I say that already?" She loops her thumbs under the waist band of her panties and wriggles out of them. "A bit of paint would brighten up this room, maybe a pale blue or even yellow? No, probably not yellow. I've read that men don't like yellow. But blue would be good, that is, if it's not too light because men don't—"

I press my lips against hers. They keep moving, her words leaking out the sides of her mouth. Then she kisses me back.

We sit on the mattress. Melody hugs her knees. "The salmon wasn't that bad, all it needed was—"

I press my fingers against her lips.

She twists her mouth sideways. "I guess I'm nervous."

"Think I'm not?"

Melody glances at the front of my shorts. "But not all that much."

The next minutes are tentative, shy, clumsy, sweet, wonderful.

Afterward, we lie on our backs, covered in sweat.

Our first time. Now's when women engage in confessions, express their hopes for a long relationship, set down rules. Or at least Adele did. She smothered me in rules. I brace myself for what Melody is going to say.

She rolls on her side and tickles my chin. "About that dessert…"

"We just had dessert."

She pinches my cheek. "Strawberry shortcake with whipped cream—go get it, buster." She thumps my chest with the side of her fist.

I pad naked downstairs and return with a tray, two plates, two forks, two napkins, four pieces of shortcake, a dish of sliced strawberries and a can of whipped cream. Melody sits up. I set the tray on the floor and sit beside her. "It's a do-it-yourself dessert."

"The best kind," Melody says.

She puts a cake on her plate, spoons on strawberries, adds whipped cream, turns the can toward me and sprays my bare chest.

"Hey, what the hell?"

She runs her tongue through the whipped cream, straightens up and gives me a goofy look. "Yum."

Not what I expected from this woman.

I grab the can, cover her left nipple with a mound of whipped cream and lick it off.

She stuffs a strawberry into my navel, giggles, eats the strawberry.

Then we get really creative.

Smeared with strawberries, shortcake and whipped cream, we make love again, sticky and sweet smelling.

Melody immediately falls asleep afterward and makes little hissing sounds through her mouth. From time to time she smiles. A good dream? About me? I hope so.

I'd wanted to tell her before she fell asleep that I was falling in love with her, but I couldn't get the words out.

Did I ever feel this strongly about Adele? Probably, but there has been so much ensuing anger that all the soft moments have been lost.

I have to tell Melody how I feel about her because the day after tomorrow is the big day, and I don't know what could happen. It's hard to believe the time's almost come. Right now my plan seems stupid, childish, over-engineered. Rescue ancestors? Blow up a government building? Get the blame placed on the Ramseys? Yeah, sure.

Willy and I could go to prison. Or get shot by a guard at the site, or whacked later by the Ramseys or one of Drucker's goons. Or the caper could fail, Clementine would be away from Back There too long, and—poof!—no more Ebenezer, Dad or Uncle Sid. No more Jeffrey Beekle.

I don't want to die without letting Melody know I love her.

Chapter 28

SCORPIO Oct. 23 – Nov. 21

*Prepare for a busy day. Expect to encounter good
people and bad people. To lie to someone you love is a
sin; to lie to an enemy is often a necessity. Tomorrow
will come and go. Keep your chin up.*

For breakfast I make scrambled eggs that are actually pretty good.
Melody and I don't mention the night before, the ancestors who visit
me, blowing up government buildings or shooting my stepfather. We
share the newspaper, exchange tidbits of news and soft glances, just
like an old married couple. A feeling I could get used to.

We both smell of strawberry shortcake.

After a communal shower, Melody drives off to pick up Dawn
from her sleepover, and I head to the office.

Everything at the magazine is behind schedule without me, so Sid
asked if I could take another day away from my vacation. I agreed
because the planning is finished, the explosives are planted and the
scenarios rehearsed. Nothing's left but to worry. Cranking out a half
dozen articles will take my mind off the big day. At least I hope so.

Sherwood and Janet are at their desks, but Melody hasn't arrived
yet. I sit down and start the first article, opening with a cheesy title
that will make Melody laugh before she changes it.

Alter to Halter

After a three-month search, the Albuquerque, NM, police have located a runaway bride at her new place of work, Jenny's Unmentionables. The jilted groom was overheard saying, "Felicia's obsession over foundation garments has always…"

I finish in a hurry and make a second pass. The article is rambling, dull and implausible, even by our standards. Normally I'd delete the thing and start over with something new, but we're under a deadline. Besides, with the way my thoughts are ping-ponging between last night's bliss and my fears over the upcoming caper, this is probably the best I can do.

I hear a squeal and look up. Dawn is racing toward me. I lift her up and sit her on my knee.

"I had an oversleep," she says.

"Uh… right. Was it fun?"

"We watched cartoons and ate macaroni and cheese."

"Sounds great." I bounce her up and down. "I wish I'd been there."

Dawn giggles. "Grownups don't have oversleeps."

"Sometimes they do," Melody says and gives me a sweet smile.

"That's silly," Dawn says. She grabs the firetruck off my desk and hops down from my lap.

She tugs off her shoes and socks, pushes the firetruck back and forth and makes engine sounds.

I say, "My father was a firefighter."

Dawn doesn't respond. She's moved on the way a four-year-old does, absorbed in the moment.

I imagine my father playing fireman with this same truck when he was a little boy.

If Grandpa Ebenezer hadn't given Dad the truck, would he still have become a fireman? Does that ever go through Ebenezer's mind?

I sure as hell hope not.

Melody shakes my shoulder. "You look far away."

"I'm getting my mind ready for my next prize-winning endeavor."

"It doesn't have to be a prize-winner endeavor, just on time." Melody lets go of my shoulder. "If I leave Dawn here, will she bother you?"

"Not a bit. I like having her around."

I type:

Keep Your Chin Up!

Which third-tier television personality with a buzzard's neck has lost his latest battle with plastic surgery? A close friend of the afflicted actor reports that the skin beneath his chin "droops like a sack of soggy oatmeal." In addition..."

Janet bends down and peers at the screen, smelling faintly of vinegar. "I hope that's not a real person you're describing," she says. "You know how much your uncle hates lawsuits."

"Nope," I say, continuing to type. "Totally made up."

"I like the oatmeal image even though it's a touch cruel," Janet says and pats my shoulder. "I'll miss you."

I stop typing and look up. Is this something about the caper? Can Janet see into the future?

"What does that mean?"

"It means my job is almost finished here."

"You're retiring?"

Janet again pats me on the shoulder and drifts back to her desk.

I watch her go. I hope she's not retiring. We'd all miss her, me more than anyone.

I finish the sagging-neck article, reread it and give it D minus. This is as good as I can do in my shaky state of mind. I start a new one that Melody will certainly reject, but Sid will love it and overrule her.

Toe Sandwich!

Killer eats victim's toes! Last week, horrified police

officers raided a thatched-roofed shack outside
the mountain village of Bolivar, Guatemala, and
discovered a cannibal killer surrounded by the
rotting corpses of eleven toeless victims. "Never,"
said police chief Garcia G. Garcia, "have I seen..."

Sherwood stops by, coffee cup in hand, reads over my shoulder, chuckles and says. "When Melody sees that, she'll throw a wild pitch. I doubt she's a fan of edible toes and—"

"Shh!" I say and point at Dawn, seated cross-legged on the floor, spinning the front wheels of the firetruck with her fingers.

She looks up and raises her bare left foot. "I have toes."

Sherwood studies her for a moment.

Dawn adds, "Jeff says barefoot people are more smarter."

Sherwood sighs. "Just 'smarter' suffices. 'More' is redundant."

He's not comfortable around kids. Or adults.

He turns back to me. "Thanks for interrupting your vacation to help out."

"No problem."

"Do you have anything special planned for the rest of your time off?"

Anything special? "Uh... no."

"Too bad," Sherwood says with a sigh. "Our lives are dull. We get our thrills from our stories, but one of these days I'd like to do something out of the ordinary, something spectacular, something that brings the crowd roaring to their feet. What about you, Jeff?"

I lean back and lace my hands behind my head. "You mean like blowing up a building?"

"Something like that."

"Maybe I will."

Sherwood shrugs and shuffles back to his desk, trailing sighs, and dripping coffee.

Melody comes over and scoops up Dawn. "I've decided to finish the editing at home because I need to take this little girl back for an early nap. She and her friend stayed up giggling most of the night."

Melody is having trouble keeping her eyes open, and I suspect she's really going home to give herself a nap. She, too, stayed up giggling most of the night. I want to tell her I love her. I want to grab her in my arms and twirl her around. Dawn, too, who's already falling asleep. I want to scoop them both up and run away to someplace safe.

Melody leans closer and whispers, "Take me with you."

Did she read my mind?

"You mean, run away?" I ask.

Melody straightens up. "Run away? No. Take me with you tomorrow. I want to help."

"We've been through this a thousand times."

"Then this makes it a thousand and one."

I shake my head. "Too dangerous."

"I'm not looking for danger, just to be useful," Melody says. She shifts Dawn to her other hip. Her eyes are already closed. "I have a question: Why did you set up the ancestors' collection point at the top of a hill?"

"You know as well as I do. It's because it's a… uh… safe spot."

"Exactly," Melody says with a tight smile.

I give this some thought. "But plans never work out the way they should,"

"Which is exactly why you need my help. I'm great at coming up with ideas. You've said so yourself. Besides, I have a lot of useful skills. I can rock climb, throw a slider, drive a stock car and—"

"And I don't believe we'll have a critical need for a race car driver."

Melody makes a face. "I could call in the bomb threat."

"Willy will do that."

"I could serve as a lookout or just snoop around in general."

I shake my head. "I have three ancestors who are much better qualified for the job because they're invisible. Why keep pressing me on this? You have a child to think about. What would happen to her if something happened to you?"

Melody bites her lower lip. Tears form. "What will happen to me if something happens to you?"

"Nothing's going to happen to me." I lower my voice to a whisper. "Everything's planned out like clockwork. The team will move in, do the job, and get the hell out."

"You just said that plans never work out the way they should."

"What I really meant was—"

"And if you fail, the other thing will happen."

Melody said that in a shaky whisper.

"What other thing?"

Melody drops onto a chair and cradles Dawn on her lap. She's sound asleep. "Didn't it ever occur to you that I read the rules?"

"What rules?"

"The ones on that website that I sent you a while back. I know that Clementine will disappear forever if she's not rescued. Ebenezer will disappear too. So will your father and Sid. And so will you."

Uh, oh.

"You've known that all along?"

"Yes."

I take a deep breath, close my eyes, then open them. "I kept this from you for your own good."

"Let me decide what's best for my own good," Melody says. "So now you know why I must have a role tomorrow, no matter what happens. You're worth the risk."

"No, I'm not."

"That's a stupid thing to say."

Melody sounds tough now, angry, determined, the kid who on a dare broke her front tooth skateboarding down a library steps. No more tears.

I say, "There's no job for you."

"Because you didn't write me into your plans, that's why."

"Not true," I say.

But it is true.

"You promised you'd never lie to me," Melody says.

"I'm not lying."

"That's another lie."

"No," I say, "it's—"

"You're getting ready to lie again, aren't you?"

I say nothing.

Melody stands up, settles Dawn on her hip and starts toward the front door.

"Wait! Melody! Don't go!"

She doesn't look back.

I'd promised myself I would never lie to this woman.

"Damn it!"

Janet looks up, shakes her head and gives me a sympathetic look.

I finish the disgusting toe article, don't bother with a second pass, and email it straight to Melody.

I'm searching around for another topic—'Man Born with Gills But Has Never Learned to Swim'? 'Olympian Sprinter Loses Leg in Tragic Salad-Spinner Accident'?—when Drucker phones.

I say, "What in hell do you want?"

"Jesus, kid, what's got into you? I called to see if you got anything new."

I lower my voice to a whisper. "In fact I do. I was just about to call you. My contact phoned a minute ago to report that Hank's got an explosives expert coming in from Chicago. They're going to blow up the building late next month and make it look like a terrorist strike."

"You're shitting me."

"Nope."

Drucker is quiet for a moment. "Actually, it's makes sense that Hank would blame the explosion on terrorists. Anyway, the other reason I called was because I've got the paperwork for our friend."

He means my fictitious contact in the Ramsey gang. "That was fast."

"A courier will have it at your office within the hour."

"I'm supposed to be on vacation. How do you know I'm at work?"

"I know everything," Drucker says. "So all your guy has to do is fill in his name, sign the papers in a couple places, and he's safely in the Witness Protection Program. I got his case expedited through my lady friend. The FBI's going to handle everything, so our only move now is for me to meet the man. Call me the minute he's back in town, got it?"

Drucker hangs up.

What's that douchebag up to? No one gets into Witness Protection this fast, and they sure as hell don't do it without revealing their identity and criminal history. Also, it's not the FBI who runs the program, but the U.S. Marshall Service. Drucker's lying to me.

Which I suppose is fair since I've been lying to him.

Time for more lies. I call Hank on the burner phone.

"Yeah?" he says.

"I just found out something very important. There's—"

"Meet me in the alley. Fifteen minutes."

I start the silly salad-spinner article, delete it, start it again, delete it, then go outside in time to see Hank and Freddie climbing out of their black SUV at the end of the alley. The two swagger toward me. Their massive, bald bodyguard hovers a ways back, yawning and scratching his private parts.

Hank says, "Talk. I'm busy."

"The Feds are going to try to blow up the OASIS building."

Hank doesn't speak for several seconds. "No shit?"

"That's what my OASIS contact says."

"How come? The place cost $42 million to build."

"The rooms are lead-lined, right?"

Hank nods.

"And no windows, right?"

Another nod.

I say, "Didn't you ever ask why?"

"Yeah," Hank says. "And never got a straight answer."

"It's a test site for all future federal buildings. It's to protect them from terrorist bombings. Without windows, there's no flying glass, and it turns out that lead is phenomenally good at protecting against bomb blasts."

Hank ponders this for a moment. "Makes sense, I guess."

"And I've got some great news for you. My contact says that, if the building withstands the test explosion without too much damage, then OASIS will not only renew the five contracts you lost, but give you additional ones. Of course, you'll have to set up a new construction company with a new strawman owner, and…"

And I stop talking. I'd expected Hank to look pleased. Instead he's scowling.

"They'd fucking better start treating me right," he says. "I coughed up two million bucks."

"OASIS took a kickback?"

"Don't look so surprised, kid. That's the way business gets done. I left a suitcase filled with $100 bills in an airport locker for John Smith."

"You're sure it's him?

"Of course I'm sure. Can you picture me parting with two million dollars and not knowing exactly where the fuck it's going?"

I can't. But I can picture expensive suits, expensive shoes, expensive watches, and web sites advertising posh homes in foreign climes. I also picture massive eye bags.

I say, "You still haven't met the guy?"

Hank shakes his head. "Nope."

Well, I have.

After Hank and Freddie leave, I stumble back upstairs to the office. Now I know why Drucker can afford expensive clothes and watches, and why he's been so scared that Hank will learn his identity. Drucker's afraid that Hank will demand his $2 million back. As much as I dislike Drucker, I don't want him whacked. Will blowing up the OASIS building make things worse for him? Or better? Better if I can get Hank and Freddie sent to prison.

A big if. The more I think about my plan, the less confident I feel. Melody's right, it'll take more than my word and Drucker's word to pin the destruction of the site on Hank. It'll take hard evidence. What that would be, I don't know. I suppose I'm in for another sleepless night.

I can't think of anything to write, either. I fold my hands across my lap and stare at my screen.

Sherwood hovers over Janet, complaining for the tenth time about how someone sideswiped his Prius during the night. Janet says, "Tsk, tsk," and keeps on typing. Eventually, even she loses patience with him. She stops typing, looks up and says, "It's not the end of the world, dear. It's just a scraped fender. No one was hurt. And who knows, maybe some good might even come out of it?"

Some good might even come out of it? Janet's sunny take on life.

Then I start typing:

A Happy Accident

Emily Elliott, a third-grade teacher from Moose Hoof, Idaho, was sideswiped while driving home from work recently and briefly knocked unconscious. She woke up reciting a string of numbers. That evening she used those very same numbers to buy a single lottery ticket.

She won $11.4 million.

Appearing the next evening on the local television station, Ms. Elliott waived the giant mock check overhead with both hands and shouted, "Grover Cleveland Elementary School can take my job and..."

And I stop typing. What comes next? Should I mention the guy who hit her? What if he drove off without stopping? What if she tracked him down, but instead of pressing charges, gave him a big hug and a check for $1 million?

But how would she find him? From the paint traces taken from her car? Unlikely. Better, why not put the guy in a construction truck, and say that witnesses to the accident saw the company name on the door?

I place my fingers on the home keys, then pull them back.

A construction company truck with its name on the door? Witnesses?

Beautiful!

There's the hard evidence I need.

Chapter 29

SCORPIO Oct. 23 - Nov. 21

If you run into a dead-end, go back the way you came and start over. Laughter is the best medicine. One garden gnome is one too many.

I finish the sideswipe article and hurry home to find Willy leaning under the hood of his gleaming red 1998 Mustang. He keeps it spotless. The garage, too. He painted its floor gray and the walls white, then organized my stuff—the ski equipment, the lawn mower, the garden tiller, the boxes of college textbooks. This is a guy who keeps his clothes in piles on the floor, the clean mixed in with the dirty.

He looks up when he sees me approaching. "What's up?"

"What are your plans for tonight?"

Willy wipes his hands on the rag dangling from his belt. "I planned on watching *The Treasure of the Sierra Madre* for the hundredth time. But from the look on your face, I'm guessing that ain't gonna happen."

"Are you up for helping me steal a truck?"

"Do you even have to ask?"

"Even if it's from the construction site where you stole the explosives?"

Willy is quiet for a moment. "You know that's a Ramsey outfit, don't you?"

"Of course."

"Why not boost someone else's truck?"

"It has to be theirs," I say. "I'll explain later. Besides, you once told me the site was wide open."

"Not exactly wide open, but the security is piss poor. No surprise there. Everyone knows better than to steal from the Ramseys. Except for you, of course."

"Can you hot-wire a pickup?"

Willy shrugs. "New ones aren't easy, but yeah, probably. But the drivers I met when I was working for the Ramsey's didn't always bother to return the keys to the guard shack. They'd just toss them into the glove compartments or under a floor mat. Like I said, only an idiot would steal a truck from the Ramseys." Willy sits on the workbench. "What's this all about?"

I climb up beside him. "I need hard evidence showing that the Ramseys destroyed the OASIS building."

Willy wipes his hands on the rag again. "So?"

"So I plan on sideswiping a parked car near the OASIS site, then sticking around long enough for witnesses to read 'Netterfield Construction' on the door. Afterward, I'll abandon the truck at some country road where you'll be waiting. You'll sabotage the truck to make it look like it broke down, and then we'll get the hell out of there."

"I don't get to go along?"

"Nope," I say.

"That's a bitch."

"Do you have any dynamite and detonators left over from when we planted the explosives?"

"Yup. Colette insisted on extras."

"We'll leave a detonator in the truck to make it look as if it's been dropped, and use the dynamite to leave strong enough traces of explosives for a sniffer dog to detect."

"How do you know the truck will be searched?"

"I'll get Drucker to arrange that. He's convinced I have a contact inside the Ramsey organization, and I'll tell him that's where I got the tip."

Willy jumps down from the workbench. "When do we go?"

"Midnight."

"Good. That'll give us enough time to watch the movie."

As we walk inside, I phone in an order for two pizzas, then as an afterthought add two salads—Melody and Willy's girlfriend have been getting on us for not eating enough greens.

We're both wide awake after *The Treasure of the Sierra Madre*, so instead of catching some sleep we watch *The Attack of the Killer Tomatoes* for the hundred-and-first time.

A little before midnight, Willy and I put on dark clothing, load the Mustang's trunk with tools and head west. I drive and fret. Willy sleeps and snores.

It takes an hour and a half to reach the strip mall that the Ramsey construction company is building twenty miles east of the OASIS site. I park a quarter-mile away. We walk to the site and lie down just inside the tree line. The lot with the construction vehicles is just beyond the wire fence, with a guardhouse in the middle. The skeletal building sits a hundred yards farther on.

For the next three hours, we scan the yard with our binoculars and watch the guard shack. A guy comes out at exactly 2:00 A.M. and shambles through the yard, swinging his flashlight back and forth. He makes two more rounds, also on the hour.

"We've got his routine down," Willy says.

"It seems so."

As soon as the guard's closes the door to his shack, I pull on my backpack, climb the fence and drop into the construction yard. It's bumper-to-bumper with backhoes, bulldozers, pickups, dump trucks and tall cranes. I slip from vehicle to vehicle, keeping them between me and the guardhouse until I reach a row of eight pickups.

I start with the first, rummaging through the glove compartment, checking under floor mats and shining my penlight under the seats. No luck. Same for the next and the next and the next.

My phone vibrates.

It's Willy. "What's happening, buddy?"

"No luck so far. It looks like you might have to hot-wire one of them. Any movement from the guardhouse?"

"Nope. I can see the goober through my binoculars. He's curled up on his desk, fast asleep."

"Any trouble cutting the chain across the rear exit?"

"Piece of cake," Willy says, an expression he's picked up from Melody.

I wish she were here. No, not here. But I wish I were with her someplace safe.

"Two more to go," I say.

I ease open the driver's door to the seventh truck. Still on my knees, I rummage under the driver's seat and find Hershey bar wrappers, a baseball cap and a sticky piece of cloth I wish I hadn't touched, even with gloves. Also a key. I grab it and climb onto the seat. The truck is a crew-cab Ford. Its interior smells of cigarette smoke and moldy upholstery. The pickup's had years of hard use, so no one will be surprised when it's found broken down. I sit up, slip the key in the ignition and feel my phone vibrate.

Willy whispers, "The guard's changed his routine and is heading your direction."

Willy sounded worried. Not like him.

I slip out of the cab, ease the door closed, crouch down and watch.

The guard swings his flashlight back and forth.

It's my old friend Cedric, moonlighting at a second job. He has a pistol in a holster.

Make a run for it?

Too late. I lie on my back, squeeze under the truck and press my nose against a rusty muffler.

Cedric stops right beside the truck. He's wearing tooled cowboy boots with high heels.

I hold my breath, pull my phone out, turn on my side and text Willy:

Create a diversion.

I hear a zipper opening.

Cedric pisses up against the left front wheel, farts, pisses, farts again.

Something goes clank off in the distance.

It sounds like a rock tossed on a steel roof.

Cedric zips up.

Another clank, another rock.

Cedric takes off running.

I crawl out from under the truck. My phone vibrates.

Willy says, "He's heading my way."

"Stay out of sight."

"You think?"

I don't move.

Willy calls ten minutes later. "He's gone back to the guardhouse. Give me fifteen minutes to get to my car."

I wait a quarter hour, then climb into the truck. A minute later, I hear Willy's noisy Mustang racing up and down the road in front of the construction site, creating enough racket to cover my escape. I start the engine and creep as quietly as possible toward the rear exit where Willy cut the chain. Once I'm through the gate, I speed up, head for the nearest road, and phone Willy. "I'm out. Go home and get some sleep. I'll see you tomorrow at the drop-off point. Don't forget to bring a detonator."

"Right."

"And the dynamite," I add.

"You sound like Colette."

"Do you want to hear me sing like her?"

"I'd rather eat vinyl siding."

After fifteen miles, I park at the edge of a gravel lane, slather myself with mosquito repellent, grab my backpack and walk into the woods. I pull a blanket from my pack and settle down on a bed of pine needles. It's uncomfortable but not as uncomfortable as getting caught sleeping in a stolen truck.

At nine the next morning I wake up shivering, eat the three pieces of cold pepperoni pizza I'd brought, drink the lukewarm coffee in my Thermos, and walk to the truck.

I find Colette waiting for me, her boots resting on the dash.

"What are you doing here?" I ask.

"Getting in on the action. Also to help out."

"I don't need help."

"You always need help."

I pull my Red Sox cap down low over my eyes, then put on wraparound sunglasses.

Colette snickers. "No goofy gardening hat? You looked so cute in it."

I ignore her and drive toward Winstonville, a town just five miles from the OASIS site.

Colette says, "I'm disappointed you didn't bring along that hunky Willy."

"I'll tell him what you said."

I drive slowly up and down Main Street in the hope that people will remember the truck.

Colette says, "Better be careful a cop doesn't see you."

"I'm watching for them. You should too. But I doubt the truck's been reported missing yet. Willy says nobody works at the site on Saturdays."

Colette says, "You'll also have to be careful when you return the truck."

"I won't return it. I'll abandon it after Willy's plants a detonator in it, leave traces of explosives and sabotages the engine."

"Clever," Colette says. A rare comment from her.

I turn into a curving side street, slow down and check for houses with cars parked in front.

Colette says, "Willy's dishy, but so are you. Melody's a lucky lady."

"No, I'm a lucky guy. I don't deserve her."

"Yeah, you're right. You are a bit of a dickhead."

"Where do you learn expressions like 'dishy' and 'dickhead'?"

Colette shrugs. "But you're a good-looking dickhead. In fact, you remind me of my Polish count—same curly brown hair, same height, same blue eyes."

"Uh..." I lift my foot off the accelerator. "Was the count...?"

"Your great-grandfather?" Colette says with a giggle. "No, I met him after Giselle was born."

I continue coasting. "Then who—?"

"I've always wondered that myself."

I pass a dented Honda Civic parked in front of a tiny ranch house. The owner is mowing the grass.

Colette says, "What about that one?"

"Nope, he's a working stiff, and I'll bet that's his only car. He would collect insurance but might not have a way to get to his job. What I'm looking for is an ugly McMansion with an expensive car out front and a spare in the driveway."

"Good luck at that."

I turn the corner and find an ugly McMansion with an expensive car out front and a spare in the driveway.

I slow to a crawl. A middle-aged man in tan shorts is out front, setting out a row of garden gnomes in peaked red hats. His knees are knobby and pale. He lifts his nose when he sees my dented old pickup.

Or at least I imagine he does.

The BMW parked at the curb isn't a convertible like the one owned by the odious Beckworth Parker-Primgate, and it's black, not blue, but that's close enough. A gray Lexus sits in the driveway.

"Hang on," I tell Colette. As if she has to.

I speed up and swing the wheel to the right.

My aim is perfect. The pickup's front bumper grinds across the left rear panel, across both doors, across the front fender and as a bonus rips off the front bumper.

Colette hoots.

The owner shouts, shakes his fist and comes running down the yard.

The guy can't hear her, but Colette shouts, "Eat my shorts!"

Does she watch the 'Simpsons'?

I hesitate long enough for the guy to read the writing on the door, then I step on the gas. The engine roars. We fly down the street, both giggling.

"What a hoot!" Colette says.

Then I slam on the brakes.

Dead end.

"Merde!" Colette shouts.

Stone fences block us on three sides.

I turn the truck around, head back and step on the gas.

Again I slam on the brakes. The tires squeal. The truck slides sideways.

The BMW's owner has backed the Lexus across the street to block it. He stands next to the banged-up Beemer and shakes his fist.

"Merde!" Colette shouts.

I look left, right, left again.

No choice. I gun the engine and swing up onto the lawn.

I crush a festively flowered chaise longue, send a pink watering can flying, and crunch a row of big-bellied yard gnomes—*thump! thump! thump! thump!*

Then I swing back onto the street and barrel away.

Colette peers out the rear window. "Did you run over those hideous little statues on purpose?"

"Yup."

Colette turns around and presses her feet up against the dash. "Well played."

Chapter 30

SCORPIO Oct. 23 – Nov. 21

There is no place like home. Question your motives, then question them again. Today you must expect the unexpected. Learn to accept criticism with grace and to accept praise with even more grace. Break down doors and confront the past.

Colette and I meet Willy at the prearranged site at a country road, plant the detonator under the seat and sprinkle dynamite residue on the truck bed. Willy tinkers with the engine to make it appear that it broke down, then drives us back to Concord in his Mustang. With me as intermediary, Colette and Willy conduct a lively conversation. I edit out her inappropriate remarks.

I wake up the next morning not believing that the big day has arrived. I want to bury my head in my pillow and go back to sleep.

Willy and I eat breakfast in silence, then climb into the rental van and drive west. For once Willy doesn't sleep, but smokes one cigarette after the other. I park a mile down the road from the OASIS site, and Willy and I get out and walk toward the employee parking lot. Colette, Hiram and Ebenezer show up on schedule and float beside us. When we reach the wooded area near the lot, I send Hiram to check for guards near the manhole to the right of the building.

Willy's station will be fifty feet away and just inside the tree line. Hiram comes back and reports that the area is clear. Willy heads out, and I start up the hill, with Colette scouting ahead. Hiram and Ebenezer drift alongside me.

Butterflies flit past, and swallows wheel in tight circles. It's a sunny Sunday afternoon, a time for a backyard cookout, a Red Sox game, a drive down to Cape Cod to stretch out on a beach... or a day to blow up a snazzy new government building.

I crawl over the crest, take out my binoculars and scan the site. Nothing has changed since Colette and I scouted the location a few days earlier. I check the blocks of deserted barracks beyond the OASIS building. No one to be seen, no vehicles on the cross streets and no movement, just flocks of crows flapping and squabbling on the barrack rooftops.

My phone vibrates. "I'm here," Willy says. "Everything's set."

His voice is low, sleepy, untroubled.

I say, "We're ahead of schedule,"

"Do I have time for a nap?"

"Don't even joke about it."

I turn my binoculars back on the OASIS building. A willowy woman with a gray ponytail steps out, followed by two short men with tool belts. She does all the talking and they do all the nodding, which makes me think that she must be Sheila, the site manager, probably in on a Sunday to catch up on paperwork. When the time comes, Willy will call her with the bomb threat. A week ago, he'd obtained her cell number from OASIS, claiming it was a family emergency.

I want to shout down to Sheila not to fuss with her paperwork because in two hours the whole place will be a smoking pile of rubble.

In two hours—hard to believe. Nothing seems real now that the day has come. I've spent nights tossing and turning, rehearsing this and that, looking for what could go wrong, then falling asleep and dreaming that this and that and everything has gone wrong.

The two workmen go back inside. Sheila yawns, studies her phone, yawns again, then steps into the building.

Colette drifts up the hill. I had sent her to reconnoiter the rear of the building, Hiram to investigate the barracks, and Ebenezer to count cars in the parking lot. Hiram and Ebenezer grumble about taking orders from me, but Colette doesn't. The good soldier.

She settles gently onto the grass, folding her legs underneath her. She's wearing a black shirt, baggy French army trousers and a U.S. Army helmet. She takes it off and shakes out her dark curls. She says, "No one's behind the building or in the construction trailer."

"What about the OASIS van?"

"Nowhere in sight."

After we get the ancestors out of the building, I can't have the OASIS vehicle rushing around vacuuming up escapees. The thing sprouted wings in one of my nightmares and flew up the hill. But Ford Transit vans don't fly, and in real life they can't climb rocky slopes, which is why I chose this spot as the ancestors' collection point. It'll be a haul for Hiram and Ebenezer, but Hiram assured me that ancestors weigh a lot less in their current state than their former state—his words. I asked why this was but didn't get an answer.

Hiram glides up the hill and settles down next to me. "The barracks are empty, but you knew they would be, didn't you? You sent me on another make-work assignment."

I ignore him.

Ebenezer slips up the slope and sits close to Colette. She shifts away. He says, "I counted three SUVs, one pickup, and six sedans in the parking lot."

"Which means at least ten people are inside," I say.

"Some might have ridden together, so we don't really have an accurate count, do we?"

"At least we know the minimum," I say.

A red-tailed hawk circles overhead, cutting wide sweeps against the cloudless blue sky, with each turn climbing higher on a column of hot air. As a kid I'd watch them for hours circling above the marsh. Total freedom. Just riding the rising wind. Bliss.

I don't want to be here.

I want to be home. I want to be sitting on the rear deck, drinking beer with Melody and Willy, waiting for the charcoal to get hot, watching the hawks circling.

I want to be anywhere but here.

Colette says, "What time is it?"

A nudge.

I check my watch: "It's almost two."

I wait three minutes before calling Willy: "Time to knock out the power."

"Here goes."

I hear a weak explosion. Or imagine I do.

The light over the building's entrance goes out.

A sirens wails.

No one comes outside. They're waiting for the generator to kick in.

A half minute later, the light over the entrance comes back on, and the siren tapers off. The backup generator is up and running.

Now we wait for the corrosive *glurp* I poured into the gas tank to knock out the generator.

Five minutes, ten minutes. Fifteen.

I check my watch: 2:18. Too long. The lawnmower that Willy and I tested died in three minutes.

I stare down the hill and wait.

And wait.

Willy phones me. "Not good."

"Not good," I repeat.

More waiting.

Hiram says, "What a cockup."

Ebenezer says, "Someone's coming up behind us."

I drop to my stomach, look back, see no one.

Is it a guard? Was I spotted on a security camera? Or is it someone out for a stroll? A birdwatcher maybe, some little guy with a goofy plaid hat and a little gray mustache.

No, it's Melody.

"Melody, what in hell are you doing here?"

She lies down beside me, panting after her jog up the slope. "You need me."

"The hell I do. Things will get ugly. This isn't the place for a single mother."

"Don't play that card, buster." She punches my shoulder, hard. "You sound like one of my brothers." She checks her watch. "The lights are still on. Aren't you behind schedule?"

"Go home!"

"Fuck you!"

Did I just hear Melody swear? A first.

"Listen Melody, get back in to your car and—"

"You said you picked this spot as the ancestors' collection point because it's safe, right?"

"Uh... right. But—"

"So it's safe... even for a single mother." Melody lifts her binoculars and peers down the hill. "Everyone else has a job. Give me one, too."

I don't have time to argue. "Okay." I point down the slope. "Keep watch on the building's entrance and see if anyone enters or leaves."

"That's not much of an assignment."

"It's make-work, little lady," Hiram says. "Jeff's good at that." Hiram turns to me. "The generator's still working. Don't you have a backup plan? You're always lecturing us about backups and double backups and—"

"Look!" Melody shouts. "The light over the front door has gone out!"

The generator has failed.

A minute later, a man and a woman come through the front door.

Both hold flashlights, both squint in the sunlight. Next come three men in white shirts and ties, a women in jeans and two men wearing tool belts. A young couple scramble out, clutching each other's hand—the office romance? Sheila is the eleventh and last. All climb twenty few feet up the slope, sit down and stare at the building. Sheila lights a cigarette and shouts into her phone.

My stomach tightens. Sweat drips from my armpits.

"See any ancestors escaping?" I ask Colette.

She shakes her head.

Melody says, "Jeff, what's happening?"

"We'd hoped that some of the recently abducted ancestors would be in good enough shape to get out of the building as soon as the power went out, but none has."

"We'll have to carry all of them," Colette says. "That'll take time."

I check my watch. We're already thirty-three minutes behind schedule. "Colette, are you ready to go inside?"

"Uh… sure."

She's not all that confident. Neither am I. What if they've installed a second backup generator? What if it isn't electricity that has the ancestors trapped inside but something else? What if Colette goes in and can't get back out?

Stupid plan. Stupid, stupid plan.

"You don't have to go," I say.

"Yes I do," Colette says, jumping to her feet. "If I don't come out in ten minutes, then… well… take it from there, Jeff."

Take it from there.

Hiram, Ebenezer and Colette drift down the hill. She slips through the front wall. Hiram and Ebenezer hover near the door.

I tell Melody what's happening.

She says, "What's got you so worried?"

"Everything."

She squeezes my hand. "Sorry I was so cranky yesterday in the office."

"That was cranky? You don't do cranky very well. I'm sorry I shouted at you just now." I stand up, reach down and pull Melody to her feet. "With the electricity out, the surveillance cameras are dead and won't spot us. Besides, there's no one inside the building to monitor them. We'll just have to stay out of sight."

I call Willy and tell him what's happening. He says, "Looking good."

I raise my binoculars and watch Ebenezer drifting back and forth in front of the entrance. Hiram takes off his hat, wipes the inside with his red handkerchief, puts the hat back on, does it again.

Melody leans against me. "What's happening down there?"

"Not a damn thing."

Stupid plan. Stupid, stupid plan.

I want to be in the newsroom. I want to be in bed with Melody. I want to be anywhere.

We wait. Five minutes. Ten. Fifteen.

I hear a faint shout from down the hill.

Hiram waves his hat.

Colette glides through the side of the building and gives me a thumbs up.

Then she, Hiram and Ebenezer slip through the front wall of the building and disappear.

I lower my binoculars and let out my breath. "They're in."

Melody rises on tiptoes and kisses me on the cheek. "Clockwork, it's going like clockwork."

I phone Willy with the good news.

"All right!" he shouts.

Melody and I hug.

My burner phone buzzes. "Oh, shit!"

"What?" Melody says.

"I sure as hell don't need this right now."

"What?" She tugs my arm. "What?"

I hold up the phone. "It's Hank."

Chapter 31

I put the phone to my ear. "Hank, my man. I was just getting ready to phone you. Have you picked a time and location for your sit-down with my OASIS contact?"

"Yeah, that's why I called. Make it five o'clock, the Old Ironsides parking lot, in that black SUV you've seen me in. Except I want to meet the guy today and not tomorrow. So get your ass moving."

I look down the slope: no Colette, no Hiram, no Ebenezer. What's holding them up? "Today might be a problem," I say.

"A problem? A problem is what I say is a problem. Phone the jerk and tell him there's a change of plans."

"He's not taking calls this afternoon on account of his daughter's dance recital. She's playing the part of a hummingbird. It all has something to do with environmental degradation."

Hank is silent.

Melody giggles.

Hank says, "Are hummingbirds endangered?"

"No idea."

"Yeah, well, who gives a shit anyway? Get ahold of the prick as soon as you can and get back to me right away."

"I sure will. You're the boss."

"Bet your ass."

I shove the phone back into my pocket.

And we wait.

Willy calls a couple times. He actually sounds worried.

Then Hiram slips through the front wall, followed by Ebenezer.

I squeeze Melody's shoulder. "They're coming!"

"What do you see?"

"Hiram's walking in front and Ebenezer's in back. It looks like they're carrying someone between them, but I can't see who it is because it's not one of my ancestors."

The two stumble up the hill and set their invisible load down.

Hiram is gasping. So is Ebenezer. Hiram is skinny and out of shape, and Ebenezer is overweight and out of shape.

Hiram says, "The hill's steep. It's like carrying a dead horse."

"You told me ancestors weigh a lot less now than they did… uh… before."

"Yeah, they do. But I'm still bushed."

"I didn't know you could get tired?" I say.

"Well now you do."

"Who'd you bring?" I ask.

"An Asian woman wearing a New York Yankees cap. She's in tough shape because she's been here a long time. We brought her out first because it'll take her longer to recover."

Hiram and Ebenezer float down the hill and soon return with another ancestor that they lay beside the woman.

Ebenezer sniffs his fingers and makes a face.

"Who is it?" I ask.

"A gray-haired guy in a business suit," Ebenezer says. "Totally out of his head. He keeps trying to sell me life insurance."

"How many others are inside?"

Hiram and Ebenezer exchange glances. Hiram says, "Forty?"

"Closer to fifty," Ebenezer says.

"More than I'd planned on," I say.

"You should've listened to me," Hiram says, "If you'd—"

"Where's Colette?" I ask.

"She's searching the building, floor by floor, room by room,"

Ebenezer says,. "She scouts, we carry."

I turn to Melody. "This is going to take a lot longer than I'd anticipated."

"Which," Hiram says, raising his forefinger, "is—"

"Go!" I say. "Get moving!"

Hiram and Ebenezer glide back down the hill.

"The schedule's slipping even more?" Melody asks.

"Afraid so."

I call Willy and fill him in.

Hiram and Ebenezer bring back an invisible accountant from the 1920s and set him down next to the others. "Colette hasn't found Clementine yet." Hiram says. His voice is tense. Sweat streaks his forehead.

I didn't know he could sweat.

Hiram and Ebenezer carry up another ancestor. Hiram says, "She speaks a foreign language, maybe Russian. She keeps pointing to herself and saying 'Alyona.'"

"That Eleanor's great-grandmother."

"Who's Eleanor?

"Someone I met recently. Long story."

Hiram and Ebenezer glide back down the hill and carry up a female contortionist from Ringling Brothers and Barnum & Bailey Circus, still in a knot.

Next is a French shop girl. Ebenezer straightens up and presses his hands against his lower back. "She says she once saw Colette dance in Paris."

"No sign of Clementine," Hiram says. His voice shakes.

I can identify the next person they lug up the hill because he's one of my ancestors. He's never visited, but I recognize him from the Ancestor Wall. He's my great-great-grandfather on my mother's side, a trim, handsome man in his late twenties, killed by a Confederate bullet at Gettysburg. He rolls his eyes and mumbles something.

"A late abductee," Hiram says. "He'll soon be well enough to slip

Back There." Hiram's armpits are wet, and his hands tremble. "No Clementine," he says for the tenth time. "Colette has searched the whole building but hasn't found her yet." He starts down the hill, stumbles, falls, jumps up, falls again.

Something I've never seen before.

Hiram and Ebenezer make a couple dozen more trips, getting more and more tired, complaining more and more.

Melody says, "How many so far?"

"I've lost count. Maybe forty, maybe more."

"No Clementine?"

"No Clementine."

Melody looks at her watch. "We're an hour and forty-nine minutes behind schedule."

Side by side, Ebenezer and Hiram roll something up the hill. "Would you believe it?" Ebenezer says with a gasp. "A sumo wrestler."

Ebenezer sits on the grass and wipes his face with his handkerchief. "That's everyone except for Clementine."

Hiram sinks to his knees and covers his face with his hands. Tears leak through his fingers. "Where is she? Where is she?"

I pat his back as best I can. "Colette will find her, Hiram. She won't give up until she does."

I sure as hell hope that's true.

We watch the building below and wait.

Sheila and two men test their flashlights and reenter the building. *Damn it!*

I report this to Willy.

He says, "The site manager's must have already ordered an emergency generator, so we've gotta get moving."

"Soon," I say. "Soon."

"I sure as hell hope so."

Willy's voice is high and tight.

We wait another fifteen minutes.

Willy calls again. "Time to get moving."

"Just a little longer."

"Jeff, we can't let—"

"I know, but... hold it!" I shout. "Colette's coming!"

She staggers up the hill with Clementine on her back.

Hiram and Ebenezer rush down the slope. Colette lays Clementine down. Ebenezer seizes her under the armpits and Hiram grabs her by her good leg and her peg leg. "Clementine!" Hiram shouts. "Clementine! Clementine!"

Hiram and Ebenezer struggle up the hill and lay her at my feet. Her eyes wander. She doesn't recognize us.

Hiram kneels beside her. "My Clementine! You're safe!"

She rolls her head back and forth.

He squeezes her hand in both of his. "I'll never stray again. I'll never say an unkind word to you again, I'll never..."

He's sobbing so hard he can't continue.

Clementine blinks her eyes. *"Mi amor!"*

Uh, oh!

I glance over at Colette.

She's grinning.

More declarations of love from Clementine. *"Mi amor! Mi amor!"*

Hiram looks up at me. "I didn't know she could speak Spanish."

"Maybe she used to teach it and never told you," I say.

More likely she learned it from her Guatemalan lover.

"We all have our little secrets," I add.

"Mi amor!"

"My precious," Hiram says, rubbing her hand.

Colette stops chuckling and slaps her hands together. "Okay everyone, let's get back to business. I checked the building four times, top to bottom. All the ancestors are out." She points toward the place on the ground where the ancestors have been deposited. "A few have already slipped away."

I turn to Melody. "Clementine's been found, which you must have guessed by now. We're behind schedule, but everything's moving along fine. Colette says some of the recent abductees have already recovered enough to go Back There."

"Where is that exactly?" she asks.

"Beats me."

She nods as if this whole business is the most natural thing in the world. Or not in the world.

I call Willy. "All the ancestors are out, but the three OASIS employees are still inside."

"I'll phone Sheila with the bomb threat," Willy says. "That'll get their butts moving. If not, then the warning explosion sure as hell will. Good job, Jeff."

"Thanks. I was hoping things would work out like this, but you never know what can—"

"Look!" Melody says, grabbing my elbow and pointing down the hill. "There's a vehicle coming from around behind the building. Is that the one that snatches ancestors?"

"It look likes it," I say. "They were probably out somewhere trolling for ancestors when the site manager ordered them back." I raise my binoculars. "But the slope's way too steep for a Ford van to... *Oh, shit!*"

It's not a van but a toothy red Hummer on big fat wheels. The monster can climb slopes, bump over rocks and logs, snatch ancestors.

The Hummer sits idling to the right of the building, probably to give the techies in back time to scan their instruments for escapees.

Melody says. "Now what?"

"Good question."

Chapter 32

I shake my head. "I hadn't expected OASIS to upgrade their vehicle."

"Well, you sure as heck should have," Hiram says. "And if you'd brought a firearm as I advised, then you could run down the hill and—"

"Okay, okay. I get your point."

Ebenezer points down the hill. "It's moving."

The Hummer rumbles along the blacktop lane running between the two nearest rows of barracks.

Willy phones me. "Is that what I think it is?"

"Afraid so."

"Any ideas?"

"You didn't bring extra explosives, did you?" I ask.

"Wish I had. Maybe we'll just have to wait and hope everything turns out okay."

"Maybe." I stuff my phone into my back pocket.

When was the last time that worked for me?

Melody says, "How close do they have to get to detect an ancestor?"

"Ebenezer said he was about a hundred and fifty feet from the van when he was snatched."

"Then the Hummer's out of range."

"For now."

I turn to Hiram. "How many have you and Ebenezer carried out?"

"Forty-five, maybe more."

"How long would it take to transfer them to a safe place?"

"Hours," Hiram says. "But where's a safe place?"

I look around. "I don't know."

Melody says, "We have to disable the Hummer."

"No kidding? Did you bring a grenade launcher?"

Melody puts her hands on her hips. "Don't take that tone with me!"

"Sorry."

Melody says, "But I could—"

"Hold that thought." I wave my phone. "It's Willy."

Melody makes a face and walks away.

Willy says, "I could run in front of the Hummer and distract them for a while."

"But not for long enough," I say. "And you'd have to leave your post—without you, there's no explosion."

"Right," Willy says. "Right." He hangs up.

Ebenezer says, "You could erect a perimeter wall of rocks and logs."

"That would take too long."

The Hummer goes a few feet and stops, a few more feet and stops, then turns into a cross road and disappears behind a row of trees.

I scan the area with my binoculars. If the Hummer heads away from us, it might give the ancestors enough time to recover and disappear. If not?

I review my options.

I have none.

Willy phones. "What's she doing?"

"Who?"

"Melody."

I look around. "Uh…she's not here."

"I know, because she's following the Hummer."

"She's what?"

"Following the Hummer in her car."

"She can't be!"

I raise my binoculars. "I don't see the Hummer. Or her. No, wait, there they are! I'll phone Melody and get back to you!"

I call. My fingers tremble.

No answer.

I try again.

Again no answer.

I phone Willy. "She's not answering me. You try."

I give him her number.

A minute later he calls back. "No luck getting through. By the way, Melody's driving like a maniac."

"She's raced stock cars," I say. I put my phone away. My hands are still shaking.

"What's she doing?" Colette asks.

"No idea."

Join her? Stay here? No, join her.

I stumble down the slope.

What will I do when I get there? Try to wave the Hummer down? Stand in front of it?

It would just drive around me.

Should I let it hit me?

If I have to.

I stay inside the woods to so the OASIS employees won't see me.

Melody's old Toyota creeps closer to the Hummer.

I wave my hands. "Drop back! Drop back!"

She's too far away to hear.

I stumble, fall, jump up.

My phone chimes. Answer? Yes? No?

Yes.

"I can see you, Jeff."

"Melody, what the hell are you—"

"You've abandoned your post," she says. Her voice is sharp. "What if an OASIS guard catches you and hauls you away at gunpoint? There goes the whole operation."

"I just had to make sure you were—"

"I can take care of myself, buster. Now get the hell back where you belong!"

The line goes dead.

I slow to a jog, then stop. Melody is right. I have abandoned my post.

Stay? Keep going? Return to the top of the hill where I belong?

What in hell is she up to?

The Hummer speeds up.

Melody speeds up.

She pulls up alongside the Hummer.

Oh shit!

I break into a run. "Melody, don't!"

She rams the Hummer's left front wheel.

Wham!

Her right front fender peels back. Her bumper drops off. Her car bounces backward, rolls, stops.

Silence.

The Hummer stops. The driver gets out.

Melody doesn't.

Don't let anything have happened to her! Don't let anything have happened to her!

I see myself lifting Dawn onto my lap. Mommy is in the hospital. But she'll be all right.

Or she won't be all right.

Your Mommy has gone far away, but she's happy there and will always love you.

The Hummer driver leans down and peers into Melody's car. He taps on the window.

The door swings open, and Melody steps out.

I stop running.

Melody shouts at the driver, waves her arms, goes up on her toes, points at her car, at the Hummer, at her car, waves her arms again.

The driver takes two steps back.

Two techies climb out the rear doors. The woman shouts at Melody. The man joins in. Now everyone is shouting.

Melody kicks the Hummer's door, bangs her fists on the driver's chest, kicks the door again.

The driver shouts at Melody.

She shouts at him.

The male techie shouts at her.

Melody steps back and begins to sob.

The woman puts her arm around Melody's shoulder.

The two men look away.

Willy calls. "I can't see Melody and the Hummer anymore. I hope that bang isn't what it sounded like."

"It is. Melody slammed into the Hummer."

"Is she okay?"

"Yes."

"Gutsy lady."

"She sure is. But she's only bought us a few minutes. In fact, the driver and the two technicians are climbing back into the Hummer."

Melody reaches through the window and grabs the driver's arm. He shakes her loose and starts the engine.

"They're moving," I say.

"Not good," Willy says.

Melody glances my direction, then disappears into the woods.

The Hummer goes twenty feet, stops, starts, stops again. The driver jumps out, bends down and examines the left front wheel. He shakes his head, gets back in and pulls away. The wheel shudders and smokes. The Hummer jerks and weaves and squeals to a stop.

"Willy, the Hummer's out of action. Melody hit the front wheel in just the right spot."

"How did she know to do that?"

"Her dad had an auto repair shop."

"Melody knows everything," Willy says, then hangs up.

I slip my phone into my pocket, then turn and rush back up the slope.

Colette glides along beside me. "When Melody tried to tell you her idea, you didn't listen, did you Jeff?"

I shake my head. "I'm afraid not."

"You cut her off, didn't you?"

"I'm afraid so."

"Women who fought with the Resistance never got the recognition they deserved. You owe your girlfriend one big apology."

"You're right."

Colette smirks.

I reach the top of the hill out of breath.

Willy calls again. "I'm trying to phone in the bomb threat, but the site manager's not answering."

I hadn't taken this into account. "Not good," I pant.

"No shit?"

"Keep trying."

Even without the bomb threat, the warning explosion should clear the building. But I don't want to take any chances. Redundancy, Colette preaches.

I sit on the grass, catch my breath and wait. Nothing to do until I hear from Willy. If he can't get through to Sheila in the next few minutes, I'll order him to set off the warning explosion.

My Civil War ancestor is now sitting up and chatting up a woman I can't see. It sounds as if he's trying to arrange a date.

A few minutes later, Melody jogs up. Her face is flushed and her hair a tangle. She's grinning.

I'd intended to give her hell, but I melt as soon as I see her. I jump up, lift her off her feet, spin her around and hug her so tightly she lets out an "*Oof!*" I kiss her sweaty forehead, give her another spin, set her down and release her.

"I should have listened to you," I say.

She punches me on the shoulder. "Next time, buster."

"You're a hero."

She shrugs. "I just did what had to be done."

More of that big grin.

Colette gives Melody a hug she can't feel.

Hiram and Ebenezer join in.

"You're brave and smart and pretty," I say. "A real femme fatale. In fact, I think…"

My phone rings. It's Willy.

"I got through with the bomb threat," he says.

"Did the site manager believe you?"

"Not until I told her I was with the Ramsey mob."

"Good job."

"Oh yeah, some guy just drove up. He's a big slouchy dude, dark hair, wide shoulders, maybe fifty, eye-bags the size of kangaroo pouches."

I turn to Melody. "Drucker just showed up."

"Is that a problem?"

"Drucker's always a problem."

Chapter 33

Sheila and two men burst out the front door and stumble up the slope to where the OASIS employees are seated in a cluster. She waves her arms and shouts. They drop their coffee cups and cigarettes, jump up and scramble farther up the hill.

I turn my binoculars toward the Hummer. It crawls a few feet, shudders, stops. The left front wheel wobbles and smokes. Still out of action.

Willy phones. "Here goes Baby Boom!"

A dull thud rumbles up the hill.

The OASIS workers hurry farther up the slope, Drucker right behind them.

"That's it, Jeff?" Hiram says. "I've heard a jackrabbit fart louder."

"That was the warning explosion. Wait for the big one."

I keep my binoculars on the front entrance in case anyone else comes out. No one does. I give it five more minutes before calling Willy. "It's a go."

He says, "And here's Big Poppa!"

Kaboom!

The building shudders. The ground shudders. A concussion wave rolls up the hill, ripples across the grass, shakes my insides.

Bricks fly. Boards fly. Chunks of metal fly.

Things crash and tumble. Things spin end over end.

Dust swirls upward, dances, twists, envelops the building.

Hiram slaps his hat against his knee. "Whoopee!"

Melody hugs me.

Colette sings 'La Marseillaise' and kicks her right leg high above her head.

Willy shouts into his phone. "All right!"

The OASIS crew groans and covers their ears.

Sheila sits down and buries her face in her hands.

Drucker shouts, curses, kicks a rock.

Clementine mutters, "What was that noise, *mi amor?*"

Hiram kneels down and helps her sit up. "Everything's all right now, chickadee. You're safe. I've destroyed the building where they kept you prisoner."

"My hero," she says.

Willy hurries up to me, grinning and jumping up and down the way he does at Red Sox games.

"Tell him he's stamping on Milton Lecker's stomach!" Ebenezer shouts.

I take Willy by the elbow and pull him closer.

"Now he's on Lana Thompkins's head!"

I tug Willy off of her.

He punches my shoulder and points at the Hummer at the bottom of the hill. The driver and the two technicians are examining the damaged wheel. One gives it a hard kick.

"Dead in the water," Willy says. "Great job, Melody."

I turn to Melody. "Great job. I have to apologize again for—"

She grabs my arm and points down the hill. "Look!"

The dust has thinned to a gray haze.

You gotta be kidding!

The building is still standing. Long vertical cracks run down its front, and chunks of brick and concrete are scattered over the ground, but the building is still standing.

"Damn it!" Willy shouts.

I can't believe it. All that planning, all that work. "Colette, what in hell went wrong?"

"Nothing."

"Nothing? *Nothing?*"

"In the summer of '43, we dynamited the Gestapo headquarters in Lyon, and it looked just like this afterward, but the whole thing collapsed a few minutes later. Expect the same."

"How can you be so sure?"

Colette puts her hands on her hips. "Because I am, that's why!"

"Uh-huh."

Her face turns red. She shakes her finger at me. "Don't speak to me like that! I was risking my life blowing things up half a century before you were even born!"

"Okay, okay," I say. "Sorry. You did your best. We couldn't have gotten this far without you. Now there's nothing to do but wait." I turn my attention back to the building. "If it is getting ready to collapse, let's hope no one is stupid enough to go back inside."

Drucker does.

"Goddamn it!" I shout.

"What?" Melody says.

I point down the slope. "Drucker just went inside."

"Why would he do something so stupid?"

"Because he's Drucker."

"Maybe he'll come right back out," Melody says.

"Maybe."

And if he doesn't? It's my bomb, my plan, my responsibility.

What did Dad think after he found out he'd left a firefighter inside a burning building?

He probably didn't stop to think but rushed right back inside.

I have to get Drucker out.

But I don't budge.

"If Drucker gets crushed in there," Hiram says, dragging his words out, "well, dang it, good riddance."

"The man abducted me and a lot of others," Ebenezer says. "His scheme jeopardized the existence of thousands of people, living and otherwise. Maybe millions. The world's a better place without him."

True, but…

I'm sure Dad wasn't scared. I'm sure he didn't hesitate. I'm sure he didn't speculate on how much time he'd have before the burning house collapsed.

Still I don't move.

Clementine hovers next to me. She's wobbly but recovering. Hiram holds her hand. She says, "We are all God's children, but I can't forget that Drucker's a liar and a bully and responsible for the abduction of dozens of us. So don't do anything foolish, young man."

Did Dad sense he would be dead in ten minutes? Do people in situations like that somehow know?

The firefighter had ignored Dad's order to evacuate the house, but Dad rushed back in to save him anyway. And died for his effort. A few minutes later, the missing firefighter staggered out unhurt.

I didn't tell Drucker to go back inside. It was his choice. What in hell was he thinking?

But it's my bomb, my responsibility.

I kiss Melody on the forehead.

She grabs my arm. "Jeff, don't!"

"I have to!"

I pull free, run down the slope and join Sheila. She's sweaty and red-faced. "Where did Drucker go?" I ask.

"Inside," she says.

"I know he went inside. But where specifically?"

"Who are you?"

"Uh… I'm from the company that installed the generator. We got a call that it failed."

I'm panting. My words come out in bursts.

She looks me up and down. "Where are your tools?"

"I'm the crew boss. The others are on their way. They'll bring them.

Where did Drucker go?"

She turns back toward the building. "To his office."

"Where is that?"

She points at the building. "Right corner, second floor. Why do you want to know?"

"Why did he go inside?"

"He went for his laptop. He says it holds some critical data. I couldn't stop him."

"That doesn't make sense," I say. "Everything should be fully backed up."

"Drucker doesn't make all that much sense."

"Flashlight."

"What?"

I hold out my hand. "Give me your flashlight."

"Why?"

I snatch it from her hand and tear down the slope.

"Hey! Hey, come back! I'm responsible for everyone and—"

And I don't hear the rest. The blast blew the front door partway open. I push inside and turn on the flashlight.

I wave the beam back and forth through the swirling gray dust. I can see only about fifteen feet. My eyes water.

There, to the right, are the stairs to the second floor.

I bound up them.

"Drucker! Where in hell are you?"

No answer.

At the top of the stairs, I swing right and run along the hallway.

I trip over a chunk of something, jump up, trip over something else and slide several feet on my hands and knees. The flashlight rolls away and goes out.

Shit! Shit! Shit!

I crawl forward, patting the floor for the flashlight.

"Drucker! Where in hell are you?"

No reply.

The walls creak, groan, threaten.

Something crashes down to my right.

"Drucker!"

No answer.

There. There's the flashlight. I crawl up to it, switch it on and see a three-foot hole right next to my elbow. I shine the light down to the floor below. I crawl backward, get to my feet and ease sideways past the hole.

I turn right. No, wrong way. I reverse direction.

"Drucker?"

I cough, spit, cough some more. Dust coats my hands, my face, my clothes, my tongue.

The building creaks and groans and rumbles. A chunk of something falls from the ceiling. I step around it.

Where in hell is Drucker's office?

I shine the flashlight into the office to my left. A filing cabinet lies on its side. Rubble covers a steel desk.

I check the next room. No one.

I shove a third door open far enough to get my head inside. I shine the flashlight around. "Drucker?"

No answer.

I kick away the rubble in front of the next office and step inside. Light comes through a big hole in the wall.

Drucker is standing behind a desk. A backpack sits on top. He's covered in gray dust—his hair, his face, his shoulders. He rushes around to the front of the desk and stands in front of the backpack. He says, "What the hell are you doing here?"

"I've come to get my pal out of a building that's about to collapse, that's what."

Drucker looks around the room as if nothing were wrong. "No, I meant what are you doing at the OASIS site?"

"I… uh, came to make sure the ancestors were getting decent treatment."

"How in hell would you be able to find out?" Drucker says. "Do you think you could just come waltzing onto the site and—"

Crack!

The building shudders.

We both look up at the ceiling.

Drucker dusts off his shoulders. "I came in here for some extremely important documentation. But mostly personal stuff. That's what's in the backpack. It's holds my only photo of me and my younger brother, the one who was killed in Afghanistan."

"I'm sorry to hear that, Drucker. It must have been a terrible loss for you."

"I never quite recovered."

"Goddamn it, Drucker, I checked you out online—you're an only child." I shove him aside, jerk open the backpack, grab three packets of $100 bills and wave them over my shoulder. "These are family portraits only if you're related to Benjamin Franklin."

Drucker says nothing.

"Well?" I say. "I'm waiting."

Drucker still says nothing.

I turn around.

His pistol is pointed at my chest.

"Put the money back," Drucker says.

I do.

"Raise your hands."

I do.

Now what? Bargain? Threaten? Go for the gun?

I start with bargaining. "Maybe we can work something out to our mutual benefit."

"That's a cliché."

Drucker grabs the backpack off the desk. He looks undecided about what to do with me. Drucker's a sleazebucket but not a killer. At least I hope not.

The building creaks.

"Why don't I just walk away?" I say. "Pretend I was never here."

Drucker grunts. He doesn't believe I'd do that. He shouldn't.

"Or you could give me a cut," I say, "and we'll walk out together and go our separate ways."

Another grunt.

Something crashes down nearby. The room shakes. A chunk of something drops from the ceiling and bangs off the desk.

Drucker jumps, turns to look.

I twist the pistol out his hand, step back and aim the gun at him.

He looks me up and down, then laughs.

Laughs?

"What now?" he asks.

"We're leaving. Right this minute—without the backpack."

"You gotta be kidding. There's over $150,000 in there."

"You have even more cash at your other office."

Drucker raises an eyebrow. "What makes you think that?"

"I have my own spies."

Drucker takes a cigar from the inside pocket of his sport coat. "Mind if I smoke?"

"Get moving, goddamn it!"

I'm screaming now.

Drucker tucks the cigar into the side of his mouth. "And if I don't?"

"I have the gun, remember?"

Drucker laughs. "You won't shoot me. You don't have the *cojones* to shoot anyone. In fact, I'll bet you've never even fired a gun."

Drucker lights a match, touches it to the end of the cigar and grins at me.

Never even fired a gun?

I see Mike raise his hand to hit Mom again. I see her turn her head and raise her right arm against the next blow.

I feel the heavy gun in both hands. I hear Mom whimper.

I hear the building creak.

I hear Drucker chuckle.
I hear the gun go off.
I hear Drucker yelp.

Chapter 34

Mike sat against the wall and kicked his left leg, just like Willy's collie did when a car ran her over.

Then Mike stopped.

Mom said I'd done something terrible.

Uncle Sid arrived and told me I'd made a mistake but everyone makes mistakes. Uncle Sid wiped the gun with his handkerchief. He said it was to get rid of my fingerprints. He told me to go to my room, but I watched from around the corner. He shot Mike, and I wet my pants.

Mike kept his eyes open but didn't move.

But Drucker moves. He hops around clutching his calf with both hands. "You shot me, you bastard!"

"Mike died," I say. "You won't."

"Mike? Who the hell is Mike?"

I shine my flashlight on Drucker's leg. "It's just the proverbial flesh wound, if you'll forgive the cliché."

"It hurts like hell!" Drucker screams. He falls down, grabs the desk and pulls himself to his feet, lets go, falls again. "It hurts too much to walk, you asshole!"

"That's the idea."

Drucker's eyes bulge. "You can't leave me here! You can't come waltzing in, shoot me in the leg, then bug out!" Drucker grabs the backpack off the floor. "You want my money? Okay, take it, but then you've gotta promise you'll—"

"Get on," I say. I toss the pistol through the hole in the wall, then turn my back to Drucker and crouch down.

"What?"

"Get on," I say, looking over my shoulder. "It'll be a piggyback ride. Remember them from the school yard? Weren't they fun?"

Drucker eyes me up and down. "I don't fucking believe it."

"Believe it."

Crack! Wham!

"That," I say, "is the building getting ready to fall down on our heads. Get on. Now!" I hand Drucker the flashlight.

He takes it and climbs onto my back. He moans when I grab his injured leg.

He's a lot heavier than I'd expected.

"Drop the backpack," I say. "I can't carry that, too."

"Not a fucking chance."

I start to put Drucker down.

"Wait! Wait!" He grabs several packs of $100 bills, stuffs them inside his shirt and drops the backpack.

I stagger out the room and down the hallway. Drucker shines the flashlight ahead of us. A great hunk of ceiling falls nearby, and a dust cloud rolls past. We cough and curse.

"Can't you go any faster?" Drucker says.

"Sure. Just let me put you down first."

No response.

We come to the hole.

Drucker shines the flashlight through to the floor below. "Careful! Careful!"

I ease sideways past the hole, stagger toward the stairs and start down. I take one step, bring the other foot down to the same level, get my balance, take another step.

Finally, I reach the bottom and set Drucker down. I bend over, gasping and coughing.

"Don't leave me here!" Drucker shouts, hopping on his good leg.

"Just catching my breath." I take a couple more deep gulps. "Get on."

Drucker climbs onto my back.

I stagger down the hallway, lurching against one wall, then the other.

More crashes and rumbles.

"The whole damn building's coming apart," Drucker says.

"You think?"

I set Drucker down at the front door.

"Don't leave me!"

I push the door all the way open. "Would I do that to a pal?"

Drucker climbs onto my back.

I step outside. A cloud of gray dust swirls out behind us.

The sky is blue, the air fresh and delicious. I squint in the sunlight, pause, take a few deep breaths, then start up the hill. My legs shake, my back aches, my arms tingle.

I hear applause.

The OASIS workers are on their feet, coming down the hill, clapping.

"Look at that," Drucker says. "You're a goddamn hero."

I stagger up to my admirers. "Move! Back up!" I shout. "The building's getting ready to collapse!" They stop clapping, turn and run farther up the slope. No one offers to help carry Drucker. I'm guessing they don't much like him.

I keep climbing.

Sheila rushes up to me. "What happened?"

"Drucker gouged his calf on a piece of broken pipe."

"It hurts like hell," Drucker says, his voice high and whiny. He's mortified to be seen on my back.

I go another few feet and drop him on the grass.

"Ouch! Ouch!" he screams.

Sheila says, "I have a first aid kit in my Jeep." She scurries off.

I flop down beside Drucker. I'm soaked in sweat, and my back muscles threaten to seize up. I wait for my breathing to steady, then say, "Before I grabbed your gun, would you have killed me?"

He shakes his head.

"I didn't think so," I say.

Drucker massages his leg. "But I would now if I still had my gun. I looked like an idiot riding on your back."

"You are an idiot."

The building snaps and pops. Sirens sound in the distance.

I turn to look up the slope. Willy and Melody are jogging toward me. I signal them back. No need for Drucker to know they're involved in this.

They stop. Willy gives me a thumbs-up, and Melody blows a kiss. They turn back.

Colette drifts over. "Another couple hours and everyone will be safely Back There," She says and gives me the V for victory sign, then drifts back to the spot where the ancestors lie recuperating.

Another couple hours? Hard to believe it's almost over.

Sheila returns, kneels beside Drucker, and opens her first aid kit. He pulls up his pant leg.

It's a clean flesh wound, a lucky shot. And painful, I hope.

Drucker confirms this. "It hurts like hell."

"I'm sure it does," Sheila says and pats his shoulder. "Be a brave little fellow."

"Go to hell."

Sheila laughs. "You were just lucky the generator repair technician showed up when he did."

"Who?" Drucker asks.

"Me," I say and make a zipper motion across my mouth.

Drucker tilts his head. "Gosh, I sure as heck was lucky," he says, putting a happy lilt into his voice. "If this nice man hadn't been here, well, shucks, I'd be up the creek without a paddle and—"

"I just thought of something," Sheila says, leaning back on her heels and looking up at me. "I didn't call the generator company."

"I misspoke in all the excitement," I say. "I came out here on a routine maintenance call. Just a big, happy coincidence."

Sheila nods then finishes bandaging the wound. Again she pats Drucker on the shoulder, and again he grumbles.

"There, that wasn't so bad, was it?" Sheila says. "But you better have a medical professional look at your leg. There should be an ambulance along pretty soon."

She jumps to her feet and shouts at two OASIS workers who've drifted too close to the building.

Two squad cars screech up, lights flashing, sirens screaming. Four policeman jump out, eye the building, then climb the hill to where the OASIS employees sit in a cluster.

Drucker eases his pant leg down over the bandage. "Why in hell are you here?"

"I've already told you—to make sure the ancestors were getting treated right."

"I've already told you that no one would've let you inside the building."

"My plan was to wait in the parking lot and chat up a few employees after they got off work."

"They wouldn't have cooperated," Drucker says.

"I'd have told them you'd sent me to interview them."

"In the parking lot? Cut the crap, Jeff. I know what you're doing here. I don't know how you pulled it off, but you're responsible for the explosion."

"Me?" I say with a loud chuckle. "Why in hell would I do that?"

"Maybe Hank ordered you to, or maybe you just like blowing things up. But more likely, you're playing hero to your ratty goddamn ancestors." Drucker reaches into his jacket and takes out a cigar. "Blowing up a federal building is a terrorist act. That'll get you twenty."

In twenty years I'll be in my fifties. So will Melody, with Dawn a college graduate.

I say, "You can't prove anything."

"Oh yeah?" Drucker says and takes out a book of matches. "When I get done with you... what the hell!"

The facade of the OASIS building tilts forward, hesitates, tumbles, smashes to the ground.

Kaboom!

The ground shakes. Chunks of concrete fly. Bricks fly. Dust spirals upward.

The OASIS workers jump to their feet.

A firetruck wails up but stops a distance from the building. Firefighters jump out and watch.

Another firetruck arrives, then a third. All stay back.

The dust clears.

The whole front of the building is exposed, like the back of a dollhouse.

"How about that, Drucker? I can look right into your office. I think I see your backpack with the $150,000. Want me to carry you back in to get it?"

"Fuck you."

The firefighters clamber into their trucks and back them farther away.

Colette floats over. "It won't be long," she says.

"It won't be long," I tell Drucker.

"You're a demolition expert now?"

"No, but Colette is."

"Colette? Who in hell is Colette?"

I don't answer.

The building trembles. A desk tumbles from a second-floor office and smashes to the ground, followed by a filing cabinet. A toilet bowl falls from the fourth floor, stops halfway down and swings back and forth at the end of a pipe.

"I can't fucking believe it," Drucker says.

The roof creaks, shudders, folds in the middle, pauses, then plunges, breaking the floors below one by one with a sound like rolling thunder.

Kaboom! Kaboom! Kaboom!

A dust cloud rolls up the hill.

Drucker swears. Crows wheel and squawk overhead.

After a few minutes, the dust settles, leaving a jumble of broken concrete, steel beams, crushed desks, chairs and filing cabinets.

"Maybe I'll be able to pick through the rubble and find my money," Drucker says in a far off voice.

"Maybe," I say. "If someone else doesn't get there first. If they do, they might steal it, or they might raise questions about how you—"

Whoosh! Boom!

Red-orange flames burst from the rubble and spiral up into the sky.

"Gas!" Drucker shouts. "The goddamn gas line went!"

Another explosion. *Boom!*

"Those wild and crazy Ramsey twins," I say. "When they set about to destroy a building, they sure as heck know how to get the job done, don't they? Sorry about your cash, though."

"Fuck you!"

Drucker pulls himself to his feet, cries in pain, wobbles, falls on his butt. I reach down and pull him up. He grunts and hops away on his good leg, pissing and moaning.

I call Uncle Sid. He answers on the first ring. "What's up?"

"The Ramseys just blew up a federal building."

"You're kidding?"

"Nope, and the FBI will soon be on their case. Hank and Freddie won't bother you again."

"You're sure?" Uncle Sid asks.

"One hundred percent."

Long pause. "Did you have something to do with this?"

"Could be."

"I owe you, Jeff."

"No, Uncle Sid, I owe you, and I always will."

Chapter 35

I lower myself onto the grass and massage my aching neck. My eyes burn from the smoke, my throat and nostrils are on fire, my hands and face are sooty, and I'm sore all over.

What a day, what a clusterfuck. But everything has worked out. After a fashion, anyway.

A hand grasps my shoulder. I look up.

Melody.

I stand up, lift her off her feet, give her a twirl and set her down. We step back and hold hands.

I want to pour out my soul. I want to tell Melody that she's brave and funny and beautiful and that I want to spend the rest of my life with her.

I pull her in close, give her another big hug, release her.

Just blurt out how I feel? Or start slowly and ease into a conversation about commitment? I don't want to scare her.

And I don't want to scare myself.

I clear my throat. "Some explosion, huh?"

Stupid, stupid, stupid.

We turn to look at the smoldering rubble. The firefighters have moved nearer, dragging hoses, shouting back and forth, sending long arches of water onto the flames. A siren gets closer. Then another. And another. Maybe one is an ambulance for Drucker.

Melody says, "Are you going to make a habit of this, blowing up federal buildings?"

"Only if you stick around to help."

A hint at long-term commitment. A really stupid one.

"Sounds like fun," Melody says. "It'll make me feel like a spy or something."

"You'll make an especially fetching femme fatale."

Did I actually say that?

Dumb, dumb, dumb.

A lump grows in my throat. God, I love this woman.

Melody points at Drucker, hopping around on one leg, showing off his bandage to anyone he can corner and no doubt making up some story of cunning and heroism.

"What happened to him?" Melody asks.

"I shot him in the leg."

Melody raises an eyebrow and purses her lips. "I'm sure he deserved it."

I love you. I love you. I love you.

I clear my throat, once, twice, get ready to profess my love, then say, "Uh... you and Willy better disappear before the cops try to interview you. I'm bugging out as soon as I get my strength back. I'll drive you home."

"Thanks, but Willy's prying my fender out with a jack. He says my car's drivable, but he'll ride along with me just in case. I'll drop him off, then pick up Dawn from the sitter." Melody goes up on tiptoes, kisses me on the cheek and whispers in my ear, "I love you."

Then she scurries off, not looking back.

I shout, "I love you too!"

Did she hear?

Colette slips up beside me and pumps her fist. "All right!"

Clementine, Ebenezer and Hiram float over. All four look pale, exhausted and... smaller?

Smaller! Or is that my imagination?

Clementine takes Hiram by the hand, gives him a soft look and says, "You saved me."

He smiles at her, pats her hand, then turns to me. "I like Melody."

I thought Hiram would scold me for admitting to a woman that I loved her.

"So do I," I say. "A lot. Melody's good for me."

"And you're good for her."

Again, not what I expected from Hiram.

"Although divorce is always a sin," Clementine says, dragging her words out, "I still can't be too hard on you. I've always found Adele prickly and cold, and it's absolutely unforgivable that she doesn't want children."

Again, not something I expected to hear.

"You've made us proud," Hiram says with a trembling voice. He pushes his hat up in front with his forefinger. "When word gets Back There about today, you're going to be a hero. I'm reminded of Sheriff Baxter Blackwell in *The Tale of the Crooked Trail*, who saved a whole town from destruction by—"

"I read that novel," Ebenezer says. "It was actually pretty good, except that the sheriff had to kill a slew of people to get the job done. Jeff used his wits. I couldn't be more proud of him."

"And me of you," I say. "All of you. We worked as a team. Otherwise, we'd have failed."

Colette bites her lower lip and wipes away a tear with her forefinger. I've never seen her cry.

Or shrink. She's definitely shrinking. So are the others.

Should I point this out? Or can they feel this happening?

And just what in hell *is* happening?

"Are you all right?" I ask.

My four ancestors exchange glances, wobble, grow smaller.

Hiram moves his lips, but his voice is faint, his words jumbled. He wobbles and goes in and out of focus. Now I can see right through him. Colette, too. And Clementine and Ebenezer.

I bend down. "Hiram, can you talk louder? I can't hear you."

Hiram squints, shakes his head. He doesn't understand what I said.

I turn to Clementine, but she's fading fast. So is Colette. So is Ebenezer.

I shout, "Can any of you hear me?"

Blank looks from all four.

They're smaller now. Child-sized.

Hiram is speaking but I can't make out what he's saying. Clementine, Ebenezer and Colette are also talking, but I can't hear them either. I try to read their lips. Is that 'Thanks'? 'Goodbye'? Or both? Hiram extends his tiny arm. It's translucent, a toddler's hand, little more than a ripple in the air.

Does he want to shake? It looks like it.

I reach out, but Hiram disappears.

So does Clementine. So does Colette. So does Ebenezer.

And I'm all alone.

Chapter 36

I ease back down on the grass. What was that all about? Did something bad just happen to my ancestors? Or was it good? Good, I hope.

Another siren. This time it's an ambulance. I pull myself to my feet and stumble over to Drucker. He's sitting on the ground and staring down the hill at the smoking rubble. I reach down. "Drucker old pal, let's get you some medical help."

He glances up at me, then turns away. "Not if I have to ride piggyback. I'd rather stay here and die of an infection."

"Uh-huh."

"Think I'm kidding?"

I shrug. "It's your choice."

Drucker looks up at me, away, back up at me, then holds up his hand and lets me pull him to his feet.

"If you won't let me give you a nice piggyback ride," I say, "then I'll hop you down the hill to the ambulance. Put your arm around my shoulder."

He does, then shouts, "Ouch! Goddamn it!" and falls on his butt.

"Don't go anywhere," I say.

"Where in hell would I go?"

I jog down the hill, find two EMTs and help them push a gurney up to Drucker. They load him onto it. As they wheel him to their ambulance, he describes in great detail how much his leg hurts. The taller EMT says, "Uh-huh."

The two slide the gurney into the ambulance. The shorter one with the freckles climbs in beside Drucker, removes the old bandage and whistles. "This looks like a bullet wound."

"Well, it's not," Drucker says and points at me. "I got stabbed by a piece of copper pipe when I was rescuing that dickhead. Back in Iraq, I saw dozens of bullet wounds, and this doesn't look one damn bit like them."

So many lies packed into just one breath.

The EMT doesn't look convinced but says nothing. He smears something onto the wound and replaces the bandage. "I have orders to stick around a little while, then we'll get you to a hospital."

After the two leave, I climb into the ambulance and sit next to Drucker. "We have to talk."

"No shit," Drucker says, sitting up on his elbows.

"I had nothing to do with destroying the OASIS building. It was the Ramseys. Remember how I warned you about their plans? In fact, you should check with Sheila. She'll tell you she got a bomb threat from a Ramsey gang member."

Drucker eyes me. "How do you know that?"

Good question. "Uh... she told me."

Drucker snorts. "Sure, she did. She might have gotten a call, but it wasn't from a mobster. No doubt it can be traced back to you or to someone close to you. That means the pokey for you."

"At least I'll get to share my cell with a pal."

"Here's where I'm supposed to ask you what the hell you're talking about, right?"

"Right," I say. "And here it is: Last I heard, taking a bribe on a federal contract was against the law."

Drucker snorts. "I didn't break any laws."

"No?" I say. "A mobster paid you $2 million to obtain a building contract. That sounds like a crime to me. It's the reason you made me spy on Hank. You were afraid he'd find out your identity, then make you return the money before Freddie fitted you out with concrete shoes and drove you to Boston Harbor."

Drucker chuckles.

"What's so funny?" I say.

"Don't you love irony?"

"What the hell is that supposed to mean?"

"It's not a crime if it's not technically a bribe," Drucker says with a broad smile. "The funny part—and I'm sure you'll get a charge out of this because you've got a really swell sense of humor—is that we were going to give Hank's company the contracts anyway."

I let this sink in. "Okay, I suppose that's possible. But you were doing business with a mobster. There must be some law against that."

"Not if I didn't know the construction company was mob-owned. I dealt exclusively with the front man, the jerk in Rhode Island."

"But you took a bribe, and that's—"

"It wasn't a bribe," he says, "but a bonus for my outstanding work coordinating the project."

"Two million dollars?"

"I'm worth it."

"Even though OASIS canceled the remaining building contracts?"

"That came later," Drucker says, rolling onto his side and wincing, "after you wrote your goddamn article. And I didn't kill the contracts, but my boss did. I fought like hell against it. Hank was never convinced, though. In any case, what I did was one hundred percent legit."

'Let's see what the courts think about that."

"And about your blowing up a shiny new government facility."

"If you turn me in, I'll do the same for you."

Drucker tugs at his bandage. "Go ahead. I already told you—it's was just a bonus."

"Okay, I'm sure you're innocent, Drucker, and I'm sure you're square with the IRS. A fine, upstanding citizen like yourself certainly paid taxes on that $2 million."

Drucker pokes his tongue into his cheek.

"Well?" I say.

"Let me think."

Two cops stick their head into the ambulance. The older one says, "What do we have here?"

Drucker pulls up his pant leg to show his bandage. "I rushed into the building to bring this guy out."

The cop nods. "Gutsy."

"Just the proverbial scratch," Drucker says.

"We have a few questions."

Drucker shakes his head, half rolls, groans and takes his wallet from a rear pocket. He pulls out an ID and hands it to the cop. "I'm afraid not."

He examines the ID, then gives it to the other cop. She reads both sides, eyes Drucker, me, Drucker again, then hands the ID back to Drucker. "You're both good."

We watch them leave.

"Was that your OASIS ID?" I ask.

Drucker shakes his head. "CIA. I didn't feel like turning it in when the bastards kicked me to the curb, so I told them I'd lost it. By the way, I just saved your ass." Drucker puts his forefinger behind his ear and bends it forward. "Do I hear a thanks?

I say nothing.

Drucker takes out his phone, punches a few buttons and holds it up for me to look at. "The thing still works."

"I'm happy for you."

"You should be, wiseass. I'm about ready to call the Feds."

"To turn me in?"

Drucker says, "Would I do that to my pal after all we've gone through together? Nope, it's to get the Ramseys blamed for today's noisy doings. By the way, you wouldn't happen to know if those rascally twins left any evidence behind, would you?"

"Of course not. How could I possibly know something like that?

But I can speculate. For example, what if the FBI drove eleven-and-a-quarter miles east on Route 32 and found a broken-down truck with the Ramsey construction company name emblazoned on the side? And what if there's a witness report of its having sideswiped a BMW yesterday just a couple miles from here? And wouldn't it be crazy if someone had dropped a detonator under the front seat? Or if sniffer dogs found traces of explosives?"

Drucker snorts. "This is all speculation, of course."

"Yup," I say.

"You seem to be good at speculating."

"Do you think OASIS would hire me?" I ask.

"Not in a million fucking years."

The freckled EMT sticks his head into the ambulance. "How're you doing?"

"It hurts like hell."

"Hang in there. We'll have you out of here in a few minutes."

Drucker watches the man go. "I gotta admit you did me a big favor."

"Bet your ass. Not many people would have schlepped you out of a collapsing building after you'd pulled a gun on them."

"Yeah, that too, I suppose. But what I really meant was that I'm happy to see the whole damn OASIS site destroyed. I'm sick of chasing ghosts and taking crap from my boss and dealing with those preening pricks at the Pentagon."

"So?"

"So, I've retired," Drucker says. "In fact, just last week I bought a place far away where's there no boss, no alarm clocks, no snow."

"A rich uncle died and left you stacks of $100 bills, right?"

"Something like that."

"So it seems we've reached an understanding," I say. "You'll keep quiet about any harmless peccadillo I might be falsely accused of, and I'll do the same for you."

Drucker reaches out his hand. "I might even forgive you for

shooting me, even though I you're still a first class dickhead."

I shake his hand. "Is that anyway to talk to a pal?"

Chapter 37

I drive home stunned by the way my ancestors shrank and disappeared, but also marveling that everything worked out in the end. The ancestors are safe. All their descendants are safe. Uncle Sid is safe. Dad is safe.

So am I.

And the woman I love says she loves me.

I hum, whistle, tap the steering wheel to the beat. Never have I felt such a sense of achievement, far more than when I won the Pulitzer or for anything else I've done in my life.

It's dark when I arrive at the house. Ignoring my aches and pains and growling stomach, I head down to the basement and rummage through Willy's tool chest until I find a paint scraper, a screwdriver, a hammer and a pinch bar. I carry everything upstairs to the Shooting Room.

Paint peels off the door in long brown strips. I count the nails: eighteen, their heads rusted over the years.

I pry the first nail out with the hammer and pinch bar.

I've pictured the inside of the room ten thousand times over the past twenty-eight years: a wooden table in the middle of the room, an easy chair up against the right wall, a matching brown sofa with bulging springs against the interior wall, and green flowered wallpaper with a splatter of blood at head height.

I stop pulling nails and step back. Why in the hell am I being so careful?

I drop the pinch bar and hammer, return to the basement, grab the sledgehammer, come back up and swing as hard as I can.

Wham!

The door splits right down the middle.

I swing again. And again. And again and again and again. Loud, hard whacks. Wood chunks fly. Splinters bounce off my arms. I pound the door until it breaks off its hinges and crashes inward. I bash it into kindling. I jump up and down on it. I kick pieces of wood in all directions.

I drop the sledgehammer, take a breath of stale air and flip on the light.

The two windows are farther apart than I remembered. The bookcase is on a different wall. The couch is gray, not brown, and I'd forgotten about the fireplace. A half-burned log lies in it along with a heap of ash and the skeleton of a squirrel that must have tumbled down the chimney.

The blood splotch on the wallpaper has turned brown. Twenty-eight years ago, I had to tilt my head back to see it. Now I look down at it. I put my little finger into the two bullet holes from when I missed. My third shot didn't.

I take a step back. The spot next to my left foot is where Mike sat dying. Mom was seated on the floor, farther off to my left, cringing, her arm raised, waiting for the next blow. I step farther back. This is where I stood without moving until Uncle Sid showed up and pried the gun from my hand. Everyone makes mistakes, he said. I'll take care of everything. I'm make things right.

I hear his voice as if it were yesterday.

I pick up a shoe. It's smaller than my hand. I'd kicked off both shoes because blood had splattered on them. The leather has hardened, and the toes have curled up. Dark spots dot them.

I never liked wearing shoes after that.

I set the shoe down, lean over and pick up a pair of glasses lying near the table in the center of the room. Mom's. Both lenses are cracked. I peer through them. What do I expect to see? A magical view into the past? All I see is a stain five and a half feet above the floor and green wallpaper with big white flowers. The splotch is the shape of a rose.

I set the glasses on the table, right next to a miniature ladder, the one missing from the toy firetruck. I pocket the ladder to give to Dawn.

I grab the pinch bar, pry the plywood off both windows and raise them. Fresh night air flows across my face and shoulders.

I get a pail of sudsy water and wash the windows.

I push the furniture into a corner, roll up the rug and drag it next to the trash cans behind the garage. Tomorrow I'll buy a new one. Something bright and cheerful. Something without a blood stain.

I vacuum the floor and mop it. I clean out the fireplace.

I strip off the section of wallpaper with the blood stain. I stuff the paper into a grocery bag and carry it to the stone terrace in back.

I set the bag on fire.

I watch pretty orange sparks rise into the night. They dance in the breeze, swirl and flicker out—the last traces of one Mike T. Wendel.

I stamp out the glowing ashes and go back inside.

I carry the table, easy chair and bookcase out to the side of the road. I go back inside, get a sheet of typing paper, a roll of tape and a black marker. I drag the couch to the street.

I tape the paper to the couch and write in big bold letters, "I AM FREE!"

Chapter 38

Six months later

SCORPIO Oct. 23 - Nov. 21

Learn to recognize the things that matter and discard those that do not. Friends and family are life's true prize. By listening to yourself, you find yourself. Soak a sponge in vinegar to remove crayon marks.

I kneel before the fireplace, lay strips of kindling across the logs and top them off with crumpled newspapers. Mom never lit the fire, feared fire. Dawn insists that a party must have one, however. Melody says I spoil her. Right now Dawn is dancing with Willy, her feet resting on his toes.

I lean back on my heels and wave away the smoke. It makes me think of the burning OASIS building. Also of my father. I never smell smoke without thinking of my father.

Snow is piling up in the roads, but everyone has made it to Uncle Sid's belated retirement party—Sherwood, Janet and a dozen others from the magazine.

Before anyone arrived, Willy and I rolled up the new carpet and lugged most of the furniture out of the room. Willy calls it 'Jeff's

Man Cave' and gives me hell whenever I forget and refer to it as the Shooting Room. I bought two leather couches, a floor-standing popcorn machine at Willy's insistence, and a humongous television set that made Melody roll her eyes. She contributed the lava lamp, a retro touch.

The old wallpaper's gone, and the walls are painted an off-white except for the spot where Dawn crayoned pink-and-green swirls. She says it's the merry-go-round I took her riding on. I nailed an empty wooden frame around her artwork. It hangs next to the full-length Elvis poster that Willy tacked up. Another retro touch.

The music reaches its end, the dancing stops, and Sherwood puts on one of Bach's Brandenburg Concertos. Everyone groans. Willy shoulders Sherwood aside and substitutes something from 'Saturday Night Fever.' More groans, but the guests do go back to dancing.

The room is warm and noisy and smells of wood smoke and popcorn. Uncle Sid is wearing the hideous red-and-green Christmas sweater Mom knitted for him many years back, the hem frayed and the elbows worn thin. He's cornered the magazine's graphic artist— giving her more instructions, I'm guessing. She nods, sips her drink, nods some more. He's had a hard time letting go of the magazine.

Dawn is showing her framed crayon drawing to Janet, who leans down and makes appreciative lip-smacking sounds.

The fire goes out for the third time. I crumple up more newspapers and toss them onto the kindling.

"You're doing that all wrong."

I look up. It's Willy.

He points at the logs. "Put the paper on the bottom, then the kindling, then the logs."

"Uh-huh."

He's probably right, but I keep on wadding up newspapers and tossing them on the kindling. "Too late."

Willy is holding two bottles of Perrier. We've been drinking a lot of the stuff lately instead of beer. He hands me one. The two women in our lives have us on a steady diet of wild salmon, Greek yogurt, salad, tofu and anything that can possibly be constructed from whole wheat, but from time to time Willy and I sneak off for beer and pizza.

He gestures toward Uncle Sid. "I still can't figure out why he turned the *Tattler* over to you."

"No? Isn't that obvious? I'm smart and forward-looking, a terrific organizer, a natural manager, a skilled wordsmith, a pursuer of excellence and a—"

"Bullshitter," Willy says. "What I really meant to say was why did he abandon the *Tattler* in the first place?"

Like everyone, Willy thinks that it was Uncle Sid who owned the magazine, not the Ramseys.

"Uncle Sid wanted to get away from the cold Boston winters."

"Yeah, I can identify with that."

In fact, Uncle Sid worked out a deal with the Feds to avoid prison on money-laundering charges in exchange for disclosing everything he knew about the Ramseys. He also had to give up managing the *Tattler*. The Feds confiscated it along with everything else the Ramseys owned and put it up for sale.

I bought it with the proceeds from my share of the Back Bay condo plus a mortgage on the Concord house.

"The fire's going out again," Willy says. "Now you can rebuild it my way."

I ignore him. I'm tired of advice of any kind from anyone.

Willy glances around the room. "The place looks great."

"Thanks to you."

"You helped. We're a great team at fixing up old houses."

"And blowing up Federal buildings," I say.

"That, too."

After I opened up the Shooting Room, Willy and I sanded the floors, stripped the wallpaper and painted the walls. Melody planted rosebushes around the foundation of the house and reseeded the lawn. The family home is a different place now, but the same place, too. The same place only better.

"You worked your butt off," I say. "And then you move out."

Willy takes a sip of Perrier. "I'll be back for the parties."

He lives in Lexington with Stephanie. She's his physical therapist, a short, freckled brunette with strong hands. A sensible woman who laughs easily.

They're engaged.

So am I.

In the five-and-half months that Melody and Dawn have lived with me, we've hiked in the marsh, made banana ice cream, crayoned at the kitchen table and laughed a lot. Tomorrow I'm taking Dawn sledding at the hill where Willy and I used to go.

Sherwood sidles over. "There's a woman out there asking for you."

"Who?"

"She didn't say."

I stand up and go to the front door.

It's Adele. What in hell is she doing here? She's bundled up in a long black coat with a gray fur hood that's flecked with snowflakes. She looks tired, worried, older. I haven't seen her since the day in her attorney's office when she bought my half of the condo and we started divorce proceedings.

She pushes the hood back and says, "Hi."

"Hi."

"Hold out your hand."

I do.

She lays something in my palm.

I look down. It's the six missing recorder chips.

My jaw drops.

"These," she says with a look of satisfaction, "will get you your Pulitzer back."

I bounce the chips in my hand. "I guess you didn't destroy them after all."

Adele pretends she hasn't heard. Something she's good at.

She says, "I was devastated about how Beckworth betrayed you, absolutely devastated."

Uh-huh.

"But this fixes everything," she says.

Uh-huh.

I ask, "Why are you doing this?"

She glances off to her left. "Because it's the right thing to do, that's why."

Sure, it is.

Last week my buddy Charlie called from the newsroom to report with great glee that Beckworth had dumped Adele for someone ten years younger and that he'd been fired for cornering an intern in the elevator and sticking his tongue down her throat.

"Adele, you've always been a shining example of someone who knows how to do the right thing."

"Thank you," she says.

Irony always escapes her.

Long silence.

She tilts her head to side and looks past me into the next room. "Is that a party?"

I nod but don't invite her in.

More silence.

Adele says, "Who's that pretty redhead who keeps staring?"

"My fiancée."

"Oh," Adele says and screws her mouth around. "Oh."

Melody notices us watching and slips away.

Willy puts on an old Glenn Miller recording of *Moonlight Serenade*. Only Sherwood and the graphic artist dance, both clumsily, both clinging tightly to the other. She says something that makes Sherwood tilt his head back and laugh. Have I ever seen him laugh before? Has he ever laughed before?

Adele says, "Everyone's having fun."

"It's my uncle's retirement party. I've taken over the magazine."

"After you get your Pulitzer back, every newspaper in the country will compete for you."

"Uh-huh."

We look in different directions, say nothing.

I hear someone break a drinking glass, the wind whistling outside, Dawn laughing.

Then Adele goes up on tiptoes, kisses me lightly on the cheek, steps back and gives me a wistful look. She pulls her hood over her head, pauses, then turns and leaves.

I remain there, staring at the closed door.

The memory chips feel warm in my hand. I look closer. Just six thin squares of black plastic no larger than a thumbnail, but for me they're the tokens I can trade in for a major journalism prize, recognition from my peers, and my job at the *Globe*.

An incredible turn of events.

I pocket the chips, weave through the dancers and return to the fireplace. The fire has gone out again.

I kneel down and prod the logs with a poker. Melody and Dawn come and stand nearby. Dawn is carrying the firetruck I'd given her.

She says, "Why isn't it burning, Jeff?"

"I don't know."

"Why don't you know?"

"Because I don't."

"Why don't you—"

"That's enough," Melody says and squeezes Dawn's shoulder.

Dawn looks up at her mother. "Can I have another cookie?"

Melody glances at the food table. "I suppose so. But not more than one."

Dawn scurries off.

Melody says, "A fireplaces needs two inches of ash to burn well."

I look up at her. "I have the feeling you'd didn't come over here just to tell me that."

Melody shifts to her other foot. "Was that pretty woman Adele?"

"That was Adele."

"Why was she here?"

"To return my recorder chips, ostensibly so I can recover my Pulitzer, but in reality to get back at Beckworth. He dumped her."

"No kidding?" Melody says. "That's great news!"

"Uh-huh."

The Pulitzer. I had just stepped from the shower when the call came. My cellphone lay chiming on the bathroom sink. Soap was in my eyes. I rubbed them with my towel. Answer? No, let it ring. It rang again, then again. Okay, answer it. I did. Mr. Jeffrey Beekle, I'm delighted to inform you that you've won this year's prize for investigative reporting.

I danced naked down the hall to tell Adele. She gave me a weak smile and said, "That's nice," then went back to reading. Adele always thought of herself as the better writer, the better thinker, the better person. Ten days later, she asked me to leave.

Melody waves her hand in my face. "You're off somewhere."

"Lost in thought."

"About what?"

"Nothing important."

Melody bends down and hands me some old newspapers.

I feed them onto the fire, then come across a postcard with a lone palm tree leaning over a sandy beach. The caption reads "Enchanted Nassau," which means that, of all the places on the planet from where the postcard was mailed, it sure as hell wasn't Nassau. I hand the card to Melody. "You might want to read this."

"Is this the famous missive from Drucker?"

"Yup."

Melody reads the card. "All he wrote was, 'Having such a great time that I think I'll stay.'" She turns the postcard over. "I'm not surprised there's no return address, but no postmark? How did he pull that off?"

"He's a spook."

"I'll bet he's some place that doesn't have U.S. extradition rights."

"You think?"

"So," Melody says, flapping the postcard. "It's all over?"

"It's all over."

The Pentagon and the CIA rushed to defund Drucker's project after learning that mobsters had blown up the OASIS building, that all the data and equipment were destroyed, and that the project designer had skipped town. Officially, the attack was blamed on terrorists.

Six months have passed, but it's still hard to believe all this ever happened.

I sit back on my heels and point at the food table. "I hate diming out a kid, but…"

"Uh, oh!"

Dawn clutches two chocolate-chip cookies in her left hand and reaches for a third.

Melody rushes off.

Janet drifts over. She points a rolled-up newspaper at the fireplace. "Because there were so few trees back on the frontier, they burned buffalo chips for heating and cooking." She wrinkles her nose. "The smell was awful, just awful."

The frontier? Buffalo chips? Where did that come from?

She adds, "I miss the newsroom, and I miss you."

Janet resigned the day after I blew up the OASIS building. She told everyone she was moving far away, didn't say where, but kept in email contact with me. This morning she sent me what she said would be my final, personalized horoscope. For the past six months, I've had to buy the *Tattler's* horoscopes from an online service. They lack Janet's flair, but they do save money. I've also renegotiated the contract with the printers, tightened up elsewhere, and the magazine now turns a nice profit even without the Ramseys' dirty money flowing through it.

"And we miss you," I say.

"Sherwood says you've started wearing shoes."

"I've become respectable."

"Oh, I hope not," Janet says. "He also reports that you've stopped talking out loud to yourself."

"It seems so."

"I understand perfectly. That went on much, much too long."

What does she mean by that? Does she know about my ancestral visits? Has Melody talked to her? Willy? No, neither would give away my secret.

Janet hands me the rolled-up newspaper that she's been holding. I start to crumple it.

"No, no," she says. "It's not for the fire. I brought the paper for you to read. Look at the front page. Aren't those the two ruffians who visited you in the newsroom that time?"

I unfold the paper and smooth it across my knee. Hank and Freddie Ramsey stare back. The photo was taken on a boardwalk along a sunny beach. Hank wears a broad-brimmed hat that shades his eyes. Freddie has his head tilted back, yielding a clear view up both nostrils.

Janet says, "Dangerous hooligans."

"Not anymore."

I'd read the same newspaper article two days earlier: "Mobster Twins Killed in Downtown Miami Shootout."

Janet says, "It's awful when someone dies so violently, but I have to admit that the world is a safer place."

Especially for Uncle Sid and myself. Drucker, too. "It sure is," I say.

Janet sighs. "Well, I'm afraid I have to disappear now."

"So soon?" I stand up and raise my arms to give her a hug, but she takes a step back.

Janet never lets anyone touch her.

I lower my arms. "We'll have to get together again."

"I suspect we won't."

"No? Why not?"

"I'll be far away," Janet says.

"Well, we'll keep in touch by email."

"I'm closing my account. I don't have a use for it anymore."

"No? Then give me your new mailing address."

Janet looks over her shoulder at Melody, who's shaking her finger at Dawn and telling her to put the cookies back on the plate right this minute. Janet turns back to me and smiles. "Melody is a wonderful person. Dawn, too. Your fortunes have certainly improved. You can't know how much satisfaction that gives me."

We both watch Dawn slowly relinquish a cookie, then another, then another.

"By the way," I say, "if you're worried about driving home in the snow, I'll be glad to put you up for night."

"That's a kind offer, but I didn't come by car."

"Then how did you get here?"

Janet looks around the room. "I have to say goodbye to everyone. I just hate saying goodbyes."

Again I hold out my arms to hug her.

She smiles, backs away, and joins Melody and Dawn.

I get down on my knees, lay the newspaper face up on the fire and watch it wobble, turn brown and burst into flame.

Goodbye Hank. Goodbye Freddie.

Someone will write a series of articles about how you bribed judges and policemen, terrorized Boston and murdered witnesses. The writer might even win a Pulitzer.

But it sure as hell won't be me.

I hear a squeal and look up to see Melody wiping Dawn's face with a napkin. Across the room, Willy, Uncle Sid and Sherwood are busy refilling the popcorn machine. Uncle Sid says something that makes Sherwood laugh.

Friends, colleagues, family, a wonderful woman and her wonderful child.

The only things that matter in life.

Melody waves and gives me the thumbs-up. I don't understand.

She points at the fireplace. I turn around. It's blazing.

Flames lick around the logs and warm my face. I reflect on what has happened to me recently, the good and the bad, and what I've learned about what counts in life and what doesn't.

I reach into my pocket and take out the memory chips. Nothing more than six little squares of black plastic with tiny printing on one side.

I sprinkle them across the fire.

They warp, sizzle, melt, disappear.

· · ·

Melody and I usher the last guests out at midnight and collapse into bed.

But I can't sleep, so I roll out, shove my feet into my slippers, grab my robe off a chair, tiptoe downstairs and stand in front of the Ancestor Wall just the way I used to when I was a kid and couldn't sleep. Only I no longer talk to the pictures.

I haven't put up a photo of Mom because I don't want to think of her as a dead ancestor, just Mom.

Footsteps on the stairs.

It's Dawn in hooded pink pajamas with bunny ears.

"You shouldn't be up," I say.

"Are you taking me sledding tomorrow?"

Dawn is the master of redirection. "Of course. Now go back to bed before your mother hears you."

Dawn takes my hand. "Is that man with the horse a cowboy?"

"No, he's pretending."

Dawn points at a heavily made-up Colette in an alarmingly short dress with a plunging neckline. "Who's the pretty lady?"

"A dancer. Also a hero."

Dawn points at Clementine standing at the front of a classroom, an open book in her hands. "Is she a teacher?"

"Yes."

Dawn is quiet for a moment. "Are they your friends?"

"I guess you could say that."

"Why didn't they come to the party?"

"They live too far away."

Dawn points at a faded black-and-white photo at her eye level. "That's the cookie lady."

The cookie lady? Right—that would be Janet. Dawn is pointing at a blurry picture of my great-grandfather on my mother's side, a land speculator who went to Mexico in search of gold, never to return. "Which lady do you mean?"

Dawn presses her finger against the photograph. "That one."

I get down on my knees and squint. My great-grandfather stands with his legs far apart, facing the camera, a Stetson on his head, a gun in a hip holster. He's in the center of the main street of a frontier town. A carnival is spread out behind him—a juggler, a clown on stilts, a dancing dog, a fortuneteller sitting under a sign that reads, "Look Into The Future!" and a second that says, "Fresh Apple Vinegar For Sale!"

I squint at the photo. It's grainy and badly focused, but the fortune teller does look like Janet.

A whole hell of a lot like Janet!

The woman in the picture wears a long black dress and a neck scarf, identical to the outfit Janet wore every day to the office.

I lean back on my heels.

Unbelievable! Fucking unbelievable!

Now I understand.

Melody once forwarded me an article that described a class of visiting ancestors who are visible to everyone, stay for long periods, can predict the short-term future (like fortunetellers?), and give out advice indirectly (like horoscopes?).

Hiram had grudgingly confirmed their existence.

Janet arrived when my life was in turmoil, and she left the *Tattler* the day after the ancestors were rescued. Now I know why we never learned where she came from, where she lived, or anything about her past. Now her remark about burning buffalo chips for fuel makes sense.

I should have guessed.

Janet must have been married to the cowboy in the photo, my great-grandfather.

I stand up. "Unbelievable."

"Yes, it *is* unbelievable that you two scalawags are up at this hour."

I turn around. Melody is wearing my gray sweatshirt pulled down over blue pajama bottoms. She shakes Dawn's shoulder. "How many times have I told you not to get out of bed, young lady?"

Dawn points at Hiram. "He's not a real cowboy."

"Don't try to change the subject."

"And the pretty lady is a dancer."

"Fine. Now let's get you back to bed." Melody reaches up and pinches my ear. "You, too, buster."

I point at the photo of Ebenezer, a cigar in the corner of his mouth, his thumbs looped under his suspenders, his stomach bulging. "Did I ever tell you that my grandfather went to prison for running a Ponzi scheme?"

"Now don't *you* try to change the subject."

Melody guides Dawn out the room and up the stairs.

I step closer to the pictures of my mute ancestors in their old-fashioned clothing, seated on stiff-backed chairs in musty drawing rooms, or holding a horse's reins, or posing for a wedding photo, or telling someone's fortune. People long dead. Strangers.

Melody comes back down a minute later, puts one arm around my waist and with the other straightens the photo of my father in his fireman's uniform. "He'd have been proud of you for rushing into that building to save Drucker."

I start to speak, feel the lump in my throat, close my mouth.

Melody looks up at me, squeezes my waist harder and leans her head against my shoulder. "All your ancestors must be proud of you."

I clear my throat. "I hope so."

"You still haven't seen them?"

"Not since the day we blew up the OASIS building."

"Do you miss them?"

I picture Hiram in his oversized cowboy hat, Colette in combat boots, Ebenezer puffing a cigar, Clementine limping on her peg leg, and Janet in her fortuneteller dress. "Yeah, I miss them."

I kiss the top of Melody's head. "But not so much that I want them back."

About the Author

David Gardner grew up on a Wisconsin dairy farm, served in Army Special Forces, and earned a Ph.D. in French from the University of Wisconsin. He has taught college, worked as a reporter and in high tech. He coauthored three programming books for Prentice Hall, and wrote dozens of travel articles and many mind-numbing software manuals before happily turning to fiction. David lives in Massachusetts with his wife, Nancy, also a writer. He hikes, bikes, messes with astrophotography and plays the keyboard with no discernible talent whatsoever. You can visit him at davidgardnerauthor.com.

For more exciting new fiction, visit encirclepub.com!

And if you enjoyed reading this book, please consider writing your honest review and sharing it with other readers.

Thank you,
Encircle Publications

Join us at:
Facebook: www.facebook.com/encirclepub

Twitter: twitter.com/encirclepub

Instagram: www.instagram.com/encirclepublications

Sign up for Encircle Publications newsletter and specials:
eepurl.com/cs8taP

9 781645 991441